ALSO BY CYNTHIA LEITICH SMITH
Blessed:

"[A] wild and ultimately fascinating, if at times grisly, alternate universe." *Kirkus Reviews*

"A hearty meal for the thinking vampire reader." *Horn Book*

"Sure, the vampires, werewolves, and angels provide the lure, but Smith's obvious affection for her characters makes this more than the typical cynical genre exercise." *Booklist*

"Smith's writing style is sometimes dramatic, often humorous, and always energetic… A satisfying blend of excitement and intrigue." *VOYA*

"Readers will particularly enjoy the relief from the scary omnipotence of Brad during the action at Sanguini's, chock-full of foodie treats and in-jokes for vampire and literature fans…" *Austin-American Statesman*

"As in the previous installments of this smart, sexy trilogy, Cynthia Leitich Smith doses every page with winking pop-culture references and groan-worthy one-liners … [a] darkly humorous send-up." *BookPage*

"A good read for those who hunger for the dark side, with all the trappings of a YA vampire novel." *School Library Journal*

Diabolical

CYNTHIA LEITICH SMITH

WALKER
BOOKS

First published in Great Britain 2012 by Walker Books Ltd
87 Vauxhall Walk, London SE11 5HJ

2 4 6 8 10 9 7 5 3 1

This book has been typeset in Palatino

Printed and bound in Great Britain by Clays Ltd, St Ives plc

British Library Cataloguing in Publication Data:
a catalogue record for this book is
available from the British Library

ISBN 978-1-4063-3912-3

www.walker.co.uk

For the kids in the chapel on College Street
in Montpelier, Vermont

The Draculas were, says Arminius, a great and noble race, though now and again were scions who were held by their coevals to have had dealings with the Evil One. They learned his secrets in the Scholomance, amongst the mountains over Lake Hermanstadt, where the devil claims the tenth scholar as his due.

—Dr. Abraham Van Helsing in *Dracula* by Bram Stoker (1897)

-❀❀ Miranda ❀❀-

UNTIL THE NIGHT I WAS TAKEN, demonically infected, the guardian angel Zachary watched over me. Now, I watch over him.

It's not your average long-distance relationship. Romantic entanglements between humans and angels are rare, archaic, and discussed only in hushed tones.

A romantic entanglement between a guardian and one of the murderous undead had been unprecedented. Then we fell in love.

One of the consequences of Zachary's "slipped" status is that, though *not* fallen, he's earthbound, limited to corporeal form, and banished from the ethereal plane.

Therefore, he's banished from me as well . . . at least for the foreseeable future.

Meanwhile, Zachary will continue to devote himself to counseling neophyte eternals, those who might embrace redemption like I did.

Assuming the monster lying in wait for him around that thorny bush doesn't pluck out his eyes, claw out his throat, and rip his glorious muscled body to bloody pieces.

Zachary is immortal. He wears a gleaming holy sword with a gold hilt, a weapon forged in heaven. His blood is as toxic to an eternal as holy water. Yet he's no stronger or faster than a mortal man. He can still be brutally injured. He has been in the past.

Far, far, far above, I'm curled in a plush wing chair in a tropical lobby of the Penultimate, the way station for ascended souls immediately outside heaven. I'm one of hundreds of thousands, gazing down on loved ones, enemies, and the occasional celebrity of the day, trying to make our peace before passing through the famed pearly gates.

It's usually a comfort, watching over Zachary, a way to hold the loneliness at bay. Yet at moments like this, when he's in danger, I feel every inch the predator defanged.

I zero in on the nearest lakeside dock. Where did the

fiend go? I never should've taken my eyes off it. Not that I can warn my angel, not that I'm useful in any way.

Zachary scans the shadowy trees. In his matte black cowboy shirt over black jeans and boots, he makes a dashing, romantic figure. My fingertips twitch at the sight of his golden hair, lit by the moon.

He's come from working as a waiter at a vampire-themed Italian restaurant located a few blocks south. There, the danger is pretend.

It's past 3 A.M., a few hours before sunrise on New Year's Day, on the wide hike-and-bike trail surrounding Lady Bird Lake. It's a natural border, dividing downtown Austin, Texas, from its south side. *Lake* is something of a stretch. It looks more like what it is — a dammed section of the Colorado River, lined with trees, brush, and parkland — a playground for waterfowl and boaters, famous for its bats.

You can see across it, stroll from one side of the bridges to the other in only a few minutes. Perhaps I'm biased from having resided on the coast of Chicago's formidable Lake Michigan, but, to me, it's more of a water feature than a lake per se.

I slip in my earbuds and raise the volume on my palm-size monitor-com. Now I can hear Zachary's footsteps on the sandy path and the whiz of a stray bottle rocket, punctuated by a loud popping sound.

Last autumn this park was the scene of a handful of murders—the victims found punctured, nearly emptied of blood. Locals hoped that would be the last of it.

Zachary exudes caution. He carries a heavy flashlight, though it's not turned on. He's not emitting heaven's light or showing his wings either, though he regained those powers during our brief time together. My angel makes every effort to operate incognito.

"Reso, reso, resolution," begins a stocky figure, who's somehow doubled back to end up behind Zachary. "Resolved."

Turning, my angel draws his sword from the scabbard with one hand, clicks on his flashlight with the other, and shines it in the eternal's—I mean, vampire's—face.

"Happy New Year, Mitch," he replies. "I've been looking for you."

Mitch isn't displaying his fangs, and his cornflower-blue eyes look as cool as creation. He's dressed up, too. No pj bottoms or camouflage pants tonight. Instead, he's shaved and sporting jeans with a long-sleeved black T designed to mimic a tuxedo shirt, jacket, and tie. He's also holding a cardboard sign, though I can't see what it says.

"Hap, happy," Mitch says. "Happily ever after. The end is beginning. It's the beginning of the end."

Mitch has been homeless for as long as anyone can remember and is affectionately thought of as a local celebrity. Before he first rose undead, Mitch had been pure of heart—so pure that he could identify Zachary, even in human form, as an angel. Typically, only quite young children possess that level of goodness, innocence, and faith.

Some say that Mitch used to build wells in Ecuador with the Peace Corps. Others claim he was wounded in Vietnam. What I know is that Mitch is young for our, or rather, *his* kind. He was infected only last September, and for months, he's been sustaining himself on pig's blood with the love and support of friends.

"We need to talk," Zachary begins. "About that kid you drained last night. . . ."

Mitch stares at his torn sneakers. "He was a druggie, drug dealer."

"He was fourteen. Desperate. Both of his parents lost their jobs last year. He has five younger siblings. They're struggling to make rent."

"Mean, you're mean. I mean, I didn't mean it that way. I was just saying—"

"What are you saying?" Zachary presses.

It's not like him to lose patience. My angel blames himself for the boy's death.

Painful as it is, he's not being unfairly self-flagellating. What happened was foreseeable. If Zachary had already struck Mitch down, the teen would still be alive.

I could've warned him that this would happen, that Mitch could only manage his bloodlust so well for so long.

Then again, perhaps Zachary wouldn't have believed

me. He's a confirmed optimist. He doesn't know the thick, sticky satisfaction of nursing from a savaged, leaking vein. He doesn't miss it like I do.

Mitch replies, "I, I, bye. Bye-bye, Zachary. It's time. Resolution. Resolved."

He holds up his hand-lettered sign. It reads:

HEAVEN
OR
BUST

"You're sure?" my angel asks, and I hear the catch in his voice. He may have set out tonight to remove Mitch as a threat. Yet now that the neophyte is willingly offering to end his existence, it's become a matter of resolve for both of them.

Mitch has taken lives—more than one. He's orchestrated violent, bloody deaths.

Yet I serve as proof that a killer may be forgiven. I was ten times the monster that Mitch is, a fiend to whom other fiends groveled and bowed.

At the same time, Zachary can't know whether he'll be sending his friend to the Penultimate en route to heaven or whether he's condemning a once-kind man to hell.

Zachary turns off the flashlight and tosses it aside. The blade of his sword bursts into flame. Raising the weapon, he begins, "What you're doing . . . Offering yourself to the

Big Boss, there's no better decision you could've made. You're going out a hero."

My angel said as much to me when I begged him to use his holy radiance to burn me to nothingness, when I surrendered my own demonic existence for *true* eternal life.

I can only imagine how painful tonight must be for Zachary, having to once again destroy someone he cares about. No doubt it must bring back memories.

It's archangels who are warriors born, not guardians.

Guardians are sent to earth to care.

"Good, good," Mitch replies. "Good for you. You're good, too. Hero."

Zachary's fiery blade falls on Mitch's last word.

~⧼⧽~ Zachary ~⧼⧽~

IF I SCREW UP AGAIN, I'm one toasted guardian angel (GA). We're talking hellfire and damnation. Hot. Searing hot. Chomp the serrano peppers. Chug the Tabasco.

In case there's any doubt, the archangel Michael himself materializes on the dock to tell me so. "That was unnecessarily costly and dramatic," he announces. "Zachary, how many times must we review this? Though the neophyte vampire's soul may have been temporarily salvageable—"

"He was still tainted by evil," I recite, returning my sword to its scabbard. "When he became an immediate threat to the living, I shouldn't have hesitated to destroy him."

I'm not inclined to argue. Michael is the Sword of Heaven, the Bringer of Souls, my supervisor. Besides, he's right.

I bend to pick up my flashlight and hook it to my belt.

"Once again, you have indulged your feelings at the expense of the greater good," Michael thunders. "Your friend's victim, fourteen-year-old Jorge Alvarez, didn't find out that his father got the janitorial position at Dell until after he recovered from the shock of dying. If Jorge had lived, that drug deal may have been his last."

I'm not sure about that, but it's not worth debating. The boy is dead. That's all that matters now. That and his grieving family.

I'd worried when Mitch didn't stop by over the holidays to pick up his latest supply of pig's blood. I should've assumed the worst and followed up then. But I wanted to give him the opportunity to choose salvation, and he did. Only too late for Jorge.

Sounding weary, Michael says, "You are a slipped angel, Zachary—granted, one who has shown promise. You earned back your wings and the power of heaven's light, and you have put them to good use. But that in no way should be interpreted to mean that your current status, let alone eventual full reinstatement, is guaranteed."

Another bottle rocket whizzes into the night with a bang. Michael adds, "Perhaps this assignment is too much for you."

These days, I'm only specifically assigned to watch over one vamp, a teenager named Quincie Morris. But the deal is that if I can help save every redeemable neophyte, I'll be allowed to return upstairs. I'll be welcomed home, reunited with Miranda.

The only problem? Fulfilling my mission is freaking impossible. Vamps grow in number with each passing night.

Then again, prior to me, the archangel had written off the neophyte undead completely. Devoting one GA to the cause is still better than devoting none.

"Another mistake of this magnitude," Michael adds, "and you'll have exhausted your second chance. I'll have no choice but to recommend that you be permanently exiled from Grace and that your assignment be given to a more capable guardian."

"But—"

"One more mistake, Zachary, and you'll eventually find yourself in hell."

~❀ Kieren ❀~

I HATE SECRETS. From day one, my parents made it clear that I couldn't tell anyone about our family. I can't talk about the fact that Mom's a werewolf, Dad's a human, and I'm a hybrid. Shifters are naturally born. But I can't speak out against humans who claim we're preternatural monsters. I can't fight back when bigots take away jobs. Even lives.

I have a lot at stake. Mom's wedding-planning business. Dad's professorship in engineering. Our middle-class life in the newly repaired McMansion. All that could be ripped away if our family's mixed heritage became public. When my kid sister, Meghan, was born, I had her to protect, too.

Now, I have secrets to keep from my family as well. Two biggies: (1) Quince is a vampire, and (2) Zach is her guardian angel. A secret is a burden. It's exhausting, a lie.

Zach hasn't told Quince what happened with Mitch.

I don't want to see her hurt. What's between me and Quince is more than puppy love. She may not need to breathe, but she's like air to me. If Zach doesn't tell her soon, I'll have to.

When the angel yawns, I push the issue. "So, Zach, when did you come in last night?"

The angel shoots me a reprimanding look.

"Yeah, you weren't here when I got home," Quince adds. She leans into her open refrigerator. She digs through plastic containers and aluminum-foil-covered plates of tamales and casseroles. Leftovers from the holidays. "I called your cell a couple of times. I was about to go looking when I heard you land on the roof."

"I had something to do." Zach disappears into Quince's dining room. He's carrying two glasses of iced tea. A mug of porcine blood is warming for Quince in the microwave.

"Aha!" Quince finally locates the Sanguini's take-out bag. She sets it on her kitchen counter. "I want you guys to try this proposed dish for the catering menu."

Sanguini's is the vampire-themed Italian restaurant that Quince inherited from her late parents. It's closed for

New Year's Day. Last night's party sold out at a thousand dollars a head (75 percent of which was donated to a local food kitchen). It attracted a country-and-western superstar, the latest Heisman Trophy winner, and several NASA astronauts.

Last night I walked her home at 3 A.M. (I don't normally get to stay out so late. We're out of school for winter break.) It's weird for Zach not to leave with her, too. It's his holy mission, watching over Quince.

I'm being too hard on him. It's not like he won't tell her about Mitch. He's just waiting for the right moment.

The microwave dings, and I take out her mug.

Not every guy would be as accepting of my girlfriend's liquid diet. But since I'm part Wolf, the smell of pig's blood makes my canines itch, too.

We join Zach in the dining room.

"Cold Italian pasta salad," Quince announces, setting down the bowl, "with prosciutto, chopped red pepper, chopped red onions, and cannellini beans. Nora let it sit in the fridge overnight."

Nora also left a pot of black-eyed peas on the stove. She's Sanguini's famed and acclaimed chef.

Nora, Zach, and their pal Freddy rent out rooms in Quince's 1930s home. It's not your typical household arrangement. Quince's mom and mine had been best friends since before we were born. My folks are Quince's legal guardians. But last fall, Nora offered to pitch in as an extra supervisory grown-up.

It's better for everyone. It was a nightmare for Quince, trying to pass as human in front of my parents. Meanwhile, my folks didn't want two love-struck, hormonally charged teenagers living under the same roof.

I distribute dinner plates. Zach ducks into the kitchen for silverware and napkins. Tonight, it's just the three of us. Nora went out for sushi with her son, who's visiting from Boston. Freddy is on a date with some Australian guy he met through the rowing club.

They come and go, whereas Zach is a constant fixture. Not that I mind. Usually.

If he were a full-status angel, he'd be invisible. Watching over Quince 24/7. Being slipped, he's corporeal all the time. That makes the logistics of "watching over" more complicated. Among other things, it's seriously cramping my love life.

Don't get me wrong. Zach's a great guy. An angel— literally. Don't think that revelation didn't knock this good Catholic boy off his boots.

But Quince and I need our alone time.

We settle around the antique table. Quince says grace and announces, "We're taking down the Sanguini's holiday decorations before reopening tomorrow. Enough with the fangs and mistletoe. I've had it with *The Nightmare Before Christmas*—"

"Until next year?" I finish.

She blows me a kiss. I laugh. Quince adores the holidays.

She takes a tiny experimental bite of the pasta salad. "Delicious, but I don't know. It says to me, 'corporate picnic,' 'Tarrytown baby shower.' Not 'Sanguini's.'"

"What about taking out the prosciutto?" I suggest. "You could market it as a prey dish." Sanguini's menu is divided into two sections—one for customers who call themselves "predator" and one for those who call themselves "prey."

It's partly a matter of carnivore versus vegetarian. It's partly sexual posturing.

"You're quiet," Quince says to the angel. "You're not eating. Are you feeling okay? You're not sick, are you? Can you get sick?"

"It's my job to keep an eye on you," he replies, "not vice versa."

Waiting, I take a sip of sweet tea. Tonight, it's living up to the "friend" part of boyfriend that's my job. When she needs me, I'll be here.

"Zachary," she prompts, "would you mind picking out the prosciutto and letting me know how it tastes?" For my restaurateur girlfriend, one of the toughest things about being undead is that it's a struggle for her to keep food down. She's still building up her tolerance for anything heartier than gelatin or whipped cauliflower. "Zachary?"

He covers her hand with his own. "You heard about the boy found dead on the lakefront." The angel takes a deep breath. "Well, I found Mitch on the hike-and-bike trail last night after work. It was him. I mean, he—"

"I know what you mean," Quince says, pulling away. "So you—"

"I didn't strike him down against his will," Zach assures her. "Mitch offered his soul up to the Big Boss. He said he was resolved."

"Good." Quince pushes her chair back and stands. "Good for him. We're supposed to be happy for him, right? Isn't that the drill?"

Zach winces. "There's no one way that you're supposed to feel. You—"

At preternatural speed, she bolts out of the room, upstairs and slams her bedroom door behind her. I'll be surprised if the hinges held.

"Should we go after her?" he asks.

I shake my head. "After dinner, I'll go up."

We polish off the pasta salad. Then we head to the back porch to grill up a couple of T-bones. Split a six pack. Dissect U.T. football.

Zach and I have a lot in common. As an earthbound guardian angel and a hybrid werewolf, we're both different from everyone we know. He's been cast out of heaven. I'm no longer welcome at the training pack. We both have big appetites. And we both—or so we're constantly told—have great hair. Plus, we love Quince. In different ways, but she's as precious to him as my little sis is to me.

Then there are our vampire girlfriends.

Quince had her uncertain days. Her blood-starved nights. In the end, though, she became stronger. More confident. Even in undeath, the true Quince thrives.

"When Miranda was upset, she'd run and hide," says Zach. "Mostly in girls' bathrooms."

"Quince isn't hiding," I explain at the picnic table. "She just wants to be alone."

I wish Zach wouldn't compare Quince to Miranda. From what Freddy tells me, Miranda kept a stable of human victims in her castle dungeon. She left drained bodies strewn across the alleys of Chicago. She ordered the tongues cut out of gossiping servants.

Zach pops the tab of a beer. "I never understood my girl like you do Quincie."

I've had a lifetime to get to know Quince. But he'd watched over Miranda from day one. "You mentioned before that you're a young angel. What does that mean?"

He hesitates before answering. "We new angels were created after the first atomic blast in 1945."

"And Miranda was . . . not a senior citizen?"

He laughs. "No, she's not much older than you. She . . ." He pauses. *"What?"*

I'm not sure how to phrase this. Zach may be my buddy, but he's still a holy being. "Aren't you kind of old for her?"

I've traced Brad, the vamp who cursed Quince, to the early twentieth century. He'd hit the preternatural scene by at least the 1920s. He used his experience, his worldliness, to try to seduce her. Just thinking about it makes me want to snarl. So maybe I'm oversensitive about the subject. But I need to know where heaven stands on much older guys going after teenage girls. I want to hear that my faith is justified.

Zach puts down his knife and fork. "You know dog years?"

"Is this a werewolf joke?" I like a good werewolf joke. But I want my answer.

"No. I mean, you know how dogs — how different species — reach maturity at different rates? How they have different life expectancies?"

I nod. Werebirds, for example, mature much faster than weremammals. Life cycles vary. On average, Wolves die fifteen years earlier than humans.

It's unclear what that'll mean for me, a hybrid. But odds are, Quince and Zach will be here years, even centuries, after I'm gone. It makes his answer to my question that much more important. I know that angels can slip, fall. So *how* good of a guy is he?

Zach yawns again. "In angel years, I'm about the age I look. I was born this way, fully grown. I'll look this way forever. But I'm the human equivalent of twenty or so."

Great to know. On the other hand . . . Suddenly, I can't help thinking that guardian angels start working awfully young. On-the-job training?

It's comforting that Zach's not a letch.

Except . . . how qualified is he to guard Quince? It's a dangerous world. With a more dangerous underworld. Given that Zach's slipped already, it's lucky that he hasn't stumbled across anyone more diabolical than his own girlfriend.

~&ra~ Miranda ~&er~

I WOULD PREFER TO avoid the people I've murdered.
Yet it's the second time I've spotted Tamara O. Williams
in the tropical lounge. She's forever age twenty-one, a
weredeer I killed last spring at the ritzy Edison Hotel on
Michigan Avenue in Chicago. She'd been a competitive
swimmer in high school and was a student at the Art
Institute. We both had grandmas named Peggy. I know
most of that from having memorized her obituary.

I pocket my monitor-com and scrunch down on the
love seat to avoid being seen. How could I begin to apologize? How could she ever forgive me? I can't imagine that

even Miss Manners has a suggestion for this particular social predicament.

Fortunately, the Penultimate lounges are always crowded, so there's plenty to distract her eye. I've caught a glimpse of her before and, like now, ducked out of sight.

I'm surprised Tamara is still at the Penultimate. I took every last drop of her lifeblood in late April. It's January first, and I've been here myself since the archangel Michael delivered me in early May. What from Tamara's mortal existence could be haunting her? Or is she simply still furious about my having cheated her out of a longer life?

The Penultimate isn't purgatory. That was made clear at the welcoming reception. No one confirmed or denied whether there actually *is* a purgatory, just that this wasn't it.

Incidentally, nobody said anything about reincarnation either, though I've met a few souls here who're waiting to experience it.

I tend to regard the Penultimate as a sort of ghost world, which isn't far from the truth, though our souls have risen and ghosts are earthbound.

Our spiritual forms mimic the shapes we took in life. Upon arrival, we're all a translucent blue. After a day or two, our color fills back in, though everyone retains a shimmer of blue. I'm uncertain as to whether it's the lighting or the Light.

The landscape is comfortably tropical, home to colorful birds like cockatiels, hummingbirds, and quetzals. Palm trees sway, gentle breezes blow, and bright blooms span larger than my hand. The furnishings are framed in wicker and rattan, accented by koi ponds, and everywhere I look, I see black-and-blue butterflies.

Peeking over the back of the love seat, I'm relieved that Tamara has moved on.

"Miranda Shen McAllister?" A woman in a smartly tailored blue suit offers me a warm smile from the other side of a clipboard. Her name tag reads RENATA (1868 MUNICH–1930 NEW YORK). The staff is made up of souls who've passed through but returned here because their preferred afterlives involve working in these jobs. You can tell them apart from the rest by their professional dress.

"Yes?" I speak when spoken to but otherwise have been fairly antisocial.

"A family member of yours has joined us," Renata announces. "Please follow me to the reunion desk."

A family member? Last I checked, Mom had been laid off from her job selling cosmetics and was considering going back to school for a degree in fashion design. Dad's new wife had told him she wanted to repaint the master bath in some color called Arizona Bisque. They all seemed perfectly healthy. "It's not Grandma Peggy, is it?"

Renata is already zipping across the lounge.

Upon reaching the desk, I resign myself to standing in line. I don't know how long it takes—a tsunami hit India yesterday, and the death toll has passed three thousand.

I take advantage of the opportunity to confirm via my monitor-com that Grandma Peggy is alive, well, and staring at an armadillo-shaped construction-paper ornament that I made for her in art class back in second grade. Its black button eye is missing.

Then a voice announces over the loudspeaker that the second-floor ballrooms have been opened for the tsunami victims, and I find myself at the front of the line.

Renata places a ten-gallon aquarium tank on the desk. "Here you go."

It's my pet gerbil. "Mr. Nesbit!"

"Yes, Mr. Nesbit," Renata agrees, using a quill pen to make a decisive check beside his name. "It's up to you whether to upgrade him to a larger tank. If so, we suggest you wait until he's had time to adjust to eternity. Meanwhile, you're of course welcome to keep him in your quarters. In cases like this, where a pet and owner have been reunited in the Penultimate, both typically pass through the gates together." Renata pauses. "When the time is right."

I'm in no hurry. It was explained at orientation that, though the territory of higher-ranked angels (like archangels) is more fluid, most guardians have been assigned to earth. During transitional periods, they await their next mission here at the Penultimate. They won't return through heaven's gates until after the End Days when there are no more mortal souls to guard—or, in Zachary's case, no more neophyte vampires who might be saved. Consequently, when I finally feel ready to pass through, I'll be leaving Zachary even further behind.

What's more, if he's ever fully reinstated, he might return only briefly to the Penultimate, where he'll wait for the archangel Michael to deploy him again.

"Would you like me to have Mr. Nesbit delivered to your suite?" Renata asks.

"No, thank you," I reply, signing on the line. "I'll take him."

Mr. Nesbit! I can hardly believe it. He looks perky and cozy enough, staring up at me as he chews on a toilet-paper roll. "I missed you."

Last I checked, he'd been living in a tank like this one in Lucy's dorm room at the University of North Texas. The sun has already risen in the central time zone. I wonder if she knows yet that he died.

Sweet Lucy. My human self is considered missing, and she's dedicated herself to searching for me. Her blog, *Missing Miranda,* has thousands of subscribers. She manages tie-in pages on a handful of social networks and has appeared on television dozens of times. I guess we're both unwilling to move on.

Of course, no new leads have panned out. It's often that way when a human is contaminated with vampirism. Not that anyone at the Penultimate could understand what I'm going through. To my knowledge, I'm the only formerly demonic being here. The only one ever to have repented and been forgiven.

It's a miracle what love can inspire, even in a pampered hell beast wearing haute couture.

The Penultimate population wavers between a few to several hundred thousand a day—about the same range as that from Plano to Austin—but feels more intimate because of the side-by-side, honeycomb-shaped residential towers located around a series of interior lounges, places of worship, arts venues, and businesses.

When I first arrived, other ascended souls treated me like a celebrity—many had been watching my and Zachary's love story unfold on their monitor-coms—but almost everyone who was here back then has since passed through.

These days, I spend most of my time alone, gazing down at my angel, and relishing memories of the two of us together. The way he smells, like musk and vanilla, the way he held me when we danced.

I'm more comfortable having a lower profile. People come and leave every day, and it's not as though I waltz around introducing myself as an ex-vampire princess.

~❀ Kieren ❀~

IT'S AFTER TEN O'CLOCK. No sign of Quince. I don't hear her moving around upstairs.

She and Mitch became pals in middle school. It was after her parents died in that car accident. He'd fall in step with her on the way to school.

She balked at first. Not because he was homeless. Or because his mind didn't work like most people's. She'd withdrawn from all of her friends except me. Mitch didn't give up, though. Or maybe he didn't realize she wanted to be alone.

This fall, when Quince found out Mitch was a vampire,

she started supplying him with porcine blood. Over time, Zach began counseling Mitch, too.

The angel has retreated to his futon in the attic. Freddy isn't home yet. Nora already went to bed. I knock lightly on Quince's door.

She asks, "What took you so long?"

I inch the door open. She's sitting cross-legged in the dark on her calico-print bedspread. "Should I have come up sooner?"

"I want to show you something." Quince moves off the bed. She reaches under it for a piece of torn cardboard that reads:

FRECKLE-FACED RED-HAIRED GIRL'S SMILE = SUNSHINE

Mitch was famous for his signs.

"When I saw this, I laughed out loud for the first time since Mama and Daddy's funeral. You know, Mitch helped convince me to give the world another chance."

"Like Zach did," I say, "after you became undead."

That sounded more pointed out loud than it had in my head.

Quince stares at Mitch's sign for a long moment. Then she stores it in the chest at the foot of her bed. "You're right." She reaches for my hand. "About Mitch, I'm not being a baby. I'm not mad at Zachary. I know he had no choice."

"Nobody thinks you're being a baby," I reply. "Least of all me."

~∾ Miranda ∾~

GUEST SUITES ARE ARRANGED like those at an atrium hotel. Each has one window that looks out to the heavens and another that opens to a tiered walkway above the nearest promenade and lobby lounge. Otherwise, the décor has been personalized.

When I arrived, mine featured framed theater posters—for *Chicago, Grease, Macbeth*—and shelves of fantasy novels. It's not like any room I've lived in before, yet it's exactly what I would select for myself now.

My understanding is that the respective guardians usually coordinate with interior designers, based on their knowledge of their assignments. Since Zachary was earth-bound, his best friend, the guardian Joshua, stepped in for my job. The multicolor feathered boas hanging from the coatrack? Definitely Joshua's influence.

We ascended souls don't have to sleep, but sitting cushions are provided for those who choose to meditate. I toss one onto my window seat next to where, a couple of days ago, I put my gerbil's tank so he'd have a view of the moons and stars.

At the moment, he's more interested in the tiny black-and-blue butterfly climbing up the glass. "Mr. Nesbit, now that you're here, the place feels more like home."

I don't know if every animal ascends or if only pets do because that's in keeping with the promise of heaven. Are the koi, the birds and butterflies, born in heaven or earth?

I don't know a lot of things. I've hardly explored the Penultimate beyond my neighborhood. I've heard that other areas are more in keeping with other cultural and religious expectations, though my local population is clearly diverse in terms of heritage, dress, faith, and fandoms. The African-Canadian gentleman living next door, for example, dresses like a *Star Trek* officer, and his was one of the three picture windows on our floor last month to feature a Hanukkah menorah. Likewise, some holy experiences are tailored to specific faiths—how angels manifest, for example. On this side of death, seemingly contradictory belief systems coexist more comfortably.

"Why don't we see how Lucy's doing?" I say, raising myself onto the cushion. "I bet she's already missing you."

I touch a few buttons and peer at the screen of my monitor-com. The reception isn't good, static perhaps. Possibly the weather is causing interference.

I shake the device, which seems to help, and notice that my best friend has had her hair cut. It bounces beneath her chin.

"My, you're here early!" exclaims someone I've never seen before.

He's tall, as tall as a guardian. Perhaps taller. He has no eyebrows or eyelashes or facial hair. He's bald in a good-looking way. My first thought is chemo, but he exudes health, strength. Perhaps it's an allergy or stress response or chemical reaction. He's leaning against a doorframe and watching Lucy unpack. "You were originally expected to be our last check-in, and now you're our first."

"I hope it's okay that I let myself in," she says. "The front door was unlocked."

"Completely okay. You just caught me by surprise. Have you had a chance to look around yet? It's a brand-new building, state of the art."

"Not yet." Lucy rubs her arms. "Mr., um—"

"You can call me Seth. It's nice to finally meet you in person. I can't tell you how much I enjoyed our chats on the phone."

"About the heat?"

Seth offers a wry smile. "The heat is on. It'll take a while to warm up."

Who is Seth? Is he flirting with her?

A chime resonates throughout the ultramodern building.

"Shall we see who that is?" Seth asks.

Lucy abandons her stack of sweaters—price tags still attached—and jeans on the platform bed, shoves a key into her back pocket, and follows him.

Through her window, I can see several inches—feet?—of snow on the ground. Those hills, the pines! That's not the University of North Texas. Where is she?

I use the monitor-com to look around. Five identical rooms are located on each side of the hallway, making ten altogether—three on each side to the east of the stairs and elevator, two to the west along with an opposing laundry room and kitchenette.

The furniture is metal framed and contemporary, in black, white, and gray with glass tabletops and canvas cushions. Each bedroom features an armoire, full-size bed, and dresser (against a side wall); a desk set loaded with office supplies (centered, facing the door); a Euro recliner with matching ottoman (alongside the window wall); and an empty shelf unit next to the unlit fireplace (on the other side wall).

In addition, each room has a walk-in closet and a rest-room with a toilet, sink, medicine cabinet, mirror, towel bar, and glass-walled shower with a black tile floor. Plush gray bath linens have been rolled and piled artfully on metal-bar shelves.

Back in the main living area, a digital wall clock hangs above the door. The floors are likewise tiled in black, the walls are painted snowy white, and the ceilings soar thirty feet high. The overhead lights are cold fluorescents. The outside-facing wall is made up of tinted floor-to-ceiling windows, and a dead bolt has been installed in each of the thick doors.

The only pieces of art—framed in silver lacquered metal, hanging above each streamlined black lava-rock mantel—are prints of the same painting, depicting a yellow, potbellied monster with a scaled head, red horns, red claws on his four fingers and toes, and a red tongue protruding from his bluish-green face. The colors are brightly modern to Day-Glo, and the image repeats four times in two rows of two.

If my eternal-art education is worth anything, the style is a tribute to Andy Warhol. The beast is naked, except for a diaperlike cloth around his waist to cover his privates, though he's squatting so low that it looks like his dewclaws are about to skewer them. His expression is mischievous, as if he's barely keeping a secret. The eyes suggest an ancient evil, some *thing* that's having fun. The effect is disconcerting, goblinlike . . . creepy in a way that crawls beneath your toenails and digs.

As Lucy and Seth chat about the weather ("How's the skiing?"), I zoom in to view the third floor and take note of the seminar-style room, the library, and the restrooms. The same devilish print is the artistic focal point in each of those spaces, too. I move the monitor-com focus up and get no reception for the fourth floor. It's all gray.

When did Lucy decide to transfer to a new school? I should've been paying more attention to her. However radiant Zachary may be, I was wrong to neglect my best friend.

The doorbell sounds again, and I zoom in to locate Lucy and Seth in the foyer. He opens the massive door.

The new arrival's salty blond hair looks salon styled, her clothes designer label, and her cosmetics professionally applied.

"You must be Seth!" she exclaims, rising on her toes to kiss him full on the lips. "I can't believe I made it." She glances at Lucy. "Don't you hate the weather?"

As a chauffeur begins unloading her fifteen-piece luggage set, Seth introduces the girl as Vesper Simon. I change screen functions to do an online search.

We ascended souls are unable to post messages or other content on the Web, but we're welcome to read what's out there.

Here it is. Vesper is the daughter of some financial guru worth $139.8 billion. Last year, Vesper herself was named Massachusetts It Girl by a local society magazine, and she's been romantically linked to a minor Kennedy.

The chauffeur wheels another of Vesper's trunks inside, and Seth admits, "I'm afraid I have to hit the road in a few minutes. The caretakers will arrive any moment, and they'll finish getting you settled."

Vesper yanks off her mink-lined black leather gloves. "I thought—"

"It's the nature of the job." Seth helps Vesper out of her fur jacket. "Tables to man, brochures to distribute, students to recruit. A glamorous life. I travel a lot, but I do have an office on the fourth floor, and you'll see me again before you know it."

Zooming out, I observe that the academy is a Mies van der Rohe–looking, four-story, rectangular building made of uniform thin steel columns supporting massive panes of tinted glass. What appears to be the basement is aboveground, and both the circular drive and the blackstone staircase leading to the entrance have been shoveled and sprinkled with sand.

The structure sits nestled among taller snow-blanked hills (mountains?) on wooded land alongside a fair-size lake, which is oddly not frozen. The closest waterline is about a hundred feet from the front of the structure.

It tightly wraps around the east side, though, and laps against glass and metal. I zoom in on the chiseled gray stone sign above the front door, an archaic contrast to the otherwise modern architecture.

It reads: SCHOLOMANCE PREPARATORY ACADEMY.

-ᴥ Zachary ᴥ-

I'M YOUNG FOR A GA. I've had only three formal assignments, but I've still managed to blow each of them to varying degrees.

Dan "the Man" Bianchi graduated from altar boy to small-time crooked politician. Alcohol led to drugs, prostitutes, and an early, ugly end in an upscale hotel suite. Only Nonna Bianchi and Dan's cousin, Vaggio, showed up at the funeral to pray for the boy Dan had once been. (The same Vaggio Bianchi who served as Sanguini's original chef. The Big Boss works in mysterious ways.)

Then my girl, my Miranda. A one-time North Dallas teen. She obsessed over Tolkien, dreamed of stage acting, mourned her parents' failed marriage, and played the loyal sidekick to her adventurous best friend.

One winter night I broke heaven's rules and revealed myself in full glory—corporeal, shining, wings and all—to warn her of an impending fall into an open grave. I'd worried she'd break her neck. I'd figured the appearance of an angel would reassure her. Instead, she panicked at the sight of me and fled.

Then the vamp king himself intercepted Miranda. Captured her, made her undead, and presented her to the underworld as his daughter and heir.

She lost her humanity. I lost my wings, my powers, and my full angelic status.

After some months of pointless wandering and burying my sorrow in booze and Miranda look-alikes, Michael assigned me to masquerade as my girl's personal assistant. I found her irresistible, even in undeath. Miraculously, she fell for me in return.

We joined forces to defeat the king, and in the final battle, my wings and radiance were restored. She begged me to use heaven's light to destroy her tainted form. To save her soul by ending her earthly existence. And, out of love, I did.

Now I'm supposed to watch over Quincie. She's got the bravado of Pippi Longstocking, the humor and wry dignity of a young Katharine Hepburn.

She's also wholly souled—the very first (and so far

only) one of her kind to have ever resisted taking a life. A fact that I realized only *after* trying to convince her to end it all. Fortunately, she believed enough in herself to figure it out in time.

At sunrise, I'm pleased to find my latest assignment propped on a chaise lounge on her new screened-in back porch. Quincie avoided me yesterday, but I take this as a sign that she wants to talk. Normally, she'd be chatting with Nora and hovering over the pastry team in Sanguini's kitchen.

"Does your cell phone range go all the way to heaven?" she asks, flipping through a restaurant-supply catalog. "Can you talk to other angels?"

"Good morning to you, too," I reply. "No, my phone is a Samsung. Not heaven-sent, like my sword. My supervisor Michael appears sometimes, mostly to yell at me. My buddy Joshua visits, too."

"Michael and Joshua are angels?"

"Full status," I say, bracing myself. "Josh is my best friend."

"Could you ask him if he's seen Mitch in heaven?"

There it is. Not long after we first met, I scolded her to respect heaven's mysteries. It's become a joke between us. Quincie asks, and I don't tell. I'm tempted sometimes. But I'm in enough trouble already without divulging more secrets. Granted, I confided in Kieren last night about angels and aging. I really should watch my mouth after a couple of beers. But that wasn't heaven-and-hell stuff. Certain separations exist between the living and the dead, even between the dead and undead, for a reason.

"Never mind," Quincie says, apparently resigned. "Truth is, I've thought more than once that it might become my responsibility to take my axe to Mitch. You spared me that." Brightening, she changes the subject. "By the way, how many times have I told you not to come outside without clothes on? You're going to cause a riot."

What? "I'm *not* naked."

I'm wearing the oversize white terry-cloth robe and slippers that Nora gave me for my birthday. Plus, under the robe, I've got on boxers with fanged smiley faces on them, a gift from Miranda.

Thinking Quincie is teasing, I open the *Statesman* to the sports section.

Then she points up at three middle-aged ladies, partially hidden by the vine-wrapped treetops. They're taking turns studying me through a telescope mounted on the third-floor balcony of the backyard neighbor's house.

I guess I have been coming out here on mornings fairly regularly.

I wave, which sends them squealing and ducking for cover.

~⚙️ Miranda ⚙️~

I APPROACH THE UNIFORMED DOORMAN for my honey-comb tower at the Penultimate. His name is Huan (1945 Oakland–2002 Oklahoma City), and he looks like Grandpa Shen, only plumper.

"Howdy, Miranda," Huan says. "What can I do for you?"

"I'm looking for a book, though it may not be permit-ted here. I wouldn't blame anyone if it weren't. I—"

"The title?"

I close my eyes and steel myself for his response. *"The Blood Drinker's Guide."*

"Would you like a hard copy? Or I can show you how to download the text to your monitor-com. It has an e-reader built in."

It does? I'm certain someone explained that at registration, but I was distracted by being newly dead. Since then, watching over Zachary and, to a lesser extent, Lucy and my family has occupied most of my attention, so I haven't played with the device like I otherwise might've. "How long will it take for a hard copy?"

"English language?" He hits a button on the stand and keys in the title. The guide materializes. "The macabre is fascinating, don't you think? Have you ever read Oscar Wilde's *The Picture of Dorian*—"

"Thanks!" I grab the guide. "I have emergency research to do."

"Emergency?" he echoes as I sprint toward the elevator. "Here?"

I'm tempted to grab the nearest lounge chair, but I'm not convinced everybody is as open-minded about demonic literature as Huan is. So I'm sprinting around souls floating down the promenade (theoretically, we could concentrate, dissipate, and pass through each other, but it's considered rude) when someone calls, "Your Highness!"

Everybody gawks. Though death is the ultimate equalizer, royalty still garners attention. "Princess Miranda!"

I'm not the only Miranda, of course. Yet how many of

the others used to be princesses? Everywhere I look, there are strangers, then . . .

"Harrison!" I exclaim.

Flashy in a shiny gold tux, my onetime castle servant zigzags through the crowd, raises my fingertips, and formally bends to kiss the back of my hand.

First Mr. Nesbit, and now this! I'm *not* the only formerly demonic being in the Penultimate. Like me, Harrison was undead when he met his end. He had been a prized legacy servant, the last of a five-generation line. In that role and, later, as a neophyte eternal, Harrison caused (or at least facilitated) unfathomable bloodshed.

Yet last October, he fought by Zachary's side and sacrificed himself to the holy light as enemy eternals closed in. Harrison gave up his demonic, earthly existence so that his friends and brother might live. He died as something far better than he'd ever been in life—a gallant gentleman.

I exclaim, "I never expected to see *you* here!"

Anyone else would be insulted. Harrison laughs and twirls me on the promenade. "Look who's talking! Your Highness, you were the most splendidly fearsome creature—"

I stop in place and shush him. "I'm past all that."

"Are you?" Harrison replies.

Yes. No. "We have bigger problems. Come with me."

I should apologize for ordering him around like

that—I'm no longer a pampered royal, and he's no longer my sarcastic servant—except he seems to be relishing it.

Harrison notes the book I'm carrying. "That looks familiar."

Minutes later in my suite, I've explained about Lucy and we've opened *The Blood Drinker's Guide* to the section about a certain famed count. Harrison points to the entry on the first Dracula, sometimes referred to as Dracula Prime.

Though royal eternals have long since adopted the name Dracul as an honorific, the original was a beast of unprecedented ferociousness who used sorcery to reinvent himself as a Carpathian vampire—a far more powerful and insidious breed of eternal than the prevalent undead today. It's *where* the count learned that sorcery that concerns me.

"According to the infamous, blathering Dr. Abraham Van Helsing," Harrison begins from the sofa, "Dracula Prime 'dared even to attend the Scholomance, and there was no branch of knowledge of his time that he did not essay.' It's the Evil One's school, Your Highness, a slice of hell on earth."

I pace, wringing my hands. "When you say 'Evil One,' you don't mean—"

"I mean Lucifer. Satan, the devil, the beast, the

adversary, the prince of darkness, the prince of pain, the father of lies, the deceiver, the cloven hoofed, the serpent, the spoiler, Old Scratch, Old Horny, the fallen—"

"Enough!" I exclaim.

"Angel," he adds at the same time.

I recall a sermon my minister gave back in Dallas—something about the archangel Lucifer falling like a star, he and those angels who followed him. Or maybe it was Shakespeare: "Angels are bright still, though the brightest fell."

"The Scholomance is located in the mountains of Eastern Europe," Harrison goes on. "I don't recollect there being a satellite campus in Vermont or anywhere else." He checks the index. "There's no mention of one in this edition. Did you try the Web?"

Vaguely embarrassed, I slip the monitor-com out of my sweater pocket. "I've been using this almost exclusively to—"

"Spy on your hunkalicious guardian back on terra firma? Be still, my celestial heart, I, too, have let my screen linger on his pert but muscular gluteus maximus."

Ignoring that confession, I exclaim, "I also check on my parents! My best friend Lucy! Furthermore, it's not spying, it's . . . watching over."

Harrison takes the monitor-com from me. "Whatever you say, Your Highness. Or do you prefer Your Majesty? You were, however briefly, queen."

I'd rather not be reminded of that. "I prefer Miranda."

"I don't. What's your read on this Seth fellow you mentioned?"

I pause. "He seemed friendly enough. Young, over-eager. He could be a dupe."

"Oh, dear." Harrison looks up from the screen. "According to the website, Scholomance Preparatory Academy on New Hermannstadt Street in Montpelier, Vermont, is indeed affiliated with the flagship institution in the Carpathian Mountains."

As I bury my face in my hands, he adds, "It's a feeder school to the original."

With a groan, I sink into a seated position, cross-legged on the carpet.

Harrison, meanwhile, rattles off factoids: "Students are required to live on campus. While foreign students are limited to submitting applications to the Romanian campus only, that's expected to change in the near future. Admissions are rolling. The first-ever U.S.-based classes are scheduled to begin this coming winter-spring semester on January seventh. Orientation is on the sixth." After a pause, he adds, "The website is mum on the curriculum."

I spread my fingers and peek through them. "What do you think?"

He purses his lips. "You're wise to fear for your friend."

~✿ Miranda ✿~

I'M LURKING in the reception area outside the Office of the Archangel Michael in hopes of running into Joshua, being eyed warily by a receptionist/assistant named Yasmeen (1965 Istanbul–2002 Istanbul), and flipping through old newspapers and magazines.

In 1929, William C. DeMille became the second president of the Academy of Motion Picture Arts and Sciences. He followed Douglas Fairbanks.

In 1984, a weredolphin, who'd been performing in animal form at a California water park, was outed and accused of being a Soviet spy.

In 1961, John F. Kennedy was the *Time* magazine Person of the Year. I remember when Lucy and I visited the Sixth Floor Museum on an eighth-grade field trip. It nearly moved me to tears.

After two hours, I approach the reception desk. "Excuse me, my name is—"

"I know who you are," Yasmeen replies. "You don't have an appointment."

The Office of the Archangel Michael isn't known for its touchy-feely-ness. "Will Joshua be done soon?"

Few guardians check in so regularly and in person with Michael. However, it's common knowledge that the archangel is especially interested in Zachary and that Joshua has been assigned to him. It's unusual for one guardian to watch over another. Then again, it's unusual for an angel to slip and become earthbound.

"At the Penultimate," Yasmeen says, "we encourage ascended souls to focus on making peace with their time among the living, not on socializing with guardians who have important business elsewhere."

The promenade is reminiscent of those at amusement parks. Some people appear as if they're on a mission, others like they're out for a stroll. A famous face catches my eye—a young Hollywood actor. I had such a crush on him in middle school. He's shorter in person, less airbrushed. He looks disappointed. I wonder how he died.

Of late, newly ascended souls have included the lead singer of a popular girl band that went down in a small plane and a baseball star who died on a Jet Ski.

Despite being dead, and undead before that, I still find myself attuned to news out of the U.S. However, I'm told that on the other side of the pearly gates, national alliances fade fast. Heaven is a place without borders, and there's no such thing as a language barrier. I'm not certain of the mechanics, but basically it's like everyone has a Federation universal translator. I pause on the promenade as a werecat in animal form springs by.

Behind me, a voice whispers, "Psst! Miranda!"

"Hello?" I turn all the way around. "Hello?"

A tall, feminine figure steps to my side. "I'm the guardian Idelle."

Like all angels, she's exquisite—in her case, with waist-long, dark, curly hair, full breasts, wide hips, and long, tapered fingers. She's wearing the standard guardian uniform—the white robes and strappy gold sandals.

"You're Zachary's former assignment?" she asks.

I pause. "Yes, I'm Miranda."

"Walk and talk," Idelle urges, and we merge into the crowd. "Is it true, what they say you were?"

I didn't realize "they" were talking. I glance at my hands as if I can still see the blood on them. "Yes."

"I heard another vampire connected to Zachary arrived in October."

"That would be Harrison," I reply.

"And a third only two days ago?"

Cheered, I reply. "Mitch." I didn't realize how much I'd come to root for him until after he died for good. "He's here at the Penultimate?"

"No, he's the uncomplicated sort. He proceeded through the gates right away."

Last night my angel returned to the site of Mitch's destruction. He lit a candle, said a prayer, and downed a tequila shot. If only I could reassure him that his friend died at peace.

"Three fully redeemed vampires." Idelle purses her lips. "My first assignment—an exceptional young man, a firefighter and father of two—was cursed with unholy blood, and so I was immediately reassigned. Now, I learn that he might still have been saved—"

"At least for the first year or so," I put in, oddly reminded of castle politics.

"Yes, *for that long*, I abandoned him to face probable damnation when there was still a chance that he could've eventually joined us upstairs."

A parakeet swoops between us and then angles higher, above the crowd.

"Should we be talking about this?" My minister often said that God was everywhere, but I feel his presence here at the Penultimate in a way I never did before. If he's listening, the last thing I want—me, of all souls—is to show disrespect.

It's as if Idelle can read my mind. "Michael is my supervisor, but he's not the Big Boss. He's been given a lot of leeway in running the GA operation. That doesn't mean he's infallible or omnipresent."

"You're certain that Michael can't hear us?" I'm not eager to antagonize him either.

"Not unless he's making a special effort, and if he's going to take anyone to task, it'll be me, not you."

Of all the luck! There's unrest among heaven's angels, and Zachary and I have become symbolic of their main point of contention. This can't help his chances of reinstatement, our dream of reuniting someday.

As the lobby lounge comes into view, Idelle changes the subject. "I heard that you were looking for Joshua. He's working in the stables today, which is strange. He should be watching over Zachary. I suspect Michael ordered him there to think."

I take an uncertain step forward. "The stables?"

"Straight ahead until you reach the entertainment district, all the way past the clock at the corner of Marshall Field's, and turn right at the theater in the round."

"Marshall Field's?" I echo.

"Great stores go to heaven," she replies. "Don't say that I sent you."

I've heard tales of heaven's chariots, and I know that ascended souls can sign up for group tours of the stables on Mondays, Wednesdays, and Fridays. However, this is my first time here. These magnificent black horses are definitely born of heaven, not earth. They snort and whinny and shake their manes, yet project a greater majesty.

Something is missing, though. The smell of hay, sweat, even manure.

While the Penultimate has its blessings, newly ascended souls, unassigned guardians, and the staff who serve them forgo sensory and, for that matter, sensual delights. No food, no drink, no lovemaking. Apparently, celestial horses don't eat either.

I find Joshua brushing a stallion. Instead of his guardian uniform, he's sporting a long-sleeved, western-style shirt with black jeans and boots. He's tied back his dreads with a gold cord, and his belt buckle reads: HEAVENLY.

In my undead days, I met Joshua once in passing. He was pretending to be a waiter at an Irish-themed chain restaurant in Chicago. My heart may be spoken for, but he's not someone I'd ever forget. One of the most popular odes in the Penultimate is a tribute to his lush eyelashes. Another celebrates his toned thighs.

"Miranda!" Joshua exclaims. "Hey, girl, I was going to find you later."

I seize the opening. "Listen, I need you to tell Zachary—"

"Whoa." At the stallion's snort, Joshua says, "Not you, boy." Returning his attention to me, he explains, "My cranky-face archangel supervisor just totally busted me for playing messenger boy."

"I'm sorry about that, but—"

"Now, you know that nobody is a bigger Miranda-Zachary 'shipper than me. In his time of need and misdeed, I have been Zachary's most loyal wingman. But I can't keep on—"

"I wouldn't ask if it weren't important," I begin, launching into the story.

When I finish, Joshua says, "Don't. Panic. Lucy has her own GA."

"Then can you tell her guardian that—"

"GAs aren't supposed to compare notes. As Michael says, 'Collusion could lead to interference' with our assignments' free will."

I cross my arms. "Well, whoever it is obviously isn't doing a good job of—"

"An angel may encourage," Joshua recites, patting the horse, "may inspire, may nudge, but each soul ultimately chooses its own fate."

"I can't believe this!" I compose myself as a tour

group approaches. "You're trying to tell me to take comfort in the fact that Lucy has a guardian, and you're trying to tell me that guardians are so limited as to be effectively useless." I fight to compose myself. "What about you?"

"You know I'm assigned to Zachary. Besides—"

"Zachary would *want* to know that Lucy is in trouble. He'd *want* to help her."

While Joshua digests my argument, I notice a young man from the tour group eyeing us. He looks familiar, but I can't quite place him. Then I notice his T-shirt. It reads: ARTEMIS GYROS, CHICAGO, ILLINOIS. "Oh, my God! I have to go."

"What? Why?"

"That man over there? I killed him." He smelled of lamb and cloves and rosemary. I broke his neck to get a better angle. "He's the first person I ever drained."

-\#\#⊙ Zachary ⊙\#\#-

I'VE GROWN TO LOVE this fuel-sucking car. It's a 1987 Impaler, a black SUV with red racing stripes, a classic. It used to belong to Miranda. She's so petite. I remember her sitting on a phone book so she could see over the hood. My girl had her sexy moments and her sinister ones, but sometimes she exuded cute.

I've been stuck on I-35 north behind an 18-wheeler with Utah plates for the last half hour. It shouldn't be much longer. According to the radio news, the wreck near the Buda exit has been cleared. No serious injuries or fatalities, thank the Big Boss.

I send a text message to Quincie to let her know I'll be a few minutes late for work. I spent the afternoon with a real-estate agent, talking about selling Quincie's compound outside San Antonio. Quincie inherited it from an egomaniacal vamp who most recently went by the name Brad. She decided she'd rather spend the afternoon shopping with Freddy for a catering van than road-tripping with me.

I suspect part of that decision was about her commitment to all things Sanguini's and part of it was a desire to avoid memories of Brad himself. Her undeath was his fault.

As I toss my cell into the front passenger seat, Joshua materializes in time to catch it. "Hello, earth angel! I bring news from your beloved in the great beyond."

"Miranda!" I grin. "How is she?"

Josh tells me that my girl and Harrison have been reunited. Mr. Nesbit is with her, too. It's awesome news on both counts, especially Harrison. Despite his grand final gesture, I'd honestly doubted he'd make the cut.

Josh goes on to fill me in on Lucy's transfer from U.N.T. to the newly established Scholomance Preparatory Academy in New England. "Bottom line," he concludes, "Miranda wants you to boogie up there ASAP and convince Lucy to skedaddle."

I think it over, weighing my duty to Quincie. "Lucy may not trust me."

"Dude, are you seriously telling me that you're not going to try?"

We've met before, Lucy and me, the night Miranda was taken from Chrysanthemum Hills Cemetery in Dallas. After my girl was taken, my powers yanked, I heard Lucy cry for help. I found her in the clutches of a vamp and scared him off.

I'll never forget Lucy, in the midst of her living nightmare, saying, "If there are monsters, there must be heroes. You're the hero, right?"

She'd nearly lost her life. She'd been confronted with the true demonic for the first time. Most people would've been rocking in the fetal position.

Not Lucy. She immediately started looking for Miranda. She's the one who called the cops. She's the one who gave me her trench coat when I found myself an outcast from heaven, shivering in the wind.

I excused myself, supposedly to look for clues. Then I ditched her once I heard the sirens. Back then, I had no way of explaining who I was, what I was.

I left Lucy alone on the worst night of her life.

As traffic picks up, Josh changes the radio station and an old Dixie Chicks song comes on. "Um, Zachary?" he prompts. "You're not going to send me upstairs to Miranda with a 'no,' are you? Don't get me wrong. You know I'm a fan. But she was undead royalty, and every once in a while, I see a flash of that old temper and—"

"Tell my girl . . ." I hit my signal to switch lanes. "Tell her I'll do what I can."

~ Kieren ~

"I TRIED CALLING this so-called Scholomance Preparatory Academy," Zach concludes that evening in Quince's dining room. "The guy who answered said that I wasn't on Lucy's list of approved callers. Worse, they don't allow unapproved visitors on school grounds."

I open a leather-bound text on the table. "Sounds like a security measure. If we're talking about an elite school for children of the rich and famous, that's not unreasonable."

My instincts are telling me Zach's not overreacting. But he's got to calm down.

Earlier, the angel left me an ominous message, asking that I bring whatever I had on the Scholomance. My mom raised me to become a Wolf studies scholar. I've got an impressive home library. But I could fit everything I found on the academy into my backpack.

"Or it might be a cultish isolation strategy," Zach counters. "Maybe by the time they're through orientation, the students have broken ties with the outside world."

"Let's not rush to 'cultish isolation,'" Quince says from behind her laptop at the table. "Do you have any experience with this kind of thing?"

"GAs don't engage the enemy directly," Zach answers. "That's archangel territory. I'm not knocking on Satan's schoolhouse door without more information. I learned better than that from you two."

Still, his bags are already packed, holy sword and all.

Quince begins reading from her screen. "Ground was broken on Scholomance Preparatory Academy, a private school in Vermont, just over a year ago." She glances up. "The land was bought at public auction, and the buyer tore down the main house, which gave the historic preservationists hissy fits. . . ."

I'm slowly turning yellowed pages. "The consensus is that the flagship school in the Carpathians was originally a benevolent gathering place. It welcomed sorcerers, magi, shamans, and the like. Over the ages, it may have fallen victim to corrupting forces. Some claim it's a place where good and evil cross swords. Others argue it's a school of pure villainy. However . . ."

I reach for a slimmer, more modern-looking volume and open it to a chapter I bookmarked earlier. "A handful of modern scholars—most notably a weresloth from Venezuela—have theorized that it's a neutral ground. A place where magic makers, the wicked and the honorable, come together on a joint quest for all there is to know."

"Ambitious." Quince takes a drag of porcine blood from her U.T. sports bottle. "Though not necessarily satanic. Is it possible that Lucifer lost interest in the school?"

Zach leans over my shoulder to read. "Anything's possible. But my girl sent down the alarm for a reason. From upstairs, she can see for herself what's happening to Lucy."

I move into the living room and turn on the Weather Channel. "Flights have been grounded all over the Northeast," I call. "But we should be okay on the interstates."

In the human world, Zach doesn't legally exist. He doesn't have a birth certificate, a social-security number, or any valid form of ID. So he can't get on a commercial airplane. Plus, there's the issue of our weapons.

"You're not coming along," he replies, walking in. "If Quincie doesn't ride up with me, I can't make the trip. Technically, as her GA, I shouldn't risk separating—"

"If Quince's going, I'm going."

"What would you tell your parents?" he wants to know. "What about school?"

"My parents are Quince's legal guardians," I remind him. "My high school is her high school. Nothing much happens the first week of the semester anyway. I'm a straight-A student. Quince rocked her finals last month. I'll tell my folks we're going to visit a friend of yours up north. That's the truth—"

"Technically," Quince says at the entryway.

"We drive," Zach agrees, muting the TV. "At least if something happens to me, I won't be abandoning Quincie completely. You two will wait at a hotel while I—"

"Wait?" Quince says. "What are you talking about? We're *seniors.* We've faced down monsters before. Do you really think we would let you go off—"

"Enough!" The angel throws his hands in the air. "For the love of the Big Boss, Quincie, you are my principle assignment. My wholly souled, high-risk, undead principle assignment. It's my sworn duty to protect you. If you were human . . . Forget it. If you were a freaking martial-arts-master *werebear,* I wouldn't let you anywhere near the God-damned place! I might as well renounce the Big Boss and march us both straight to hell."

That quiets her.

"What about me?" I ask. "You may be our resident expert on heaven. But I've been studying the demonic since I was old enough to read." When he doesn't answer, I add, "You need my help, Zach. If you didn't, you wouldn't have called."

We're not leaving until dawn because Zach wants to talk to Freddy first.

Meanwhile, Quince and I stop by Sanguini's. We touch base with Nora. Then we hit my house so I can pack. I don't have much cold-weather gear. No snow boots. No winter coat. I grab a couple of long-sleeved T-shirts. An extra pair of jeans.

On my bedroom carpet, Quince plays tug-of-war — using a thick, knotted white rope — with the quickly growing German shepherd pups, Pecos and Concho.

Nora will take care of the dogs while we're gone.

"Have you considered stretch denim?" Quince asks.

I pat my flat stomach. "You trying to tell me something?"

She laughs, and Pecos bounds up to lick her face. "News flash, Wolf man. You're stretchy. Shape-change-y. For those shifts when you can't start au naturel, it might be nice not to trash your whole outfit. Less painful and expensive, too."

I hold up a ski boot that fit back in sixth grade. Then I toss it back in the closet. My black cowboy boots will have to do. "You don't find tattered shirts sexy?"

"On you?" Quince replies, suddenly flirtatious. "Or off you?"

Uh . . . "Which would you prefer?"

We didn't tell Zach. But yesterday my folks took Meghan with them to a destination wedding that Mom is working in Hawaii. They'll be gone two and a half weeks. We'll call. We'll text. Quince and I will be back before they realize we've left. I hope.

"I've never seen Zachary so freaked out," she says, scratching Concho's belly. "I get that he's worried about Miranda's friend, and any place associated with the devil is profoundly disturbing, but—"

"It's the 'Miranda' in that sentence that's your answer," I reply. "Love makes people crazy." I pull Quince up and kiss the tip of her nose. "I should know."

Her half smile reminds me that we don't leave until sunrise. Temptation tugs.

Thank God that my family is off doing the hula.

Thank God that her guardian angel has other plans.

~❦ Zachary ❦~

AT 2:30 A.M., Nora comes home and informs me that Quincie stopped by the restaurant with Kieren but didn't stay to work. Quincie loves to work.

When she doesn't answer her phone, I jog to the Morales house and catch a glimpse of her silhouette intertwined with Kieren's through the Wolf's bedroom window. The world over, GAs are watching over assignments in more intimate clenches.

But my being corporeal makes sticking around seem, at most, perverted and, at least, like I should get a life.

~

At 3 A.M., Freddy pours us each a cup of coffee and adds a shot of Baileys to his. "The devil himself, eh?"

Freddy is firmly human, about forty with bleached hair and wire-rimmed glasses. Each night at the restaurant he plays Count Sanguini, leading dinner guests in a midnight toast.

He was raised in the human servant community that caters to upper-echelon vamps. As an adult, Freddy made a life for himself on the fringes of that underworld. He stuck around only because his twin, Harrison—the same Harrison who's keeping my girl company upstairs—was the personal assistant to the undead king. Freddy's not the kind of guy who could just walk away. He couldn't leave his own brother to the monsters, even if Harrison was staying by choice.

"About your plan to rescue this Lucy," Freddy begins again. "If this Scholomance Preparatory Academy doesn't allow visitors or calls, how do you plan to contact her? Do you have an e-mail address? Are you connected on some social-networking site?"

I open Quincie's laptop. "I'm not a detail guy." Or, for that matter, a Web guy.

"Hmm." He hands me a steaming mug. "Some years ago, I had the occasion to encounter an alumnus of the Scholomance's Carpathian campus—a necromancer—at one of His Majesty's galas." Freddy slides into a kitchen chair. "He was coming on to an Old Blood aristocrat. You know how it is with eternals and necromancers."

I'm willing to take his word for it.

Freddy adds, "He claimed the building's physical structure was impenetrable. Unless you're an enrolled student or a staff or faculty member, simply touching the outside—a door knocker, a chimney, or a window—is enough to trigger a fatal magical charge. That defense system is a Scholomance trademark. You can bank on it."

"How does anyone get in?" I want to know.

"An incantation making individuals immune to the charge is routinely completed for students upon admission. Faculty and staff, too, I'd assume."

I don't want to find out what it means for an immortal angel to be magically electrocuted. "Any suggestions?"

Freddy shoos me from the computer. "If it were any other demonic establishment—any other not potentially affiliated with Lucifer, that is—I'd suggest we ask for the eternal queen's assistance. But in this case, I recommend faking it."

The Mantle of Dracul
Respectfully Requests that Zachary and Kieren
Be Welcomed as Students
at Scholomance Preparatory Academy.
Your Faithful Servant,
Her Royal Majesty Sabine

"Stick to your real names. That's how you'll be iden-tified in the spell. You don't want to end up in a coma or worse because you used an alias."

Freddy is a genius. Anyone on the receiving end of that note would assume Kieren and I—like him and Harrison—had been raised off the grid among the living servants to the high-class vamps. "I'm still not sure about taking Kieren."

Freddy's hand hovers over the keyboard. "Would you like me to go instead?"

I think it over. He is a grown-up. The school's target market appears to be older teens. I look about twenty, which may be enough of a problem. Besides, as a human, Freddy is more physically vulnerable than the Wolf. "Nah. Thanks anyway."

Freddy hits a link to download the admissions application.

~~∞ Zachary ∞~~

WITH WEATHER DELAYS and pit stops, we don't drop off Quincie until after 5 P.M. Sunday. She gives me a quick hug in the living room of the historic B and B in Montpelier. "How long will you two be gone?"

"It depends on Lucy," I say. "How quickly we can convince her of what the school is really about. Whether after finding out, she's willing to leave with us."

"Why wouldn't she be?" Kieren asks. "Any sane person would run screaming."

Quincie's phone ringtone goes off. It's Pavarotti singing "Mamma."

"There's a reason you-know-who is called the Prince of Lies," I reply. "He figures out what people want most. He uses that information to tempt them." I don't say what we're all thinking: that the devil has managed to lure Lucy there in the first place.

"Howdy," Quincie says into her phone. "Damn." She bites her lower lip. "Are you sure? What was the number? Thanks." Quincie raises a finger and makes a quick call. Covering the receiver, she looks up at me. "That was Yani from the hostess desk at Sanguini's. Sabine left a message for you at work. She said it's important."

Sabine, the vamp queen. Crap. The school must've checked our references.

Quincie asks for Her Royal Majesty and hands over the phone.

I gesture at the young couple to stay put and step outside Norma & Harry's B and B. It's getting chillier every minute. "Zachary here."

"Friend Zachary, I am confused. If you have fallen, why would you go to the American Scholomance and not instead come to me?"

"Sabine . . ." She's helped me in the past, when it was in her best interests. I'm tempted to let her think that I'm a fallen angel now. It would make my enrolling at the school more plausible. But what was I just saying about lies and temptation? "I need to talk to one of the students. A friend of Miranda's. What can you tell me about the place?"

"You should stay away from it."

"Sabine—"

"*Non!*" she exclaims. "You should not have involved me. Do you know what happened to the last eternal royal who tried to deceive Lucifer?"

I couldn't care less. "Not exactly."

"Neither does anyone else! This afternoon I received an electronic letter from the school, requesting confirmation of my previous correspondence. I will not reply for twenty-four hours. Consider it a gift to celebrate the annulment of our association. I will assist you no further, Zachary. That is all."

She beeps off. The vamp queen fears the Big Boss, but she fears his adversary, too. Still, for a damned undead royal, it's a pretty generous offer. Twenty-four hours.

Back inside the B and B, it occurs to me—not for the first time—how hard it will be for Quincie to wait here alone. She's not a sidelines kind of girl.

Even if she weren't worried about me and Kieren, doing nothing is contradictory to her nature. What's more, it's almost painful for her, being away from Sanguini's.

In the living room, my young assignment is seated with her beloved Wolf on the piano bench. They're talking in hushed tones. When I come in, they stand.

"We've got twenty-four hours," I announce. "If we're

not out by then, we have to deal with Sabine ratting us out." I glance at Quincie. "Will you be okay here?"

"You're asking me?" she replies, walking us to the door.

"I'm surprised you're not putting up more of a fight about being left behind."

Quincie shrugs. "Call me crazy, but I'd rather you not 'renounce the Big Boss and march us both straight to hell.'" With that, she hugs me again like I'm going off to war. Then she gives Kieren a kiss that could melt snow.

~≈o Miranda o≈~

THROUGHOUT THE AFTERNOON, Vesper has chattered at Lucy nonstop, which is how I know Vesper took extra classes to graduate early last semester from a private girls' school in Georgia. She doesn't have a particularly Bostonian or southern accent. It's more of an affected mix.

The sheer volume of her belongings is staggering, and this is coming from me, who, as eternal royalty, used to toss away million-dollar gowns after one wearing.

In terms of gloves alone, she's unpacked pairs for driving, skiing, weight lifting, and kickboxing in leather, suede, and knit, in patterns and solids, in various colors, with fingers and without, in classic and opera lengths.

"They barely fit in my drawer with the mittens and muffs!" Vesper exclaims.

"Do you think you'll need all that?" Lucy asks, removing one of two identical uniforms from the closet. It's an ash-gray oxford-style shirt and matching pants. The embroidered logo is based on the devilish monster depicted above each fireplace.

Vesper glowers at the outfit. "Did you see the shoes?"

Zooming in on the closet, I consider the terry-cloth robe and matching slippers. They're not heavy enough for winter in Vermont. Lucy, who unpacked herself in about three minutes, opens yet another of Vesper's trunks, this one filled with silk bedding.

"Don't you love the color?" Vesper asks. "It's Persian plum. I adore the contemporary furniture and design. Monochromatic is always chic, but it can get tiresome after a while. The color will give it punch."

I don't think Vesper is a demon, just incredibly boring, superficial, and spoiled.

According to Seth, they're the only two students who've checked in thus far, because of the weather. He left when the caretakers arrived.

The Bilovskis are a married, middle-aged couple, who've been given an apartment to themselves on the first floor. It has a separate bedroom and its own kitchenette but is otherwise designed and decorated like the student quarters. The couple seems rural, polite, and in no way remarkable.

As headlights flash against Vesper's windowed wall, I zoom out to watch a compact car slow to idle in the circular front drive. A petite girl exits. Her long, blue coat looks worn. She has chestnut-colored hair under her knit cap and carries only a backpack.

Meanwhile, upstairs, Lucy, who worked as a hotel maid last summer, has Vesper's bed made in record time—skirt, mattress pad, shams, and throw pillows. Lucy tosses an extra Persian plum pillow on the black leather Euro recliner.

Vesper looks impressed. "Are you always this quiet? It's Lucy, right? Earlier, it looked like you'd been crying or had pinkeye, but it's better now."

"I got in an argument with my parents before I left home," Lucy explains. "They didn't want me to change schools. Or leave Texas. And my gerbil died. Actually, he was my best friend, Miranda's, gerbil."

Vesper seems baffled. "You were crying over your friend's dead gerbil?"

The newcomer steps out of the elevator, and the two girls peek into the hallway.

~∞∞ Zachary ∞∞~

"DO ALL ANGELS know each other?" Kieren asks from my front passenger seat.

"Nope," I say. "We're talking about a lot of angels. GAs alone solidly outnumber mortals. But with the earthly population soaring and tensions rising around the globe, it wouldn't surprise me if the Big Boss created more soon. Why?"

Kieren flicks his wrist, unleashes his claws, and retracts them.

"Are you pretending to be Wolverine for a reason?"

"The devil," he replies, "has quite a reputation. What does he bring to a fight?"

"Lucifer is battle trained. He taught Drac his tricks. He can change shape, mess with your mind, vanish at will. Or seem to. He can cater and reframe the experience of hell itself. Beyond that, who knows? He's had a lot of time to gather strength and forces."

The Wolf's scowl is formidable. "Would you recognize Lucifer if you saw him?"

It's a good question. "I'm a new angel. He fell long, long before my time."

"So that would be a no?"

Wolfish posturing aside, Kieren is nervous. I answer, "The fact that Scholomance Prep is supposedly Lucifer's school doesn't mean that we'll find him there personally. Where the Big Boss sends down GAs, Lucifer sends up demons. The devil himself has been banished from earth. He has minions but no power except what we give him. That's why he's big on temptation. Bargains."

The blizzard intensifies and we briefly lose all visibility.

Kieren is silent for a long moment. Then he says, "His minions have earthly power, though? They can hurt us?"

I turn down the heater. "There is that."

The Wolf chuckles. "Your pregame pep talk needs work."

Minutes later, we come upon a black hearse stuck in a ditch. It has New York plates. We can't see through the tinted windows, but the taillights are on.

I pull over the Impaler, and Kieren and I go investigate.

"Can we give you a hand?" the Wolf calls, turning on a flashlight.

The driver lowers his front window. He stares blankly at us through long, unnaturally black, uneven bangs. "Do what you want."

The girl sitting beside him leans forward into our field of vision. "Excuse me, who are you? I have my phone right here, and 911 is programmed into my speed dial."

When my first assignment, Danny Bianchi, was a boy, nobody would've questioned someone stopping to help a motorist in distress. It sucks that people these days often doubt each other's motives. It sucks more that they're often smart to do so.

"We're students," I reply, "on our way to a school called Scholomance Preparatory Academy. It's up the road another five minutes or so."

"Us, too!" the girl exclaims. "Hang on. Can you prove that's where you're going? Do you have your admission letters with you?"

There's cautious, and there's paranoid. Why is she so high-strung?

Freddy received a curt, officious e-mail confirming our acceptance only moments before we left. Not that I was expecting, say, a formal, embossed parchment on such short notice. But I had no intention of letting my guard down either.

Kieren glances back at the SUV. "We've got a printout of the directions from Yahoo! Maps. If you want to stay in the car, though, we can push you out."

The ditch isn't deep. Even if it were, the Wolf could handle the job solo, but like most shifters, he's careful about showing off his strength.

I mean, like most werepeople. That's what they prefer to be called, even though the term doesn't make literal sense. *Were-* means "man," so the translation is "man-people." No animal-form reference. From what I understand, it's designed to emphasize that they're people first.

The driver is ignoring us. The girl hops out of the front and, from the other side of the hood, calls, "Show me your map."

I jog to my SUV, parked ahead of them on the side of the rural road, and fetch it for her. I'm not surprised to have run into other students along the way.

Meanwhile, Kieren goes around to the back of the hearse. He waits until I wade into the ditch with him before single-handedly half-pushing, half-lifting the car up and out.

"I could've actually helped," I say.

"I know. But if you injured your back or shoulders, could you still fly?"

Valid point, though I'm hoping to get through this without doing anything as showy as flying.

As we return to the roadside, the girl has already climbed into my idling SUV. The guy in the hearse peels out, swerving on the ice.

Our new passenger introduces herself as Bridget Gregory from San Jose. She had a rough flight to JFK and decided to take the train to Burlington. She called the school to explain she was getting in late. Someone named Seth suggested that Bridget carpool with another student, Andrew, the hearse driver.

"Andrew told me he got a recommendation letter from the mayor of New York City. New York City! Can you believe that?"

"We're glad to have you along," Kieren says—his way of wondering out loud why she switched cars—"but the school is only a few minutes away."

"That is exactly what I was thinking when we went into that ditch," Bridget replies from the bench behind us. "If you two hadn't shown up, who knows? I might've frozen to death. I've wasted the last eight hours of my life in that death trap on wheels with Mr. Morose, listening to something called ethereal wave music. It's a relief to finally talk to some normal people."

It occurs to me that Bridget is chatting with an earthbound GA and a human-Wolf hybrid. Then I realize that, unlike Andrew, she doesn't seem the least enamored of the eerie. "What about Scholomance Prep appealed to you?" I ask.

"When the judge interviewed me for the admissions committee—"

"Judge?" Kieren asks.

"A ninth-circuit federal appellate judge," Bridget replies. "Some say he'll be the next tapped for a U.S. Supreme Court nomination."

"Let me guess," the Wolf says. "When you grow up, you want to be a lawyer."

"I will be a lawyer," she agrees. "Like my father."

"About the judge . . . ?" I nudge.

"He's an alumnus of the flagship school in Eastern Europe."

Of course he is. The Scholomance in Romania has a worldwide network of successful graduates.

"He promised to write me a recommendation letter to law school if I graduate, and if I want to get in to Stanford or Yale, I'll need every advantage."

"What grade are you in?" Kieren asks.

"I graduated from high school last spring on my sixteenth birthday, but you know what happens to smart kids? We get older, and nobody thinks we're that remarkable anymore. Then we're smart grown-ups, and there're plenty of those in the world. Now is the time to capitalize on my intelligence and set myself up for the future."

Bridget is either highly verbal by nature, uneasy about our destination, or trying hard to impress us. The beige sweater peeking out of her unzipped ski jacket appears new. Her diamond-stud earrings look real, not that I'm an expert. Her hair is gathered at the back in a bun and accented with a satin bow that matches her sweater. This is one preppy, well-to-do kid.

"You've put a lot of thought into this." The Wolf clears his throat. "Me and Zach are late admits, so we didn't get to interview. What else did the judge say?"

Kieren is a brainiac. Growing up, he split his time between his public school and Wolf studies. Otherwise, he could've graduated years early, too.

"I went to my interview armed with questions," Bridget replies. "We're in the first class. The school admits only ten students at a time. It's very exclusive, with an amazingly low faculty-student ratio. The majority of admits have a personal referral from someone connected to the Scholomance family. Most of us graduated from high school early." She finally takes a breath. "Maybe not you, Zachary."

Kieren replies, "Zach's education has been unconventional. Go on."

"My parents liked all that. Given my age, they weren't keen on the idea of my going off by myself and meeting college boys. A small, elite boarding school sounded ideal. When I asked the judge about course work, he said the final curriculum was still in development, but I'd be sure to leave with a solid foundation for legal study."

She reminds me of Quincie, so driven and focused from such a young age.

Is that the idea behind Scholomance Prep, to turn unwitting prodigies to evil? Is Lucifer becoming more strategic? Trying to build a brain trust?

It's a puzzle. Bridget and Kieren fit the student profile—underage, brilliant, motivated teens. I don't, but that could be explained away by my recommendation from Sabine. Connections. What about Lucy, though? She's a smart enough kid. Above average, but no Baby Einstein. What would the devil want with her?

"You don't suppose Andrew took my bags in," Bridget says, getting out of my SUV to check. "Or at least left the hearse hatch unlocked?"

I turn off the engine. It's about 6 P.M. Orientation is tomorrow. I hope to convince Lucy to leave tonight, well before Sabine calls our bluff.

"Looks like an office building," Kieren says, exiting the car.

He's right. Scholomance exudes none of the playful Goth posturing of Sanguini's. None of the old-world elegance of Sabine's castle. It looks modern, fungible, and utilitarian, which does nothing to reassure me.

Outside in the moonlight, I realize we're at the bottom of a valley, surrounded by snow-blanketed hills.

Kieren is muttering something about hell freezing over and a volcano in Iceland. He wanders over to the man-made lake. He sniffs the air and bends to touch the water.

"What is it?" I call.

The Wolf shrugs. "Something I've never smelled before."

It's not the kind of thing that full human beings say. The slip tells me he's more unnerved by our mission than he's been letting on.

Bridget doesn't seem to catch it. She loops a garment-bag strap over her shoulder. "It's probably a moose."

Kieren turns to look at me. "The water is tepid." He doesn't have to point out how strange that is for Vermont in January. The temperature right now is about twenty degrees and falling fast.

Hopefully, the Wolf and I overpacked. We each brought a duffle bag, a backpack, and a garment bag. They're not just for show. We have a change of clothes and toiletries. But we've also got my sword, Kieren's battle-axe, holy water and wafers, and an interfaith collection of religious symbols from Alpha and Omega to Zen Circles.

Plus, the Wolf has his teeth and claws.

San Diego Sun-News, April 19

HIT-AND-RUN DRIVER IDENTIFIED AS HIGH-SCHOOL DEBATE STAR

By Farid Karam

San Diego—The hit-and-run driver who struck a 2002 gray Subaru Legacy has been identified as a San Jose teenager on her way to a high-school debate competition, according to San Diego police spokesperson Jill Lowell.

Although damage to the vehicle was minor, Agnes Blistford, 82, the driver of the struck car, died of a heart attack within an hour of the accident.

Lowell said prosecutors elected not to press charges. She added, "Given Mrs. Blistford's small stature and the fact that her car was parked, we believe that the young, inexperienced driver in question did not realize that it was occupied."

It is the policy of this newspaper not to publish the names of underage persons potentially involved in criminal cases.

~%o Kieren o%~

"WHAT IN BLAZES IS THAT?" Bridget exclaims, pointing toward the building.

"Porcupine," I reply. "It's probably after the salt on the drive."

The animal—it's too small to be a shifter—is backing away from us. I'm about to warn Bridget to keep her distance. Then its hind end hits the base of the first step leading to the Scholomance front door. A light flashes. The porcupine flies, spinning off the walk.

"What happened?" Bridget wants to know next.

I recall Zach's telling me what Freddy said about the Scholomance defense system. The angel strides ahead with his bags. He sets a firm foot on the same step. Nothing.

It might be Zach's angelic-ness or immortality protecting him from the spell. Just in case, I hurry to his side. I put my foot down on the same step.

I'm fine. Bridget will be, too. I double back to grab her heaviest bag.

I'm usually charmed by snow. In Texas, it's so rare. Not so here. The blizzard is oppressive. Or maybe that's just my growing sense of dread.

Moments later, I press the doorbell and a chime sounds.

A silver-haired man with a hooked nose greets us. He's dressed in flannel, denim, and a hunting cap. "Welcome to SP! Come in out of the cold."

I pause, midstride. I study the door. It's made of metal—steel?

"I'm Mr. Bilovski, the handyman. My wife, Mrs. Bilovski, she's the cook. I'll show you to your rooms on the second floor. Then you can come down for dinner with the rest. Or, if you're starving, leave your luggage here. I'll run it upstairs for you."

"That's okay," Zach replies. His sword is wrapped in a sheet in the unfolded garment bag. "We've got it, but, Bridget, if you—"

"I'm starving," she says. "There's more in the back of

the hearse. And a dead porcupine beside the stairs." She pauses. "Watch out for lightning."

"All righty." Mr. Bilovski takes Bridget's bags. "This way to the elevator, boys!"

To the left of the foyer, I see a formal living room. Beyond that, there's a more casual lounge. I hear voices. I smell fish, bread, and baked apples coming from the back of the building. I hesitate at the elevator. My inner *Canis dirus sapiens* is wary.

"If you want to take the stairs," Mr. Bilovski says, "it's only a flight up."

I shouldn't act suspiciously. I resign myself to the elevator.

Inside, Mr. Bilovski adds, "After lights-out, this baby is programmed to wait open on the student residential floor, in case one of you needs it."

The buttons are labeled *S, B, G, 2, 3, 4,* and *R.* There's also a keypad. *B* obviously stands for basement, and *G* for ground. "Subbasement and roof?"

"Yep," Mr. Bilovski replies, hitting 2. "The fourth floor is faculty housing. The elevator doesn't typically stop there, on the roof, or at the subbasement. I don't even have the code for the roof or 4. I only go when I'm summoned and let out."

He doesn't seem like a guy who says things like "when I'm summoned."

"That reminds me, we've got a little apartment, me and Mrs. Bilovski, on the first floor. You need a bulb changed or school supplies or what have you, just knock. I'll attach a whiteboard to the door so you can leave a message if I'm busy or out."

"What's in the subbasement?" Zach prompts.

"Well, the basement serves as a gym, so we use the sub for storage. Two strapping boys like you, you'll love the gym. It's got a basketball court, eighth-mile running track, weights, and aerobic equipment—all brand-new."

On the second floor, Mr. Bilovski shows us down the east hall to the last two rooms. They're located across from each other. "These doors will lock behind you." He hands us each a key. "I've got extras, if you need them. Now, don't dawdle. The missus is serving apple pie for dessert. You'll want it hot."

After watching Mr. Bilovski leave, we look around. Besides ours, the doors to three of the other rooms are open. Inside, they're identical.

I set down my bags. I pace the perimeter of my assigned space.

Zach trails in. I gesture at the pop-art print above the fireplace. "It's an illustration from the *Codex Gigas*. Thirteenth century. Bohemia. It was first created by a monk who supposedly sold his soul to the devil."

"Subtle," the angel replies, "in an egomaniacal kind of way."

I bend, intending to unzip my duffle bag. Then I stand again. "We might as well keep the weapons packed. I'd rather not abandon them. But charging down to dinner with battle-axes won't do much for our credibility." When he doesn't argue, I add, "What're you going to say to Lucy?"

"Unclear." The angel steps out to deposit his luggage in his room. "The one time I met her in person, she seemed to trust me. Like you did, when we met."

I open a manila envelope on my desk. Looks like standard school paperwork. A welcome letter, dorm rules, code of conduct . . .

Back at my doorway, Zach says, "I've been meaning to ask for the longest time. . . . Could you recognize me as a GA right away?"

"I'm not that pure of heart," I assure him. "But I follow my instincts."

~∞ Zachary ∞~

I SPOT LUCY, taking a bite of salad greens, only seconds before she glances up and her fork clatters on the black-tile floor. Yeah, she recognizes me.

The high-backed chairs around her are filled, so I sit next to Kieren across and farther down the table.

As the Wolf leads introductions, I wave and gauge the other students. At the head of the table, a girl named Vesper looks coiffed, runway ready. The hearse driver, Andrew, is to her right. Bridget wonders out loud if she'll be the only African-American student in the class.

Lucy, slack jawed, is still staring at me.

A cute brunette in a knit cap announces, "Evelyn. Evie, to my friends. I'm the only native Vermonter so far."

Three of the ten chairs are still empty. No faculty in sight, but a rail-thin, pinched-looking woman with a pointed chin—Mrs. Bilovski—enters through the swinging kitchen door. She's carrying a tray stacked with steaming plates. Her long-sleeved, high-necked black dress would make perfect funeral attire. "Tonight, for your main course, we've got your broiled trout, broccoli, and baked beans. I'll fetch a couple more salads and ice teas for you new arrivals and more corn bread and butter, too."

The country-comfort cuisine contrasts with the sterile décor. Maybe it's my having worked at the vamp castle, then Sanguini's, but at a place like this I'd expect mini-plates, smoked fruit, pretentious hummus, and whey.

Andrew's silence is hostile. Kieren and the others are trading war stories about their journeys through the blizzard. Bridget spent two and a half hours stuck on a runway on a layover at Chicago O'Hare.

"You poor thing!" Vesper exclaims. "Flying coach was one of the worst experiences of my entire life. Then again, I expect the rest of you are used to it."

On the far end of the table, Evelyn and I are out of the loop. I ask her, "Did you graduate early like Bridget?"

"Me?" She takes a bite of trout. "More like *dropped* out early. I'm a Second Chance student."

"What's that? Second Chance—"

"Basically, I promise to make good grades, and in return, I get room and board and set up in the job of my choice upon graduation. I had no idea the school would be so chichi."

It sounds like each student was told what he or she wanted to hear, offered whatever it would take to get them to commit. "Why did you run away from home?"

Evelyn blinks at me. "How did you—"

"Sorry," I say. "I used to work in a shelter. I was homeless myself for a while."

This soothes her. "Takes one to know one, I guess."

First Bridget, now Evelyn. My image of Lucy as the lone innocent in a den of demons-in-training is busted. That changes everything.

"Zachary," Vesper calls. "What do you think? Who'll be the first of us to hook up?" The curve of her artificially plumped smile is an invitation.

I shouldn't be surprised. Beyond Lucy's, I didn't notice the students' reactions when Kieren and I walked in. But according to Quincie, one of Kieren's finest qualities is that he has no clue he's one of the most lusted-after heartthrobs at Waterloo High. And not to sound conceited, but humans overreact at the sight of GAs. They find us literally heavenly. Sanguini's manager had to institute a policy forbidding touching of the staff to stop diners from trying to play with my hair.

I settle for saying, "I don't know. I'm not looking for a relationship."

"Who said anything about a relationship?" Vesper counters, blowing me a kiss.

At that, Andrew takes his plate and glass and leaves without excusing himself.

Vesper laughs. "What a goon!"

Mrs. Bilovski brings my salad and dinner plate. Then Evelyn leans in and lowers her voice. "I guess, living together, it'll be no time before we know each other's secrets anyway. I'm a throwaway, not a runaway. An outcast."

She says it with bravado, not self-pity. I almost admit to having been cast out, too.

"Did you and, uh . . ." Evelyn gestures down the table.

"Kieren," I supply. The greens are fresh enough, the maple dressing sweet.

The Wolf tilts his head our way, but he doesn't break from the other conversation.

"Did you two ride in together from the airport?" she asks.

"We drove in together." Nora's cooking has spoiled me. The trout is too dry.

"You knew each other from before?"

The doorbell sounds. I hear Mr. Bilovski's voice from the foyer. Then he slides open the door separating the dining room and the living room. The girl student is bare-foot in a black minidress. The boy looks like he's off to prom in a thin red tie and pin-striped suit. Their eyes are dilated. They're slightly swaying, trashed.

"Party on, fools," the boy calls. "For tomorrow we all die."

Before anyone can react, he passes out.

Kieren shakes his head. "I'll take him upstairs to sleep it off." On his way out, the Wolf lifts the unconscious guy like a bag of flour.

"I'll help you," Bridget volunteers.

Following them, Vesper jiggles her phone. "I'm not getting any reception."

From the rear, Lucy pauses at my side. "We need to talk."

"Soon," I tell her. "Very."

The new girl, Willa, joins me and Evelyn for dinner. She explains that she and Nigel (the intoxicated, self-appointed prophet) took a limo from the Burlington Airport. They drank the complimentary champagne on the way. "I only had a couple glasses."

"You don't weigh much," I reply over apple pie. "You're probably dehydrated from the flight. That's why it hit you so hard." Trying to sound casual, I add, "By the way, what did Nigel mean by, 'For tomorrow we all die'?"

"He's always been dramatic," she explains as Mrs. Bilovski brings her a tall glass of water. "When we were kids, he used to dress up in robes and sacrifice lizards with sharpened Popsicle sticks. Of course, he had to cut off their heads first to make sure they'd lie still on the rock until he finished chanting. Then the pet store banned our whole family from the place, and, you know, lizards are hard to catch."

Evelyn coughs and sets down her fork.

"Nigel's your brother?" I ask Willa.

Sticking three fingertips into her glass, Willa flicks water at her face. "No, he's . . . My parents always referred to him as a guest. They raised him for as long as I can remember."

"Your family makes a habit of sacrificing animals?" Evelyn wants to know.

Willa flinches. "Only Nigel." As if reconsidering what she's said, Willa adds, "Don't listen to me. I'm tired and wasted, and that was a long time ago. He can be really sweet. Now that I think about it, he had little pretend funerals for the lizards, too."

"Just checking." Evelyn stands. "See you in the morning."

Once she's gone, Willa and I chitchat. She keeps glancing up, like she feels guilty for not helping Nigel to his room.

Finally, I ask, "Why did you two choose Scholomance Prep?"

"We didn't." Willa pushes her plate away. "My parents'

biggest financial backer is an alumnus. Last night, he took them to dinner at the MGM Grand. This afternoon, they told us to dress up, flew with us to Burlington, and then announced that we were both transferring here. Never mind *asking* if we wanted to move or change schools."

Kieren

"EVELYN, THE SECOND CHANCE GIRL, is a wereotter," I announce after closing the door to my room.

"You could tell from her scent?" the angel asks.

"Also the cute factor," I reply. "I don't mean that in a Wolfish way. You know how I feel about Quince. It's just a statement of fact. All Otters are cute."

"It's that button nose," Zach replies. "The cuteness is practically a superpower."

"She was probably able to sniff me out as a Wolf. Or maybe not a Wolf exactly. Being a hybrid, I'm harder to ID by species. But at least as a werepredator."

"If she tells people, that'll nix the surprise element you'd bring to a fight."

"Evelyn can't out me without revealing herself." I pull out the desk chair and straddle it backward. "What's the scoop on the partiers?"

Zach fills me in. "Willa and Nigel are both going into the second semester of their junior year. I suspect that Lucy is the oldest at nineteen."

"Not counting you," I say. "We're off the grid in terms of any traditional educational structure. Of course, we knew that going in. Both Bridget and Vesper mentioned they plan to eventually transfer to the Carpathian campus."

"I thought Bridget wanted to go to law school."

"She does," I assure him. "Afterward."

Zach stares at the devil-inspired art. He sips from a mug of hot maple herbal tea brought up from the kitchen. "Who *don't* you think is an innocent?"

"Innocent is a high standard," I say. "I'd rather know who's here by choice. Who fully understands what 'here' is all about." I think about it for a moment. "Evelyn came in through a Second Chance program for disadvantaged kids. Bridget, Nigel, and Willa are here because of alumni recruiting efforts. Vesper mentioned at dinner that her folks are alumni themselves.

"Andrew," I add, "is our mystery man. And given

Nigel's history with animal sacrifice, he might be an excellent fit for the school."

"The way Nigel was acting," Zach begins, moving to the window, "that wasn't hooray-for-hell drunk. That was my-life-is-over-so-I-might-as-well-get-smashed drunk."

I don't know what difference it makes. We have to warn the students. All of them. A few might already know what they're in for. Someone might sound an alarm or try to block our escape. But what else can we do? "You realize you're stalling, right?" I ask. "You could be talking to Lucy right now. We could take it from there."

"How do I convince her? How do I convince any of them to leave?"

We could've had this conversation on the road. Zach has spent most of his existence watching over his assignments. Invisible. Incorporeal. Silent. He hasn't been earth-bound for even two years. His social skills are a work in progress.

"Why not bust out your wings?" I suggest. "That's old-school convincing. Like, 'Joseph, son of David, do not be afraid to take to you Mary your wife, for that which is conceived in her is of the Holy Spirit.' Or, 'Hey, Lucy, if we don't vamoose, your soul may be taken in sacrifice by el diablo.'" Some news is easier to sell when it comes from an angel of the Lord.

Zach taps on the glass wall. "We could all stroll quietly

out of here tonight. I could maintain my secret identity through an entire crisis. I want to try that first."

"All right," I reply. "But remember, Scholomance is like the serpent in the tree of knowledge. It promises to reveal great mysteries. For Lucy, what happened to Miranda is the ultimate question. You can give her the answer. *Scientia potentia est.*"

He sets his mug on the desk. "Come again?"

"Knowledge is power."

We hear a knock on my door. From the other side, Vesper calls, "Kieren!"

When I answer, she's standing there with Bridget and Evelyn.

"Do you have cell reception in your room?" Bridget asks.

I fish my phone out of my pocket and try it. "Apparently not."

Vesper's sigh borders on dramatic. "I cannot believe this! What are we, prisoners? Don't the Geneva Conventions guarantee access to—"

"The school is remote," Bridget puts in.

"Vermont remote, not Antarctica remote," Evelyn counters.

~❧ Zachary ❧~

ON A HUNCH, I unzip Kieren's bag. His axe is missing. I brush past him and the girls into my own room. When I check my hanging garment bag, my holy sword is gone, too.

Crap. Would I recognize Lucifer? I don't know. Probably not. Would his minions recognize a sword forged in heaven? Maybe. No matter that I'm immortal. Michael will *find* a way to kill me for this. I glance at the devilish print over my fireplace.

I'd swear it's grinning wider.

Back in the hall, Kieren shakes his head at me. It's bad news. Our weapons have been confiscated. The holy symbols, too.

The girls are still fixated on the phone issue.

"I can't log on to the Web from my laptop either," Bridget says, "and I'm supposed to call my parents tonight before I go to bed."

Vesper counters, "Big deal. I'm supposed to call my boyfriend."

"Well, I'm supposed to call my girlfriend," Evelyn says, "and you don't see me having a meltdown over it."

Kieren frowns at Vesper. "You have a boyfriend?"

She winks at him. "He knew I was a flirt when he fell in love with me."

I decide to talk to Lucy first, alone. Then I'll confront the other students. After a quick shower, I'm dressed and ready to go.

"What are you doing?" a voice asks. "You had to fake being a student to get through security. Sure. But why are you still here? Grab Kieren, find Lucy, go, go, *go!*" Joshua has materialized on the recliner. His feet are propped up. He's painted his toenails silver and gold to match his fingernails and sandals.

I rub my temples. "You know it's not that simple. We can't kidnap her. I have to find the right words. I have to convince her. Then she has to choose—"

"Normally, I'd agree with you," Josh says. "Rules

good. Kidnapping bad. But oh yeah, this isn't a normal situation."

"No," I agree. "In addition to Lucy, I'm also dealing with these other kids who—"

"Are not your responsibility!" Josh exclaims, standing. "Your interference could make things worse for all of them. Did you think of that?"

What is with him? "At Drac Radford's castle, you not only supported my rescuing the prisoners in the dungeon, you demanded to know what was taking me so long."

"That was different! Michael ordered you to go to the castle. You were supposed to be there. It was your principle assignment, and it was vague. You had wiggle room. Right now, Quincie is your specific, principle assignment, and she's cooling her heels solo at Norma and Harry's B and B, watching *Dead Poets Society*, and counting the minutes until you and Wolf boy return. Go guard her."

"But—"

"Dude, look at where you are, what you're doing!" Josh points to the *Codex Gigas* illustration hanging above the fireplace. "Freaking Beelzebub is your interior decorator!" He pauses, taking in the art. "I didn't realize he had a sense of humor."

"So does the Big Boss," I say. "Consider the platypus." I move to clasp Josh's shoulders. "Look, you're the one who told me about Lucy in the first place. Miranda asked that I save her, but you passed on the message."

Josh shrugs me off. "I know, and I feel terrible about the whole thing. I've been putting off filing my latest report to Michael." He sighs. "If you don't skedaddle ASAP, when the archangel finds out . . . Zachary, he's totally gunning for your ass. Having slipped is one thing, but because of this mess, you could fall all the way down."

"That's not up to Michael," I say. "He's higher ranked than us. He puts the Word into action. When it comes to GAs, day to day, he's in charge. But whether I'm eternally cast out of heaven, that's between me and the Big Boss."

"You keep telling yourself that," Josh says. "Meanwhile, I'm praying for you."

~ Zachary ~

MIRANDA READ FANTASY. Lucy watched horror flicks. Miranda shrank in the face of their high-school queen bee. Lucy was immune to social politics. Miranda treasured a blanket knitted by Grandma Peggy and her stuffed toy penguin from SeaWorld. Lucy decorated her bedroom with the impressions of old tombstones made with colored pencils and paper. Would they have become friends at all if they'd met later in life? It doesn't matter. When you're friends with someone that long, they're like family.

Lucy opens her door before I knock on it. "You're not wearing a dress this time." She's talking about the standard GA uniform—the white robes I had on when we met.

"Sorry I never returned your coat," I reply.

"Did you bring it with you?"

I dimly recall giving it to someone at a homeless shelter in Dallas. "Uh, no."

I join her in a private room identical to the rest. My gaze rests on the print from the *Codex Gigas*. It's creepy how it's everywhere.

Lucy shuts her door. "Start talking."

"You may want to sit down."

She doesn't.

I don't blame her for being pissed. "Do you know what Scholomance Prep is? Who's behind this school?"

Her hand still on the knob, she replies, "It's a demonic institution in terms of fields of study, ownership, and origin. Or at least that's what I read on the de Nostredame group message board, heard at the Dallas metropolitan chapter meeting of the Nosferatu Studies Society, and confirmed via *Baba-Yaga's Junior Encyclopedia*. When I asked Seth whether I would find out here what had happened to Miranda that night in Dallas, he said yes."

I don't get it. Lucy may have been gleefully fascinated by the eerie—monster movies and Goth fashion, though she only dabbled in the latter. But only when it was make-believe. Dress up. In fun. "So why are you—"

"Seth promised me answers. Everyone says I have to face that I'll probably never see her again. But what if they're wrong? What if she needs me?"

"The best way to be her friend is to leave. Tonight. Would Miranda want you to stay in a place like this?"

"What do you know about Miranda?" Lucy demands. "Who are you, Zachary—if that's your real name? Why were you at the cemetery? Why are you here?"

I take a step closer. "That night, you said that if there were monsters, there must be heroes. I frightened away the vamp then, and I'm here to rescue you now."

"What?"

"If there are demons," I say, "there must be angels." Josh was right. We don't have time to debate. I've always sucked at the whole secret-identity thing anyway. I move to the center of the room, in front of the angled desk.

I show my wings. "I was Miranda's guardian angel."

Lucy recoils, her back flat against the door.

"W-was?" she finally stammers.

That would be the part she'd zero in on. I hide my wings again. "I'll tell you what I can, but—"

"Prove it." Lucy slowly passes by me. "Prove that you're Miranda's guardian angel. Tell me something that only Miranda's angel would know."

My mind goes blank. "Her parents were divorced. It wasn't . . . amicable."

"Anyone could find that out. The local church ladies knew more details."

I try again. "She had a gerbil named Mr. Nesbit."

Lucy pauses, then gestures to me to move on.

"She had a crush on Geoff Calvo. She dreamed of being an actress. She was bullied by Denise Durant. She listened to Christian rock and used lemongrass body-wash—"

"That's kind of personal." Lucy sinks to the corner of the bed. "The bodywash. But anyone in her gym class could've told you that." She shifts her weight. "Geoff went missing, too. Did you have something to do with that?"

As Kieren would say, *Scientia potentia est.* "Miranda was taken by a vamp named Radford, the reigning king of his kind. He made her undead and claimed her as his adopted daughter. An Old Blood vamp aristocrat named Sabine presented Calvo to then-princess Miranda as a gift."

Lucy laughs. "Vampire princess? Miranda? Don't get me wrong. I love—loved—that girl more than anybody, but she wasn't exactly royalty material."

I throw up my hands. "You don't believe me?"

"I believe you're a supernatural being. I believe you're a supernatural being that I first encountered in a dark cemetery crawling with bloodsuckers and am meeting again at a Scholomance institution. That says demon to me."

I'm flabbergasted. "Didn't you see my wings?"

"Vampires and demons can have wings." She nods at her skewed logic. "Like in the movie *Van Helsing*." She points to the depiction of Lucifer over the fireplace.

"Maybe not that one, but you can make yours appear and disappear. Maybe he can, too."

"Demons have scaly, dragonlike, clawed wings," I counter. "Not gleaming, white, eagle-like . . . pretty wings."

That sounded lame. *Luminous* is the word Quincie uses. I should have said that. "Vamps have wings only in bat form, and only Old Bloods can achieve that. I have a pulse. You're welcome to check. There's no way I could be—"

"Lying?" Lucy stands. "Deceitful. Hiding an ugly nature behind a . . . pretty face?"

That's it! I grab Lucy, toss her over my shoulder, and, halfway down the hall, shout, "Kieren!" Meanwhile, Lucy kicks. She yells to be set down. She pounds on my back.

Other students pour into the hall. The Wolf grabs her legs and we duck into the elevator. "Lucy already knew about the school," I say. "She's willing to risk staying to get answers about Miranda."

Kieren stares at Lucy like she's insane. "Didn't you tell her . . ."

"I tried. She just started bitching me out and—"

"Stop talking about me like I'm not here!" Lucy exclaims.

The elevator reaches the first floor and opens. Bridget, Vesper, and Evelyn are blocking our way to the front door.

That leaves Willa and Nigel, probably passed out in their rooms, and Andrew, who likely couldn't care less. I'll worry about them later.

"Put her down!" Vesper says.

"She's claustrophobic," Kieren replies, pushing through. "She'll calm down once we get her some fresh air."

"You're claustrophobic?" Evelyn asks Lucy.

"No!" Lucy yells. "Do something! Help me!" She kicks her calves free and throws her weight backward.

I let go so I don't fall onto her. Cussing me out, she hits the tile floor.

"Hey!" Kieren shouts, holding up the front doorknob. He's apparently ripped it off. "We have a problem."

"What?" Bridget calls.

"We're locked in," the Wolf replies.

~&o Kieren o&~

MY FIST TIGHTENS on the metal knob. Where's another way out?

I start searching. The door to the kitchen is bolted. Could I bust through? Not without revealing my inner Wolf.

I will my descending canines to retract. Can't panic. Can't run faster than a human. But I can run.

With the others, I canvass the building. We stumble over each other like the Scooby gang. First-floor common rooms. Second-floor student housing. The basement gym. Up to three. The seminar room and library? Both locked. Restrooms swing open. They're nothing remarkable. Nowhere else to look.

The sealed front door is the only one leading outside. Fires blaze in all of the fireplaces.

Back on two, Bridget asks, "What about fire code? Shouldn't there be a stairwell leading outside at the end of every hall?"

"Relax," Vesper says. "I'm sure the lock-in is a security procedure. This must be a smart building. You know, run by computers. The front door lock, the spontaneous fires. They're just opening-weekend glitches in the program."

"Of course there's a fire plan," Lucy adds. "They'll probably review it tomorrow at orientation." She sounds convincing. She's acting unfazed. She smells like fear.

Downstairs, Vesper plucks the sticky note from the Bilovskis' door. It reads: AT A MEETING ON 4. BREAKFAST IS AT 7 A.M.

"Four?" Zach puts in.

"Fourth floor," I reply. "Faculty housing and offices." The others are winded. I try to sound like I am, too.

Vesper crumples the note. "It could be hours before they're back."

"This is our first night in a remote building in the snowy mountains," Lucy points out. "We're hot. We're tired. We're scaring ourselves for no reason. Let's go to bed."

Midway upstairs, I toss the front doorknob and catch it in one hand.

"Can I see that?" Bridget asks.

Once we reach the second-floor landing, I set it in her palm.

"You ripped it out!" she exclaims. "And sort of crushed it."

"It's not crushed," I try to argue. "It's—"

"Adrenaline," Evelyn replies, with a dismissive wave. "People sometimes show extraordinary strength in moments of crisis. Lucy was right. We should turn in."

I count the Otter as an ally.

⊸⊷ Zachary ⊷⊷

KIEREN AND I run our fingertips along the border of his floor-to-ceiling window. We're looking for a weak spot that we know isn't there. "What do you think?" I ask.

He sets his palm flat against the pane. "I have no idea whether it's natural, artificial, or mystical. I'd bet my tail, though, that it's shatterproof."

I will my wings to appear and rise to check along the thirty-foot-high ceiling for cracks, anything. "No luck," I say, coming back down.

"I will never get used to you doing that," Kieren replies.

He braces himself with both hands against the tinted window.

I return to wholly human form and take the same position, with some space between us. "One, two, *three*."

Muscles straining, we shove as hard we can. Sweat trickles down my forehead. We might as well be trying to move Mount Rushmore.

"Hold up," Kieren says.

I let myself fall forward a bit.

"You'll want to step into the hall," he announces.

"Because?"

"I'm a Wolf. If I go all out, and the window breaks loose or—"

"Got it." I retreat to the restroom doorway instead. As Kieren centers himself to try again, it occurs to me that he was trying to protect my ego. It's considerate. Maybe in the world of teenage guys it's critical to his getting by. But this isn't Waterloo High. If Kieren's shifter strength is the key to our escape, that's great by me.

He takes a cleansing breath. Straining against the window, Kieren grimaces. His canines lengthen. His eyes go yellow. A moment passes. Fur ripples across his forearms. His T-shirt splits. Two minutes, three, and the glass doesn't budge.

"Uh, Kieren?"

He swings his head toward me. Opens his jaws.

"Good werewolf," I say. "Ease off. It's no use."

Kieren barks a laugh. "I'm not a cub." Shaking off the shift, he adds, "Maybe if I ran at it, full speed. We could open both doors. I could get a head start from the back of your room. Race through the hallway into mine, and—"

"Break both of your arms on impact. Maybe kill yourself." I hate to admit it, but . . . "We're going to have to wait and see what tomorrow brings."

Lacking any better ideas, I turn in. I'm wearing running pants and nothing else. It's warm from the fire in the fireplace, from the heat pouring in through the vents. I'd rather sleep naked, but I'm out of the habit because I have housemates.

Not long after moving into Quincie's home, I snuck down to the second-floor restroom in the buff. I surprised Nora, who was coming upstairs with a glass of water from the kitchen. She loves to tell that story.

I admit, this platform bed is comfortable. It feels a lot like my futon in Quincie's attic. Just as lonely, too. Like every night, I imagine tracing the lines of Miranda's heart-shaped face. Her blue eyes laughing at me. "It usually makes me feel better to think you're looking down on me," I begin. "Not tonight."

I've abandoned Quincie. Walked into the most obvious trap on earth. Brought Kieren with me. Blew it with Lucy. Lost a sword of heaven. Now I have six more teenagers to worry about, too.

Kieren and I should've cased out the building before

going inside. There could be fire escapes we didn't see. Hidden doors. Maybe even a tunnel like the one leading out of the dungeon at Sabine's castle.

"Try not to worry," I tell Miranda, though there's no way I can know for sure if she's listening. "There's another exit—a way to bring in food and supplies. The forces of evil would never risk the magical costs of conjuring maple syrup or toilet paper."

~⊹⊱ Kieren ⊰⊹~

"CAN I COME IN?" I whisper outside Evelyn's doorway.

"I couldn't stop you," she replies, hairbrush in hand.

"*May* I come in?" I try again.

Evelyn lowers her voice. "Are you one of those big bad Wolves or —"

"I'm only half Wolf." I lean in. "A hybrid."

At that, she grabs hold of my shirt. She practically drags me inside. "Is it common? Are there a lot of us?"

"Nobody talks about mixed-species kids." I extract myself from her grip as she checks the hallway before shutting her door. "I've met a few. Probably more than I realize." I run my hand through my hair. "You have to be careful around humans. No hospitals. No blood or urine tests. If the general public realizes that werepeople and humans can have kids—"

She nods. "I saw a werehyena skinned—"

"You were there?" I ask. "Did you know him?"

It happened about a month ago. A Hyena skin from Vermont was sold on eBay. A U.S. senator from Wyoming was quoted as saying it was legal to hunt shifters in animal form. According to a CNN/*USA Today*/Gallup poll, 44 percent of Americans agreed. Worse, 26 percent indicated it was okay if the shifter was in human form.

"No," Evelyn says. "I know the people who skinned him. My dad is the head of the New England Council for Preserving Humanity. It's a—"

"I've heard of it." I don't obsess over bigoted crackpots. But I do keep up with shifter-related news on the Web. "So you're an Otter on your mother's side."

She sits cross-legged on her desk. "From what I've heard, Mom is claiming she had a one-night stand with a stranger. 'Didn't even catch his name,' she says. But I've heard family stories about her grandmother and about my great-great-grandmother for years. 'Don't tell your daddy,' she'd scold when I was little. I didn't believe it. I didn't even know I could transform until it happened last spring at the lake."

"You went swimming," I explain. "That triggered your first shift. For wholly aquatic werepeople like Whales or Dolphins, it's automatic from birth whenever they're submerged. With Otters, Seals, and Sea Lions, the first shift doesn't happen until puberty. That's more typical of shifters in general. Hybrids probably later than most.

"Water calls y'all like the moon calls us Wolves," I add. "You don't need it to transform, but it calls. At least that's what my books said."

Evelyn studies the hairbrush. "Dad wasn't there, thank God. Mom screamed at me that I was shameful and told me to leave and never come back. How did you know I wasn't a full Otter? How did you—"

"You're an adolescent. You were drinking water in mixed company. Depending on how good your control is, you could've sprouted whiskers at the dinner table."

Her fingers fly to her lips.

"Sorry," I say, "what else were you going to ask?"

"Why do you know so much about Otters? Besides me, there aren't any others in the local interspecies community right now, and—"

"I'm a trained Wolf studies scholar. I know more about other kinds of werepeople. More about the demonic. More about a lot of things than most shifters."

"Do Wolves eat Otters?"

It's not an unfair question. "This one doesn't."

After a long moment, she asks, "Are there any religions that don't preach that werepeople are shameful?"

She's using her mother's word for it. *Shameful.* "Sure. Most Otters are Buddhists."

I cross to the recliner and give Evelyn time to digest what I've said. Then I prompt, "You mentioned a girlfriend."

Evelyn perks up. "She was doing a summer marketing internship at Vermont College, and I met her at this outdoor art exhibit on campus. It's been a revelation. That I fell in love with Ollie, that my body can do these amazing things. Werepeople are everywhere. Now that I know, I see us, smell us wherever I go."

"Ollie?"

"Olinda Ann," she explains. "Ollie is an Elk." Suddenly, Evelyn bursts out laughing. She hugs her stomach, as if trying to keep it in. "A wereelk. You know." She holds up her hands, fingers up, on each side of her head to mimic antlers. She chuckles, snorts. Then she laughs again. The gesture is obviously a private joke between the girls. "Their animal kin was megalo, megatlope . . ."

"*Megaloceros giganteus*," I reply with a grin.

Evelyn's laugh is infectious. I'm reminded of her animal counterparts—otters that I've seen in zoos and on nature documentaries. Their joy and play in the water. She's a bright spirit. I should've noticed it before. This place is caging both of us.

I've never met an Elk before, either. "How tall is she?"

"Taller than Zachary," Evelyn replies, still giggling. "Evie the Otter and Ollie the Elk. It should be Evie the Elk and Ollie the Otter."

Like most inside jokes, it's not that funny. But I like her enthusiasm.

"She has the most beautiful arms," Evelyn continues. "Long, like a dancer's. When I met Ollie, I felt safe for the first time."

Too bad Quince isn't here to hear this. Beneath her ambitious restaurateur exterior, Quince's nonbeating heart belongs to a confirmed romantic.

"I haven't seen much of Ollie lately, though," Evelyn says. "Her parents found out about me, us. You know how it goes. We're in a mixed-species relationship. They told her to keep her distance. The fact that I was my father's daughter didn't help."

"You're *not* your father's daughter," I assure her.

Evelyn beams at me. "How about you? Are you involved with anyone?"

"Quince. It's Quincie, actually. Our moms were friends before we were born. It feels like we were friends before *we* were born."

"Just friends?"

"Not since middle school, not really. For years, I tried not to let it show. Until recently, I had control issues with my shift."

"You held yourself back to protect her." Evelyn twirls her hair with one finger. "Because that's not condescending."

"Wolves are more dangerous than Otters."

"Than Elk?"

I think about it. "Depends on the Wolf, depends on the Elk."

For a while, we're both quiet.

"About the fires in the fireplaces," Evelyn begins again. "No wood, no control lever for gas. No smoke. The chimneys are sealed, but all we're getting is heat. Now that we've established that neither of us is a bad guy, do you know what's going on?"

I told Zach I trusted my instincts. "This is what we know about Scholomance Preparatory Academy. . . ."

I don't mention that Zach is an angel. I do explain that his girlfriend Miranda is Lucy's best friend. I say that Miranda sent him here to rescue her. Then I explain why.

While I talk, Evelyn brushes her hair. It seems to soothe her. Grooming is something that Otters do a lot.

When I'm finished, she says, "I can't believe I fell for such a catastrophic bait and switch." Evelyn tosses the brush onto her bed. "I guess this isn't my second chance after all." She frowns. "Do you think the magic here could make me wholly human?"

The question surprises me. "Is that what you want?"

"It used to be," Evelyn admits. "I wanted to be all

human more than anything."

Given her parents, I can't blame her. "I understand. There was a time when I thought that I couldn't control my shift because I was a hybrid. Before I mastered it, I used to wish I was a full-blooded werewolf."

Evelyn slips down from the desk. "If you were human, you wouldn't have to shift. It wouldn't be an issue."

"True," I admit. "But I always saw shifting as a blessing. For me, there's nothing better. Except being with Quince."

~❀ Miranda ❀~

IT'S JUST LIKE LUCY not to believe Zachary is an angel! Not that it would've helped her to escape in that vile place. At the moment, they're incapable of leaving. Still . . .

Curious about what the Bilovskis are up to, I try to zoom in on the fourth floor of Scholomance Prep, but my screen goes dark. I try the subbasement, and it happens again.

I shake the monitor-com. I'm about to blow Mr. Nesbit a kiss and go downstairs to ask Huan what's wrong with it when I spin back to two and notice Andrew peering into the hallway. With his black-on-black wardrobe, matching chopped hair, and studded leather collar, he looks like Lucy's type, except that she requires an actual personality.

The image is snowy, but I can make out Andrew stepping barefoot into the hall. He's carrying his sheet, rolled into a ball. He takes the elevator to the basement gym and ties one end of the sheet like a noose.

Leaping to my feet, I rush out of the suite without bothering to shut the door behind me. Minutes later, I show my screen to Huan. "We have to do something! This boy is going to hang himself!"

Huan's brow furls, but he's looking at me, not what's happening in Vermont. "Miranda, we talked about this when the guardian Zachary was injured in battle. Our ability to affect what happens on earth is—"

"Zachary is an immortal," I reply. "This Andrew—"

"There's nothing either of us can do."

I suppose this is a taste of how my angel felt when I followed Lucy into the cemetery. More than ever, I understand why he broke the rules to try to save my life.

"My monitor-com is broken," I say finally. "I can't see all of this building, and what I can see . . . The reception is awful."

This time, Huan takes the device and fiddles with it. "What is this place?"

I remember what Joshua said: if Michael finds out where Zachary is, my angel could fall. "It's a school.

A high school. Or a finishing school. It's a boarding school." I'm babbling. "Why do you ask?"

"Your device isn't broken. It can't transmit from anywhere the divine is absent."

Isn't God everywhere? "I don't understand."

"These areas you're trying to view, they're borderlands and territories of hell."

~☙ Miranda ❧~

SINCE HUAN'S REVELATION, I haven't been able to stop staring at my monitor-com. What I wouldn't give to dive through the screen and emerge fully corporeal, ready to battle by my angel's side. Unfortunately, I'm stuck here in a rattan lobby chair, my hair nearly covered in celestial butterflies. I shake my head, and they fly away.

Willa is the first student to wake up. She'd slept fitfully. Likely worse because of last night's champagne.

Willa's eyes open. She sits up abruptly and glances around the room as though she's forgotten why she's there. Then a hand goes to her forehead. She's probably trying to soothe away a hangover.

Moments later, Willa reaches into the glass shower

and turns the control handle to a lukewarm setting. She opens the medicine cabinet to reveal an array of clear gels, lotions, conditioners, shampoos, and the like. Each bottle is marked with the Scholomance logo. I envy Willa for the shower she's about to take. I adored the feel of warm water pulsing against my bare skin.

As a human girl, I allowed myself the luxury of long showers and steaming hot baths. I spent much of my meager movie-theater earnings at Bath & Body Works. Bloodletting aside, perhaps my greatest regret about my time at the castle is that I had the maids, rather than Zachary, draw my baths. Why didn't I command him to sponge off my back and shoulders and . . . ?

Willa slips out of her silky pj's, and I can't help noticing the scars on her breasts, the backs of her thighs, and her buttocks. She's had fairly recent cosmetic surgery, and a lot of it—especially for a slender girl her age.

Willa begins to hum a song I don't recognize. It's sad and wistful, and as she steps onto the black tile and turns up the water temperature, I long to talk to her. I remember what she told Zachary about her parents packing her and Nigel off to the academy. I wonder if the surgeries were her idea or something else her parents insisted on.

I shouldn't be invading her privacy. I'm about to zoom away when her eyes widen and she recoils from the glass shower wall. It takes some maneuvering with the controls, but seconds later, I see what's frightened her.

As if drawn by a finger, the mischievous-looking devil is slowly taking shape—one line, then another, drawn into the condensation on the glass.

Willa shuts off the water.

She opens the shower door and peeks outside.

The bathroom is empty.

When she checks it again, the drawing has streamed away.

Willa grabs two plush gray towels and rushes out into her room. Shivering despite the heat, she wraps up her nude form as she goes.

Catching sight of the image over her fireplace, she jerks back again.

"Stop it!" she scolds herself. "You're imagining things."

No, she isn't.

~⚙️~ Zachary ~⚙️~

AN UNGODLY LOUD ALARM sounds throughout the building. Fire alarm? Security alarm? Beats the hell out of me. I wrap my pillow around my head and get up.

I'm sweating. I kicked the covers off in the night. The fire roars on in the fireplace.

The noise stops. The digital clock says it's 8 A.M.

A wake-up alarm. It's not like me to sleep in. The stress of this place is taking its toll. I spent most of last night awake. Beating myself up over what I should've said to Lucy. Wondering how I'm going to get us out of here. Missing Miranda.

After a shower and shave, I see the note on Kieren's door. He's gone to the basement gym with Evelyn.

I wander downstairs to the first floor. The front door is still sealed tight.

I continue to the dining room. "Morning, ladies."

Andrew and Nigel haven't arrived yet. It's me, Willa, Vesper, Lucy, and Bridget, who's mysteriously gone gray at the temples. They're complaining about the heat. The alarm. The ongoing absence of a wireless network. They're also helping themselves to a continental breakfast: platters of yogurt, croissants, rolls, bagels, various flavors of cream cheese, sliced grapefruit and pears. Pitchers of orange juice and ice water.

Other than the food and drink service, I see no sign of the Bilovskis.

Last night we were served with silver and china. This morning, it's paper plates, paper cups, and plasticware. Nothing that can be made into a weapon. Much like a prison cafeteria, at least in that way.

"Are you okay?" I ask Bridget.

"Bad dreams." She glances at her watch. "Orientation starts at 9 A.M."

"It does?" Willa asks, picking apart her buttery croissant.

Right then, Kieren and Evelyn come running into the dining room.

"Andrew's dead," they announce.

Upstairs in the third-floor seminar room, I'm the first in. The centerpiece is a glass-topped rectangular table with a metal base. A podium stands in front of a chalkboard secured to the wall. DR. URSULA ULMAN is handwritten on it. I assume that's the name of the faculty member or administrator or hell beast who'll be joining us.

A chalkboard. It's a low-tech choice for such a modern setting. But evil is old. Sometimes it prefers the retro.

The framed *Codex Gigas* illustration is identical to the rest.

The clock above the door reads 8:58 A.M. A typeset place card marks each of our chairs. It's five female students on one side, from back to front: Vesper, Willa, Lucy, Evelyn, and Bridget. Three male students on the other, from back to front: me, Nigel, Kieren . . . and the next student would've been Andrew. He hanged himself with his bedsheet from the pull-up bar.

The others trail in. They're subdued. Bridget is teary. She and Andrew may not have bonded on their road trip, but she spent the most time with him.

"I didn't think he was depressed," she says. "I—"

"It wasn't your fault," Lucy assures her. Evelyn is quick to agree.

Nigel strolls in last. Blurry eyed. Hungover.

Kieren breaks the news about Andrew.

"Nine becomes eight." Nigel puffs on a cigarette. "For us, it's too late."

I scoot my chair to the foot of the table. Whatever creature is about to appear in this room, I want to face it head-on.

At breakfast, I considered telling the students to lock themselves in their rooms, at least until Kieren and I could find a way out. But what Andrew did—or what happened to him—may be proof that we're safer together.

"Didn't you say Andrew was driving a hearse?" Vesper asks Bridget. "I'd call that a tip-off. Plus, his Goth look screamed—"

"Shut up," Lucy snaps. "This isn't about—"

"It's nine o'clock," Evelyn says in a soft voice.

Everyone checks the clock. Kieren knocked on my door last night to say he'd filled in the Otter on the school. So far as I know, the three of us and Lucy are the only ones in the know. No one expected a student to die within twenty-four hours.

Everyone else is clinging to whatever explanations they can muster.

"Good morning," intones a raspy, disembodied voice. "Welcome to the Scholomance Preparatory Academy. I am Dr. Ursula Ulman."

It's coming from the front of the room, near the podium.

"Speakers," Bridget whispers. "Hidden speakers."

I have to give her credit for trying.

"You may call me Dr. Ulman. We'll be spending a lot

of time together, and I'm not inclined to stand on ceremony." The voice is clearer now.

"I see that your tenth has yet to arrive. I myself was once a tenth scholar. Those who know what that means may make of it as you will. Those who don't will likely find this orientation disconcerting. Please note that we do not provide health care, mental or otherwise."

As she's speaking, Mr. Bilovski strolls in, passes out schedules, and exits.

SCHOLOMANCE
PREPARATORY ACADEMY

SEMESTER ONE

9–9:45	Alchemy & Incantations
10–10:45	Demonic History
11–11:45	Underworld Governments
12:30–1:45	Lunch
2–2:45	Physical Fitness & Combat

"No Language of Animals?" Vesper queries. "No Weapons and Technology?"

"Next semester," the voice replies. "This one-year, year-round program is devoted to study in preparation for admission to the Scholomance in the Carpathian Mountains."

A shadow catches my eye.

"For those of you familiar with that institution, please note that while areas of academic concentration largely overlap, this campus operates by its own set of rules."

Willa gasps as the shadow solidifies. We can make out a buxom woman with short—no, pinned-up—hair. She's wearing a long, dark gown.

"There is no option to withdraw. Minimum performance standards must be met, if a student is to advance in the program. My available discretion is limited.

"Anyone who compromises the sanctity of this academic community will be punished according to the severity of his or her crimes. To further encourage compliance, disciplinary action may be doled out on a transferable basis to any or all of you.

"Rules will be enforced without appeal. We have a zero-tolerance policy, and again, my available discretion is limited."

So she keeps saying. The figure standing (floating?) alongside the podium is gray, transparent. It's increasingly clear that Ulman's face is full and oval. Her eyes must've been blue or gray. Her hair is arranged in two braids, tucked to cover her ears and accented by brocade. Lace decorates the gown at the bust and from midthigh to the floor. A lace-trimmed handkerchief is tucked at an odd angle in the bodice.

"You'll find school uniforms hanging in your closets. Plan to wear them to class, beginning tomorrow morning."

Bridget pipes up. "My parents know I'm here. My father won't let you—"

"Your father," Ulman begins in a voice perfectly mimicking Bridget's, "has exchanged a dozen text messages and two voice calls with someone he believes to be you. You promised to tell him about orientation tonight after dinner."

"That'll only work for so long," Kieren says. "Sooner or later, someone will insist on seeing one of us in person."

"By then," Ulman replies, "it will be too late."

Too late for what? Before I can ask, Ulman's image flickers. I see horns, claws.

"Are you a ghost?" Vesper whispers.

Ulman ignores the question. "Your chances of success are best in a full-immersion setting. Therefore, you will not be leaving the building or contacting the outside world until you graduate. Please note that the Bilovskis are likewise permanent residents and have no more choice in the matter than you do. They have no power to facilitate your defying school policy or leaving the premises."

She pauses. "I hope you all got your flu shots. Now, if you will please stand and follow me, I will show you the library." Ulman floats out the door.

It's as though we've been spellbound until that moment. Everyone starts talking. Bridget insists that Ulman is a hologram. Vesper mocks Bridget for being naive. Willa begins babbling something about the condemned or condemnation. Nigel stands, muttering about unworthiness. Lucy asks what we should do.

Kieren replies, "Go to the library."

He, Evelyn, and I hang back as the others file out.

"What *is* that thing?" the Otter asks.

"Probably a previously descended soul or essence," the Wolf says. "One that was taken to hell and has come back. 'Ghost' is close enough. But her variety is so rare, that's about all I know about it."

Given that Ulman has no solid physical form, we can't fight her or force her to tell us anything. "Do you think she's the teeth and claws of this place?" I ask.

"If she was a tenth scholar," Kieren says, "she may not even be evil. Just damned and resigned to her fate."

The library takes up half of the third floor. Freestanding shelves separate two work areas. Each has a glass-topped, metal-framed table and metal chairs. A few cushioned chairs with matching ottomans offer a more relaxed reading space. They've been angled artfully in the corners.

An unoccupied desk toward the front of the room is bookended by custom-designed card catalogs. The books are old, some charred along the spines. They come in various sizes. A couple of larger ones are displayed on podiums.

The students stand in a bunch. They're trying not to draw attention to themselves.

"Is there a librarian?" It's the first question I've asked.

"No," Ulman replies. "We'll require a library assistant."

Kieren raises his hand. "I volunteer." He's a whiz at demonic lore and history. If the answer to our escape were in these books, he'd find it. But this is Satan's schoolhouse. We can't trust anything we learn here, except maybe what we learn from each other.

Ulman nods in agreement. "No food or drink on this floor." Her image begins to fade. "I'll see you all tomorrow at 9 A.M. in the seminar room. Tardiness will not be tolerated. During class time, you may not leave without my express permission. Ten o'clock P.M. is lights-out. Those of you familiar with the administration are welcome to share your insights with your peers." Only the eyes and mouth are left. "You have no secrets here."

New York Weekly Harbinger,
Aug. 6, 1888
Ursula Ulman (1836–1888)

Ursula Ulman, nicknamed the Maleficent Miser and the Miser of Manhattan, died on August 4. The daughter of Russell Rippington, U.S. ambassador to France, and his wife Beatrice, she was born November 10, 1836, in New York City.

Upon her parents' death in a 1858 suicide pact, she inherited eight million dollars in liquid assets. Ulman neither married nor had children. She relocated to Maine in her forties.

Throughout her life, she pursued a conservative investment policy, primarily concerning real estate and adamant frugality. She never allowed the use of hot water. She warmed her daily gruel on the radiator. She wore only one black dress and, in an effort to conserve soap, washed only those parts of it—the hem and underarms—most likely to become soiled.

Ulman's entire estate has been willed to the Scholomance, a little-known academic institution in the Carpathian Mountains, with which she had no publicly known previous association.

~ Kieren ~

ZACHARY HAS COME to rescue Lucy and whoever else needs help. That's what guardian angels do. They work one-on-one to save lives and souls.

We may be stuck in this place for a while. I take point in front of the tinted window in the formal living room. I mostly come clean with the other students. I use the word *demonic* rather than mentioning Lucifer. I don't say anything about my Wolf or Evie's Otter heritage. I don't out Zach as an angel either.

"Did you see when Ulman changed form?" Nigel asks.

"I saw horns!" Lucy exclaims.

Not everyone came downstairs. After Dr. Ulman vanished, Willa ran out of the library and threw up in the girls' restroom. Nervous shock. Evelyn offered to sit with her in the second-floor kitchenette. The Otter will tell Willa the rest once she calms down.

"What I don't understand," I conclude, "is the assumption that, after a year here, any of us will want to transfer to the Carpathian Scholomance."

Vesper leans back in her chair. She crosses her long legs. "Once you have a taste . . . My parents both graduated magna cum laude—my father first, my mother the following semester—and they married within the next year. They've attended every alumni retreat, reunion, and continuing-education program. The knowledge, the magic. It's addictive. Then there are the contacts. Music and sports stars, captains of industry, heads of state. People who launch social-networking sites."

"Vesper's parents are grads," Bridget says to Kieren from the sofa, "but how do *you* know so much? Or should I say, you and Zachary?"

I'm ready for the question. "We have ties to the va—"

Zach coughs. "Eternal."

He's right. An insider wouldn't use the word *vampire*.

"Eternal," I correct myself. "The eternal underworld. Zach used to work as a servant to the Mantle of Dracul, and I'm dating a neophyte member of the gentry."

Neither of which is enough to explain my expertise. Hopefully, they don't know that. I'm doing my best to stick close to the truth.

"Come again?" Lucy asks.

"Zachary used to work for the Mantle of Dracul," Vesper explains, sounding impressed. "The vampire royal family. And Kieren is dating a vampire of property."

"Dating!" Nigel exclaims. "A vampire? Is anyone here *not* suicidal?"

Andrew's name hangs unspoken in the room. It seems an unlikely coincidence that he'd choose to kill himself on his first night here.

"Vampires are extinct," Bridget puts in. "Or at least very rare and—"

"That's what they want you to think," I reply. "In Vermont, Burlington is the only sanctioned hunting ground. Unless we're dealing with a rogue, eternals are the least of our worries." I take a deep breath. "When we found out about the school, Zach and I came to warn you. The students. Those who might not realize what you're getting into. To help you leave." I don't single out Lucy. "We didn't expect to become imprisoned. We didn't expect a lot of things."

I raise my chin. "Other than Vesper, is anyone here by choice?"

Vesper begins filing her thumbnail.

Lucy keeps quiet. She's standing with her arms crossed and staring at the repeated devil image above the fireplace. I keep doing that, too. It demands attention.

"I knew." Nigel pulls a pack of cigarettes out of his

back pocket. "Willa knew." He crosses to the fireplace and lights a cigarette. "Not exactly, but we'd figured it would be bad of the seriously evil variety. Her parents brought us, after all."

It doesn't make sense that someone, even a parent, could forfeit his own child in a bargain with Satan. Let alone someone else's child. Surrender their own lives? Their own souls? Fine. But that's as far as it should go. Even assuming they're into soul bartering.

Why did Andrew drive himself and Bridget to the school at all? What does the mayor of New York City, who wrote Andrew's recommendation, have to do with it? How many political leaders are tied to Scholomance? What percentage of the rich and powerful ultimately rests in Satan's palm?

"Any ideas as to how we might escape?" I ask.

"Chain saw?" Lucy suggests, apparently for the hell of it.

Bridget adds, "Did anyone bring a weapon?"

"Confiscated," Zach admits for both of us.

Vesper holds up her metal fingernail file. "They didn't take this."

"We're dealing with the forces of evil," I point out. "Not the TSA."

~∰ Zachary ∰~

KIEREN AND I go to the gym to look for any hint of foul play in Andrew's death.

As we stare at the pull-up bar, I ask, "Is that nose of yours getting anything?"

The Wolf crouches, runs a hand over the mat. "You, me, Evelyn, Andrew, and Mr. Bilovski. No one else has been here, at least not lately. Andrew's scent is off, though."

"Off?"

"I'm not sure." Kieren stands. "At the roadside, he never got out of the limo. In the dining room, he exited around the other side of the table. Plus, it was crowded in there."

"This was a mistake," I say. "Lucy is no safer because we came."

"Isn't it up to me to decide that?" Lucy replies, exiting the elevator. "It's been a crazy couple of days." Her smile is slight, cautious. "We could start over. You said you watched over Miranda. You guarded her every day of her life."

She strides across the track toward us. "I saw for myself a vampire in the cemetery. I'm willing to believe a demon could be interested in her. But I somehow doubt one stuck around 24/7, 365 days a year, for her entire earthly existence. Much as I love my best friend, she wasn't that fascinating on a cosmic level."

At the pull-up bar, Lucy adds, "So, prove it. Prove you're Miranda's guardian angel. Try again. Try harder. Tell me things about her that only her angel would know."

Kieren shifts his weight. "I'll head upstairs. I want to talk to the Bilovskis."

As the Wolf leaves, Lucy pushes herself up on the nearby balance beam. She's wearing loose enough jeans that she can swing her leg over.

"Careful," I warn her. "You don't want to break your arm again."

Lucy bites her lower lip. "A lot of people know that. I wore a cast for—"

"You started your period when you were nine years old. You were home alone, though your mom, Susan, was just next door. She went over to borrow an egg from Mrs. Chopra and stayed to chat for a while. Susan had never told you about menstruation. She hadn't started until she was fifteen. It never dawned on her that you'd start so young. You called over there, but a boy answered. I forget his name. He was a cousin, visiting from Washington, D.C. So you hung up without saying anything."

"I forget his name, too," she says. "That all happened to me, not Miranda."

I stand with my back to the bar and raise myself to sit next to Lucy. "I know, but after about ten minutes you called Miranda. You told her all that. I was watching and listening, like I always did."

Ultimately, Lucy will have to decide for herself whether or not to believe me. To have faith in what I'm saying, to choose her fate.

"The worst fight you girls ever got in was about Geoff Calvo, the varsity soccer star. After second hour, in the girls' restroom, you said it was a waste for her to pine for him. You argued that he didn't even know her name. You were tired of hearing her go on about a guy she knew only from a distance. You said it was Miranda's way of not taking a chance on someone who might actually like her back. You thought she lived a narrow life. It frustrated you, especially when she second-guessed some of the risks you took."

"I can be a loud mouth," Lucy admits. "That morning—"

"Her dad had moved out for good, but you didn't know it. For the first time ever, my girl screamed at you to shut up." I'm uncomfortable on the beam. I don't get off, though. I want to stay at Lucy's level. "You never would've brought up Geoff if you'd known what was going on with Miranda's family at home."

"But I did know," Lucy says, biting her lip. "Or at least there was this rumor that Mr. McAllister had been seen kissing some woman in the Holiday Inn parking lot."

Lucy didn't used to hold so tight to her regrets.

But at least now she's finally listening to me.

~⚬ Kieren ⚬~

THE SCHOLOMANCE KITCHEN is stocked with modern appliances. I don't see a door leading outside. "Afternoon, Mr. Bilovski. What did you do with Andrew's body?"

Mopping the kitchen floor, he looks up at me in surprise. "Me? What makes you think I did anything with it?"

"It's gone," I reply. "None of the students moved it. Dr. Ulman—"

He shakes his head.

Play it that way. I start opening drawers and find only plastic and rubber utensils. No knives. "What about notifying the police, his family?"

"I mind my own business." He returns to the task. "You should, too."

"What *is* your business?" I ask, checking the counters. Paper plates and napkins. Flour and sugar. Spices and rice.

"I'm the handyman," he tells me. "Mrs. Bilovski is the cook."

That's not good enough. "You know what this place is. Get help for the rest of us. Say you need something from town and—"

He wrings out the mop. "We're beyond help ourselves, beyond salvation." His weathered face crumbles. "We believed his lies and lost it all."

Transcript of Call:
Vampires Quincie Morris and Queen Sabine
1/6, 3:45 P.M.

Sabine: Did I not make myself clear to Zachary? In light of his foolish behavior, I am severing my relationship not only with him, but also with his various teenage neophyte associates. You included. I hereby command you to leave me alone. In reward for your compliance, I am willing to waive your future taxes. That is how serious I am.

Quincie: Chill, Sabine. No one is asking you to prom. It's just that he and Kieren aren't back yet, and I—

Sabine: This is not my problem. I am hanging up now. I should have refused this call.

Quincie: Wait. You don't have to lie to the Scholomance.

Sabine: If I am not to lie, then what would you have me say?

Quincie: Say *nada.* Don't reply to the e-mail at all. Ignore it. Delete it.

Sabine: What if I find myself confronted in light of my

lack of response? What do you suppose I tell Lucifer's minion then?

Quincie: Tell him that it must've gotten caught in your spam folder.

Sabine: *You* are suggesting this strategy? You who keep company with an angel of the Lord? Is that not a sin?

Quincie: It's the electronic age. If that's a sin, hell's about to get a lot more crowded.

~⚬ Zachary ⚬~

LUCY AND I TALK until dinner. I'm not sure she's sold on my story, but it's a start.

The atmosphere at the meal is somber. None of us mention being locked in. Or the still-blazing fires in the fireplaces. Or our specter of a teacher. Or Andrew's suicide. Or the fact that we're cut off from the outside world. We don't talk at all.

Evelyn and Bridget keep obsessively checking their phones, though, like they hope that the lack of reception is a temporary glitch.

Vesper has begun tapping her fingernails on the closest available surface.

Mrs. Bilovski silently serves bread bowls of clam chowder with oyster crackers and fresh cracked pepper. Plastic soup spoons.

Finally, Bridget stands. "None of us really knew Andrew. I wish he'd given us a chance, but it's too late now. Nigel and Willa never even met him. But . . ." She raises her iced tea, and I can almost imagine the lawyer she'll be someday. "To Andrew."

"To Andrew," Vesper echoes without her usual irony.

"To Andrew, to Andrew, to Andrew," the rest of us chime in.

I notice how carefully Kieren and Evelyn make a point to carefully sniff their food before anyone takes a bite.

That evening, I hole up in my room. I'm hoping Joshua will appear.

Kieren stops by to report that the new normal has started to sink in. The girls have been speculating on why Andrew killed himself. "Nigel is binge drinking and chain-smoking," the Wolf adds. "On the way here from the airport, he had the limo driver stop and buy him two cases of beer, a fifth of vodka, and an entire suitcase of Lucky Strike cigarettes."

Not helpful. "How do you think Quincie is holding up at the B and B?"

Kieren kneels on the floor. He's trying to stare up

the fireplace shaft without getting burned. "Better than we are."

Most GAs know their assignments better than anyone else, but I've never been able to observe Quincie from an incorporeal vantage point. I wasn't even assigned to her until she was seventeen and already undead.

The Wolf adds, "We've been gone too long. Her stress meter has kicked up a notch. She's working on a plan B. She has Frank open. There's a to-do list involved."

Frank is Quincie's nickname for her planner book, a present from Kieren. He buys the refills, too. No matter that everyone else on the planet is tech obsessed. Quincie likes flipping through the pages. She likes the feel of the leather cover on her fingertips.

Giving up the idea of a chimney escape, Kieren grins. "I'm also guessing Quince is the reason that Sabine hasn't ratted us out to the administration."

I'd almost forgotten about Sabine. With everything that's happened, I lost track of time. We've spent our first night and whole day here. How many more lie ahead?

The Wolf touches the olive shell hanging at his collarbone, the one Quincie gave him for Christmas. "About the last twenty-four hours: it's felt longer than my nearly three weeks at the pack."

Apparently, not all the answers are in his books. "Time passes differently. . . ." I pause. That's not quite right. "It's perceived differently—in heaven and hell—than on earth."

Kieren draws his thick eyebrows together. "You're saying we're *in* hell?"

"Or damned close to it. Even without Lucifer pulling strings, that may be enough to mess with our heads."

Suddenly, the entire building goes pitch-black. "What now?" I ask.

"Lights-out at 10 P.M.," Kieren replies. "You want the flashlight? I brought it in from the car." He doesn't rub in how much better he can see in the dark.

"No, you hang on to it."

I stay up until well past midnight, waiting. No Josh.

~❀❀◎ Miranda ◎❀❀~

EARLIER, HARRISON SET UP a hammock in my suite because the place "needed more whimsy," and Mr. Nesbit has been running around, chewing on the ropes. As I focus my monitor-com on Quincie, the gerbil scampers up my leg and into my sweater pocket.

At the B and B, Quincie is seated behind her laptop in front of an antique desk and chatting with Freddy on the phone. "We're talking nothing. *Nada.* I sent a dozen messages to both of them, and I've received one ridiculously generic text from each."

Quincie's oversize T-shirt reads FAT LORENZO'S, and her strawberry curls are twisted up with a scrunchie.

Listening, she cocks her head. "They said that they were busy getting acclimated to school and having fun, and they'd get back to me later."

A brown bag labeled GREEN MOUNTAIN BUTCHER SHOP has been left empty on the dresser. Quincie continues, "I didn't get too personal. You're the one who said that their communications might be intercepted."

This afternoon, Quincie called Hawaii to tell the Moraleses that Kieren and Zachary had decided to go fishing. Then she changed the subject to the luau wedding.

I adjust the controls on my monitor-com. Back at the academy, Lucy sits cross-legged in new candy-cane pj's on the tile floor in front of the coffee table in the casual lounge. She's alone, it's dark, and she doesn't try to turn on the overheads.

Instead, she sets a lighted lavender votive candle in front of her. "I should have a mirror," she whispers. "Or a bowl of water. But it's not like I expect you to talk back."

The flame illuminates her face. "Howdy, Miranda," she begins again. "I've been looking for you. If Zachary is telling the truth, then you already know that."

Her eyes well up. "I'm sorry I dragged you out that night. I knew you didn't want to go. We should've stayed in and watched movies. Chick flicks, whatever you wanted." She lowers her voice even more, almost mouthing the words. "I'm so, so sorry."

I can't comfort her. I can't tell her that I'm safe here with Mr. Nesbit.

"I believe Zachary—story, wings, the whole enchilada. Or maybe I just want to believe because this place is scarier than I thought it would be." She tucks a stray hair behind her ear. "Can't argue with the view, though. I'm guessing by the way he talks about you that y'all are an item." She wipes away a single tear and laughs. "That's one hunky immortal boyfriend you've got."

At the knock on my door, I reluctantly turn off my monitor-com. "Coming!"

It's Harrison. No one else visits me. I collect Mr. Nesbit, deposit him in his tank, and cross the apartment again to open the door. "Harrison, I was looking down on . . ."

The girl is attractive and slender. She has slightly drooping blue eyes.

"Who're you?" I ask.

"Cissy!" She holds up a back issue of *Eternal Elegance*. "I'm your biggest fan!"

Yikes! I snatch the magazine from her. On the cover is a photograph of me, wrapped only in a sparkling crimson scarf. A long, flowing, transparent scarf. "I'm not this . . . thing anymore." I'm also not so naked on a public basis.

"I know!" Cissy exclaims, bouncing in place. "That's the best part. Can I come in?" She skips by me. "I adore your suite. It's incredibly normal. I asked Harrison if it looked like the wine cellar or your third-floor nursery in the castle."

Mystified, I watch her peruse my shelves. "You know Harrison, the castle?" I ask.

"Since before I died," Cissy replies, picking up a copy of *The Lion, the Witch, and the Wardrobe*. "Not well. I'd hear him and the other servants talking about you when they'd come to drop off meals in the dungeon." She grins. "This will sound weird, but the hamburger gravy was delicious."

Nora's hamburger gravy. That cinches it! Cissy was one of many among the Mantle of Dracul's bleeding stock, humans kept captive for the convenience of thirsty eternals. Other than the stark cells and terror and blood-letting, their lot wasn't all bad. I wonder if Cissy ever had a chance to try Nora's quiche Lorraine.

"Don't worry," Cissy says, returning the book to the shelf. "You didn't kill me. I died as a party favor at your debut gala. I was one of the prisoners chained to a courtyard wall. The vampire who drained me was a guy wearing a necklace made of baby teeth."

She's talking about Victor, an eternal aristocrat—and she's chatting casually under the circumstances. I toss the magazine onto the coffee table. "You're not upset about that?"

If this weren't the Penultimate, I'd assume that she's come to avenge her death.

"At first I was upset, but then I became curious about you and the guardian Zachary—now *he's* heaven in blue jeans—on my monitor-com."

Cissy clasps her hands together. "So, bygones, princess! I feel like we're old friends. Besides, we're in paradise now! Well, almost. This is our new beginning. It's like we're made of light. Can't you feel it? The warmth? The Light?"

Not exactly. I feel split, as if the best of me remains on earth with Zachary. I feel helpless and frustrated and occasionally furious that he's in danger. Most of all, here at the Penultimate, I feel like I don't belong.

Deflated, my ADD poster child of a fan girl retrieves her copy of *Eternal Elegance.* "Can I at least have your autograph?"

~❦ Zachary ❦~

NOT ALL ANGELS ARE INNOCENTS. I surrender to the dream; I'm grateful for it.

I revel in Miranda in my arms, by my side. Her delicate fingertips circle the cherub tattoo over my heart, and she hooks a slim calf around my thigh.

"My angel," she sighs. "Zachary."

My lips trail lower. I whisper songs into her sweet skin.

My girl. How can I love her? How many ways? I'll try them all before dawn.

"No!" She pushes my hands away and scrambles off the bed. "You *can't* tempt me!"

Passion gives way to confusion. My murky, dreamlike state begins to fade. We're in my room at the school. She's reaching for a sheet to cover herself.

"Miranda?" She can't be here. It's impossible. Isn't it? If Ulman rose all the way from hell, could my girl have journeyed here from heaven?

"Never touch me again!" Miranda exclaims. "Never! You failed me, Zachary. Without your interference, I would've died a natural death in that cemetery. Every life I took is on your head. It's a miracle you didn't cost me my soul."

"I tried to save you. I *did* save you." Or at least I helped her save herself. "What's wrong? I don't under—"

"You're home now, Zachary," she announces, draped in gray cotton like some Egyptian priestess. "Here at Scholomance. You're far beneath me and still slipping. You're dragging me down. You, with your drunken nights and look-alike whores, how could I love you after—"

"Miranda." I toss aside the comforter cover. "I thought I'd lost you forever. I was grieving. You have to understand."

"You are the one who has to understand, Zachary. I no longer love you. Our time together is over. This relationship just isn't working for me anymore."

When I reach for her, there's nothing there. The sheet she took is tangled with my other bedding. I become aware of an insistent knocking on my door.

I let Kieren in. "Who were you talking to?" he asks.

For a moment, I wonder how loud I was. Then I remember that Kieren has the keenest ears in the building and is staying across the hall. "Would you believe it was Miranda?"

"No," he says. "I wouldn't. What do you think it wants?"

For me to give up on her. For me to give up on the idea of ever returning upstairs. "I don't think it's a coincidence that Lucy came here to the school or that we came after her," I say. "I think this is some kind of sting operation. That it's personal, to all of us."

To me, maybe most of all.

⤙ Zachary ⤚

THE MORNING ALARM is as piercing as it was yesterday. So help me, I'm going to hunt it down whether it's mystical or mechanical and obliterate the damn thing.

Breakfast today is much like Monday's, except that Nigel's not hungover. He's buzzed. Eyes dilated. I don't have to be a shape-shifter to smell it on his breath.

Kieren, Evelyn, and I elect to skip the SP uniform. The idea of sporting Lucifer's logo makes my stomach roll. We show up in the classroom a few minutes before 9 A.M. in our regular clothes — T-shirts and jeans.

Vesper and Willa get creative with their uniforms. I'm not surprised, given the way they'd griped about the dress code last night after dinner. Both girls are wearing their SP shirts open and tied at the waist over silky undershirts. Camisoles, I think they're called.

Everyone else looks fairly regulation.

What I don't get is that the supplied clothes all fit perfectly. Maybe the other students indicated their sizes on a form, but Kieren and I didn't.

Today Ulman's manifestation at the head of the classroom is less dramatic. She appears in the same formal gown. I wonder if she died in it.

"Today is the first . . ." Ulman's dead eyes widen. "What is this?" She extracts the lace-trimmed handkerchief from her bodice. "Did the uniforms require further explanation?"

"From a fashion perspective?" Vesper asks. "Do you have any idea what gray on gray does to a girl's complexion?"

Other than Kieren, our declared legacy is the most composed student. Her camisole is forest green. Willa's, coppery. To Vesper's credit, I could swear that she'd been trying to give Willa something normal to focus on.

Ulman waves the hankie at Willa. "We reviewed the policy at orientation."

Ulman's ghostly image wavers again. It briefly seems as if she has four arms—two of her own and two of the devil's as depicted in his logo and signature art.

Before I can think more about it, Willa slumps forward on the table.

"What happened?" Bridget asks as the others rush to help.

"Oh, my God!" Vesper exclaims. "I think she's dead."

"She is dead," Ulman confirms.

In a hollow voice, Nigel mutters, "Eight becomes seven. Who'll go to heaven?"

"Shut up!" Lucy yells. "Never, never rhyme again."

"It's true," Evelyn says in a hushed voice. She has two fingers on Willa's wrist.

"Let's all sit back down," I suggest, sounding infinitely calmer than I feel, "before someone else dies."

That was one hell of a show of power. Ulman didn't utter any words, use any ingredients, or sacrifice anything. I can see why she got this job.

"Bring her back," Nigel screams at Ulman. "Do it now!"

"My available discretion is limited." Her gaze lingers a moment on Vesper, each of the shifters, and finally, me. "Be thankful that I didn't punish all of you."

I can't help wondering why she chose Willa.

Everyone sits. Kieren leans forward as though nothing tragic has happened. "This is Alchemy and Incantations class," he says. "Is there a syllabus?"

Ulman dodges the question. "Today's assignment is straightforward. A resurrection spell that, if successfully completed by the end of class, will result in Willa's being brought back to life with no lingering ill effects."

"You don't mean that she'll be returned undead?" Kieren asks. "As a vampire, a zombie, a revenant—"

"I mean," Ulman says, "she will be fully reinstated as a living human being."

"At what cost?" I put in.

"It's a beginner-level spell," Ulman replies, which doesn't answer my question. "A team project. Choose the words that resonate with you. Chant them as a group. Mr. Bilovski is waiting in the elevator with a list of ingredients."

Her image begins to recede. "That's all I know. This isn't originally my lesson plan. However, it meets prevailing standards. The curriculum is prescribed."

Ulman is somehow simultaneously passive-aggressive and aggressive-aggressive. But is she the devil? And if so, how can she be so powerful aboveground?

"I'll return at 10 A.M. for Demonic History," Ulman says. "Take care that you're not tardy or in further violation of the dress code." She doesn't have to add, "Or else."

Kieren is on his feet. "We have to hurry, people. We—"

"We can't use demonic magic," I say. "That way leads to—"

"The only chance that Willa has," Vesper argues.

"If Willa had died a natural death," Kieren begins again, "I wouldn't consider trying to undo it. But Dr. Ulman struck her down magically."

"Besides," Bridget says, "if a dress-code violation is a capital offense, who knows what'll happen if we blow off our first Alchemy and Incantations assignment."

Lucy gestures to Willa's body. "What about . . ."

Evelyn scoops up the dead girl and gently lays her on the conference table. The Otter shouldn't be revealing her strength like that, but everyone's too upset to notice.

"Should we leave her here alone?" Bridget asks. "What if something happens?"

"What worse could happen?" Vesper mutters.

Nigel laughs, but there's no humor in it. "You had to ask. You just had to ask."

"We don't have time for this," Kieren announces. "You heard Dr. Ulman. We have forty-five minutes." The Wolf glances at the digital wall clock. "Make that forty-one minutes."

Bridget pauses, clearly reluctant to be left alone with the body, torn between her sense of propriety and her rising fear.

"I'll stay with you," Nigel offers, regaining his composure. "She's counting on us, me. I've composed incantations before."

"I'll stay, too," I say, recalling Willa's stories about Nigel's sacrificing lizards with sharpened Popsicle sticks.

The shifters trade a look, like they're weighing

their respective abilities. Then Evelyn offers to remain behind, too.

I glance at Kieren for confirmation. "You're just going downstairs to fetch some eye of newt or something, right?"

"That's the theory," he replies.

~❦ Kieren ❦~

LUCY BOLTS OUT OF THE CLASSROOM. Vesper and I dog her heels.

From behind, I hear Nigel saying, "We should start by free-associating words related to our goal. Like *revival, restoration, resurrection . . .*"

He's either the most manic of the group or the sanest.

That said, saving Willa isn't half as important to any of us as it is to him. I don't think they're *together* together. But sometimes that just deepens the ache.

Mr. Bilovski holds the elevator door. "Mornin', kids. I've got your list here."

INGREDIENTS

Lavender candles
River rocks
Eye of dragon

We ride down. When the elevator opens again, we're faced with a shadowy subterranean space. It's not a natural cavern. It looks like a warehouse with a blue-gray rock floor and ceiling. The room may have been blasted out. Or conjured.

"Did you two catch the elevator code Bilovski keyed in for the subbasement?" Vesper asks. "It's 666."

I should've guessed. I make a mental note of it.

The storage area is filled with long rows of high metal industrial shelves. We pass shelves of school supplies, toiletries, cleaning and laundry supplies, prepackaged food.

Everything it would take to run a boarding school for at least a year.

Moving on, the selection gets more interesting. Whole animals and individual organs in jars of formaldehyde. Fetal pigs, octopuses, toads, ape brains.

Lucy moves in for a closer look. "Are those human fetuses?"

Vesper shakes her head. "Demon. See the little horn buds?"

"Forgive the dust," Mr. Bilovski calls. "It was all

I could do to get the shelves assembled and stocked by New Year's." Punching a button, he adds, "I'll send the elevator back to fetch you. Mind your step. Wild—" The doors close.

"Anybody else wonder how he got that job?" Vesper asks, tucking in her Scholomance Prep shirt.

It's a rhetorical question. The three of us weave deeper into the storage area. We pass containers of sweetgrass, salt, tobacco, honey, cedar, sage. Candles are an easy find. They're stocked in all colors, sizes, and scents. I identify jasmine, vanilla, cinnamon, coconut, caramel, pumpkin, lime, salt, gardenia, the required lavender, lilac, apple, eucalyptus, and a few more unpleasant-to-nauseating things I can't quite place.

"I hear water," Lucy says, pointing. "From over there."

Me, too. An underground stream, probably connected to the lake that wraps around the building. I hear a clicking noise, too, like nails—or claws—on rock. The overhead lights are the same fluorescents as the ones upstairs. But beyond this area, it's dark.

I should've brought my flashlight.

Most of the jars are labeled in broad, clear strokes. Like from a Sharpie.

"Dragon's eye," Vesper reads.

The iris is a flaming orange. The pupil, a long slit. I'm fascinated by the size. I'd been assuming that we were looking for the eye of a Komodo dragon, like at the San Antonio Zoo. This is bigger.

"Dragons are real?" Lucy asks.

I nod. "Or were. In Asia, Europe . . . In Persia, a long, long time ago."

As Lucy reaches for the bottle, I add, "Careful. Every aspect of this is delicate. Forget what Dr. Ulman said. Nothing we're doing is 'beginner level.'"

"We can handle it," Vesper insists.

I hope so. The last time anyone in my life attempted a major spell, the roof of my house blasted off. That involved far less risky Wolf healing magic.

At the end of the row, we come upon the stream. No place where you'd expect to find river rocks. But here they are. I hold the candles. The girls stuff their pockets.

"We're being set up," Lucy says. "Dr. Ulman planned to kill one of us this morning. She'd already dictated the ingredients to Mr. Bilovski and told him to wait. These stones were planted here for us to find."

"You just figured that out?" Vesper replies.

Lucy ignores her. "So, it's a test. Hell of a way to open classes."

"Speaking of hell." I inhale brimstone. "Something's coming." I would've noticed it sooner except for the competing candle scents. The clicking is closer, too.

We sprint for the storage area.

"Please tell me you mean *someone*," Vesper says.

A low *woof* echoes through the chamber. "You two should go," I say.

"What is this," Lucy scoffs, "some kind of sexist—?"

A slobbering, growling hound lands on the top of the nearest shelf. Its paws are bigger than my face. Its canines? Six inches long. The eyes are reddish like a vampire's.

The monster looks like a cross between a bulldog and a hyena, only larger, more formidable. This thing isn't undead. It's never been what we'd consider alive.

I hand the candles to Vesper. "Go! I'll buy you some time."

The girls trade a glance. Hesitate. Under other circumstances, I'd admire their loyalty. I hate having to reveal my secret. But I've got no choice.

I call up my Wolf within. "Hurry! Get out of here." My fangs aren't as fearsome as the hound's. But they're convincing.

Lucy's mouth drops open. "You're—"

Vesper grabs her arm. "Come on. He knows what he's doing."

The girls take off for the elevator.

Fur ripples across my body. My bones grind. Ache to rearrange. My elbows pop out of joint, and I suck in a breath. I've been in fights before, but only once in Wolf form. I'll be better off midway. Moving on two legs. It's more familiar.

I fight to manage the shift. Pace it. Maintain my control.

The hound crouches, snarling lower. That can't be good.

My jeans strain. My shirt splits.

A second hellhound leaps onto the same shelf. Saliva drips in long strands from bared teeth. Agile, muscled, the beast didn't even need a running start. The scent of brimstone is overwhelming.

Demon dogs usually appear in churchyards, cemeteries, along hillsides. In gateways to hell. I might've had a chance against one. But two? I can't placate them by acting submissive. I can fight and die. Roll over and die. Run and take my chances.

Paws slam into my back. A third hound pounds me into the stone floor. My nose breaks. Blood pours into my eyes. Claws tear open my right shoulder.

I try to push up, but it's no use. The monster must weigh more than three hundred pounds. The claws hit bone. Snarling, the other two hounds leap down. One lunges for my leg. It sinks its canines through the denim. I can feel it chewing.

The other huffs at me, like it's thinking. I fight to do the same. I've read of them in England and Latin America, in Tennessee, on Long Island. Along what used to be U.S. Route 666. They're often harbingers. It's said that if you see them once—maybe three times—you'll die soon. Three at once doesn't bode well for me.

I hear a whistle from deep within the cavern. The monsters freeze. They cock their heads. Waiting. I try to twist free. A paw shoves me down again.

I hear distant footsteps. Hoofsteps? Scraping the rock, they come closer. The hound pinning me shakes its head. Panting. Drool drips onto the back of my neck. More whistling. I recognize the song as "Auld Lang Syne."

Shouts drown it out. My rescuers stampede the hounds. I smell smoke. I hear Zach, Evelyn. I'm not sure who else. Blood floods my eyes. The hound at my leg yelps.

Suddenly, I can't hear it anymore. I can't hear the voices. Or the whistling. I'm losing consciousness. I can't feel anything.

~ Zachary ~

WE'RE BACKING into the elevator—waving flaming mops in defense—and the burliest of the devil dogs attacks. Jaws gaping, fangs eager.

I slam my mop into its muzzle and knock it into the beast at its heels, and both go tumbling. They turn on each other and draw more blood. We're forgotten.

Almost. The third charges—frothing and furious. A formidable paw blocks the doors from closing. I kick it—hard—and break claws.

There's a yowl, and the doors shut. Lucy punches the button for the third floor.

Inside, Evelyn and Nigel adjust their hold on Kieren.

We're all breathing heavily. The Wolf looks awful. He's cut, mauled, and bitten. Blood masks his face. He's passed out.

If Kieren were human, he'd be dead. He may still die.

What would I tell Quincie? I'm supposed to be watching over her 24/7. The least I can do is keep the boy she calls Wolf man alive.

Kieren's wholly regained his human features — not that it matters. Vesper outed him as a werewolf to the others when she and Lucy went running for help.

I peel off my T-shirt and tear it in half. "Here," I say, handing a piece to Evelyn. "Press this against his forehead."

I tie the remaining material like a tourniquet around his calf. The muscle looks gnawed. Shredded? The shoulder, worse. But it's the head injury I'm worried about.

Fortunately, shifters heal fast.

"He needs a doctor," Lucy says.

"No chance of that," Vesper replies, blinking at my abs. "Unless one of you has a medical degree that you haven't mentioned. What time is it?"

"It's 9:56," Nigel answers. "Willa is dead for good." The edge in his voice says he's not looking for sympathy, at least not from us.

That's just as well right now. We don't have time to grieve.

Evelyn says, "We should let Kieren rest in his room until—"

"Until Dr. Ulman kills him or someone else for tardiness," Lucy puts in. "No, he has to be sitting in his chair by the time Demonic History starts."

As we pass the second floor, Vesper exclaims, "Keys! We've got to grab some extra uniforms. We don't just have to be back by 10 A.M., we have to look the part."

Right, because defying the dress code is what started this particular nightmare. It takes some doing in the cramped space, but I manage to fish my key out of my front jeans pocket and toss it to Vesper. Ditto Evelyn and Nigel.

It's decided that Vesper and Lucy will ride back to the second floor, grab the extra clothes, and dispose of the mops. On the way down, it was Bilovski who handed them to us from a supply closet. He's the one who suggested we light them in the nearest fireplace and use them as weapons. I don't trust him. But the look on his face said he didn't have a choice about being here. That he's trying to help, the best he can.

The others exit onto the third floor, and I lift the Wolf in a firefighter's carry.

"You know, he might be a werecat," Nigel theorizes as we hustle through the hallway. "Vesper only saw him shift partway and—"

"Wolf," Kieren mumbles. "Definitely Wolf."

"That's disturbing," Nigel says.

"You got a problem with werepeople?" Evelyn wants to know.

"No," he assures her. "I have a problem with the fact that one of us has the strength and speed of a werepredator, and this goddamned place has already knocked him off his paws."

"One of us?" I echo. "There's an 'us'?"

"Of course," Evelyn says, studying Nigel. "Us versus them."

At least that's good news.

In the conference room, Willa's body is gone. So are the supplies we'd gathered in hopes of crafting a spell to revive her.

"I tried," Bridget says breathlessly. "I followed Nigel's directions. I laid out the stones in a circle and lit the candles. I pricked my finger. I did the chanting and waved my arms, but nothing happened. Willa didn't so much as twitch."

In our rush to save Kieren, we left Bridget alone with Willa's body and the task of trying to bring her back to life. That spell would've been completely beyond her even under ideal circumstances.

"The Bilovskis took Willa away," Bridget goes on. "They grabbed all the ingredients, too. It was before time ran out. I told them we still had a few minutes. I said I wanted to try again. But Mrs. Bilovski said that if I tried to fight them, Ulman might—"

"No one is blaming you," Evelyn says, shooting a warning look at Nigel.

Meanwhile, I'm getting Kieren settled in his chair. He's fading in and out of consciousness. The shoulder is bad. I think I can see bone.

Lucy rushes in with gray hand towels. "Use these!"

I do, pressing them against the wounds. They're wet and clean. I'm able to clear some of the blood from his face. "Kieren? Hey, buddy, can you hear me?"

The answer is a low moan.

"Twenty seconds," Nigel warns, glancing up from his wristwatch.

Modesty is forgotten as Vesper dumps spare uniforms on the table. "Hurry!"

Evelyn, Nigel, and I rush to change. When Lucy raises Kieren's arm, he growls, low and menacing. I pause to help her slip the oxford over his T-shirt.

"He's seated," she says. "Dr. Ulman might not notice that he's still in his jeans."

"Zachary," Bridget exclaims, "hurry!"

Staring at Lucifer's logo, I pause with my own oxford in my hands.

"Just put it on," Lucy says. "It won't change who you are."

I don't think I can do it. It's the devil's uniform, his image.

"For your mission," she adds. "For Miranda."

It's the right thing to say.

"Three seconds," Nigel announces. "Two. One."

"Welcome to Demonic History." Ulman nods toward Kieren. "Alas, the mongrel revealed." After a pause, she adds, "Please note that you have all failed your first Alchemy and Incantations assignment."

"What happened wasn't Fate," I say. "It was your choice."

"My available discretion is limited," she counters. "Insolence will not be tolerated." With that, Ulman makes the same murderous gesture toward me that she did earlier toward Willa.

Nothing happens. Apparently, this particular spell doesn't work on GAs.

Flustered, she tries once more. No dice.

I shrug at my fellow students like I don't understand either.

"Welcome to Demonic History," Ulman says again. "Why don't we begin with a story? The setting is a garden. The hero is a weresnake."

I vicariously attended school in North Dallas when I was watching over Miranda. Supernatural trappings aside, the rest of the morning at SP doesn't seem that different.

A teacher, students, nobody bothering to take notes.

❦ Miranda ❦

SNOWFLAKES FALL LIKE LACE CURTAINS. I can barely make out Quincie, who's carrying a substantial-looking, battery-powered bullhorn that she ordered on the Internet and had delivered overnight to the B and B.

She's picking her steps carefully down the sidewalk toward Main Street. Quincie didn't have any time to shop for the trip. She's wearing her Teva sandals over a pair of kneesocks. She has on earmuffs and a long knitted scarf, on loan from the concerned lady at the B and B, but they're for show. Quincie didn't even bother to bring a coat.

I'd guess the temperature is hovering at about twenty degrees, but cold has little impact on eternals.

Quincie pauses to peek into the window of a crêperie.

She's stopped in there before for cocoa and to satisfy her professional curiosity. Over the past couple of days, she's called Sanguini's probably ten times.

Quincie is tapping her free hand against her leg. The average passerby wouldn't think anything of it. Yet I recognize the mix of uncertainty, frustration, fear, and preternatural energy. Her only love greater than the restaurant is the Wolf.

When Quincie doubted herself, Kieren's faith in her remained unshakable. No matter that there had never been a wholly souled eternal before. No matter that every expert on the demonic had decreed it impossible. To Kieren, if it was unprecedented, then she was obviously the first, and he was correct. I, on the other hand, was a pawn of the undead king, who did nothing but stoke my appetite and egg me on.

Still, she is the good vampire, the best, and at my worst, I was very, very bad.

At the foot of the hill, Quincie waits until a truck passes and then positions herself in the middle of the street. Traffic is steady. People here aren't easily scared off the roads by snow. Quincie raises the bullhorn, flips it on.

"Attention, Joshua!" she begins in an amplified voice. "Calling the guardian angel Joshua! This is Quincie P. Morris! I want to talk to you!"

I cannot believe she's doing this. It's simply *not* done!

Did she try calling him privately first? Not that it would've worked, but—

"Attention, Joshua!" Quincie shouts again. "I am talking to the guardian angel Joshua, best friend of the guardian angel Zachary! I am tired of waiting around."

The exceedingly polite Vermont drivers have no idea what to do. Traffic is backing up in both directions. Bundled pedestrians are pointing from the sidewalks.

"Howdy, Joshua! This is Quincie. I know you know who I am. I know you know what's going on at Scholomance Preparatory Academy."

A lone driver honks, giving others permission to do the same.

"Yo, Joshua! Quincie again. Do you want me to tell these fine Vermonters about the devil's school? Hello, Vermont! Satan seeks to corrupt your children."

The honking is in earnest now, and a few cars move slowly past her.

"Calling Joshua! I'm not going to give up! I could stand here yelling for the next century. You know what I am. You know I'm capable of it."

Talking on his phone, a businessman in a gray sedan hits a patch of ice. Quincie dodges, barely avoiding injury. The driver beeps off his cell and keeps going.

"Hello, Joshua!" Quincie begins again, unfazed. "It's me, Quincie!"

"Miss!" exclaims an approaching police officer. He blows his whistle and signals with his hands to stop traffic coming from both ways. "What are you doing?"

Quincie ignores him, her bullhorn still poised. "Do you want me to get arrested, Joshua? Or institutionalized?"

As the officer crosses to her, I zoom in and notice that it's Joshua himself. His dreads are blowing all over the place. I think that's illegal, impersonating an officer, though the Montpelier Police Department doesn't have jurisdiction over guardians.

"Excuse me, miss," Joshua says. "I have to ask you not to stand in the street. You're endangering yourself, your fellow pedestrians, and drivers in passing vehicles."

She grins up at him. "Hey! You're the guardian angel Joshua."

Quincie has never met Joshua before, and, though I don't watch my angel every moment, I don't recall Zachary ever describing him.

"Am not," Joshua snaps back.

"I can tell!" she replies, waving the bullhorn. "Look, I'm not some random person. I ID'd Zachary back in Austin, and he was way less obvious."

Joshua seems stymied. "Less obvious how?"

Now, he's as much as admitted it, which Quincie figures out a half second before he does. "First of all, you're a breathtakingly beautiful man, and second of all, you're a breathtakingly beautiful black man in Vermont. And you appeared after I called to you. This is the whitest place I've ever been, and I'm not just talking about the weather."

Clearly flattered by the "breathtakingly beautiful" part, Joshua extends his arm and escorts Quincie toward the sidewalk.

"No wonder Zachary has his hands full, watching out for you." He leans in conspiratorially. "Now that you know who I am, if I drop by Sanguini's sometime, will you slip me a plate of West Texas rattlesnake ravioli?"

"Depends." She looks him in the eye. "What's happening with Kieren and Zachary?"

"Sorry," he says. "I'm not allowed to say. And even though you're not my assignment, I can't let you get run down either. Zachary would kick my ass." When Quincie holds her ground, he adds, "Come on, I have to clear out of here. I'm not supposed to be identified as an angel on the mortal plane. That's roughly what got Zachary busted in the first place. If my supervisor finds out that I—"

"Please," she says. "Do they need my help? Is it bad? Is Kieren—"

I don't know what she planned to ask. Is Kieren still alive? Is Kieren still safe? Is Kieren still obsessed with her? But it doesn't help when Joshua replies, "His injuries are healing better than expected, and—"

"*What* injuries?" Quincie usually confronts her problems with a mix of humor and bravado.

Without reply, Joshua glances to make sure no one's watching and disappears.

Alone on the sidewalk in the falling snow, Quincie looks momentarily deflated. "Fine," she mutters to herself. "No rattlesnake ravioli for you."

Yet Joshua has answered her question. He told her, albeit not in so many words, that Kieren is hurt.

THE ARCHANGEL MICHAEL

The Sword of Heaven
The Bringer of Souls

To: Joshua
From: Michael
Date: Tuesday, January 7

Regarding your D-665A form filed and dated today, this is an acknowledgment and record of your admission to having revealed yourself in human form to the vampire Quincie P. Morris on Main Street in Montpelier, Vermont.

You are already well versed in the seriousness of this infraction.

I have decided to let you respond in this matter. The time and date of your hearing is yet to be determined. However, I recommend that you begin preparing your defense immediately.

~⚙️⚙️ Kieren ⚙️⚙️~

"IF YOU DON'T NEED ME HERE," Evie begins, "I'm off to lunch."

I'm temporarily out of commission. That makes her shifter senses more valuable than ever. I doubt her Otter nose can detect every poison. Or, for that matter, demonic blood, which can be even more dangerous. But we've both been doing our best.

I'm stretched out on my bed. I try not to wince as Lucy cleans my head and face. My entire body radiates pain. My head, calf, shoulder, nose. I feel the bones and cartilage resetting. My face is so swollen, I can hardly see.

Evie ducks back in. She's holding open a trash-can liner. "Shirts, please. Since we only have two uniforms each, Bridget and I are going to try to remove the stains."

Zach, who's been hovering, peels his off.

I tell Lucy, "You can grab one of my Ts and change in my bathroom."

"I'll bring you back some food," the angel says. "It might help to eat something, if you can keep it down."

"Tell Nigel we're confiscating his beer," Lucy says, dropping her oxford in the bag. "We'll need it for Kieren. At least for a few days."

On her way out, Evie asks, "What about the vodka? Can you use beer to sterilize—"

"I'm thinking painkiller," Lucy explains. "Vodka might be overkill. Ask if anyone has aspirin or ibuprofen. Whatever."

"Be right back," Zach says.

Lucy rakes the towel across my mangled calf muscle.

I bite my fist and draw fresh blood.

"Oh, God!" She rolls up a hand towel. "Bite this instead. Sorry, we can't risk—"

"Infection. You don't have to apologize. I appreciate your—"

"The least I can do. Vesper and I never should've left you like that."

"You went to get help," I say, wincing. "If you hadn't, all three of us might be hellhound chow. Besides, I told you to go."

"You *growled* at us to go." Lucy wraps a long orange

scarf around my leg. It's one of many Vesper donated for the cause. "On the off chance that it matters, I've always been a big believer in werepeople rights. I used to make a lot of noise about it." She pauses. "I used to make a lot of noise about a lot of things."

"Then Miranda became your cause," I say. "I don't blame you. My girlfriend, Quince—Quincie—vanished for a couple of days last fall. I scoured Austin for her. I couldn't sleep. I couldn't think about anything else."

"What happened?" she asks.

"The vampire who infected her locked her up during the final stage of her transformation. When I finally found Quince, she was undead."

After a moment, Lucy asks, "Is that what usually happens with missing people?"

"I don't think so. I don't know. Quince doesn't associate much with other vamps. She's different from the rest. The only one never to have taken a life. That's why we think Zach was sent to guard her."

Lucy stiffens beside me. "So, Miranda *killed* people?"

This is why I hardly ever talk. When I do, I say the worst possible thing.

"Miranda didn't ask to become a vampire," I say. "She sacrificed herself. She found forgiveness. If God forgives her—"

"We should, too." Lucy's smile is wan. "It's just

Miranda, you know." Lucy begins playing nurse again. "You don't know. Miranda was dreamy and sensitive and half-lived in the fantasy worlds she read about. She hid from bullies and got teary at the sight of roadkill. I can't imagine her hurting anyone, let alone taking a life." Lucy pauses. "I can't imagine her ever forgiving herself if she did."

I'm grateful that's something Quince will never have to face.

Lucy gestures for me to roll on my side. When I do, she gasps. "Kieren, you lost a chunk of flesh. It's just . . . gone."

"It'll grow back," I say, my teeth clenched.

She gets up to wash her hands. "I envy you your claws."

Glancing over my mangled shoulder, I can tell she's serious. Lucy is a fighter. That's good. Willa wasn't. I wonder if that's why Dr. Ulman picked her off.

"Give me your room key," I say, "and your hand."

Lucy fishes the key out of her pants pocket. She presents her right palm to me.

I slip the key between her first and second fingers. "Make a fist."

Turning her hand at an angle, she does.

"Now, you have a claw of your own."

~ Zachary ~

LUNCH IS TOMATO SOUP with sour-cream topping, BLTs—
apple-smoked bacon on whole wheat—and freshly fried
sweet-potato chips. I give it a solid B for effort.

"Kieren is a wounded werewolf," Vesper begins.
"Andrew and Willa are dead. What do you think Physical
Fitness and Combat will be like?"

"The fact that Kieren is a Wolf has nothing to with his
being here," Evelyn says. "He was born that way."

"Does the fact that he's dating a vampire have something to do with it?" Vesper asks, between sips of soup.

"Kieren already told you," I reply. "We came to
help—"

"How's that working out?" Vesper asks, putting down her sandwich. She turns to Nigel at her left. "You don't seem that broken up about Willa. Wasn't she your sister or something? Shouldn't you be catatonic right now?"

Nigel dabs his lips with a napkin. "Willa was not my sister. Her parents are not my parents. They locked me in my bedroom at night and nailed the windows shut. They used an ankle monitor to track my every step."

I can't help wondering whether they had their reasons.

"You shouldn't say bad things about the dead," Bridget scolds.

"Technically, I'm talking about her parents," he replies, "and—"

"You shouldn't say bad things about people who just lost a child, either," Bridget adds, waving her fork. "Even if they don't know it."

Physical Fitness & Combat is a bust. Ulman is annoyed that no one is dressed in gym uniforms. When Lucy quickly protests that we never received them, Ulman restrains herself from killing anyone; by the time we return to our private rooms, two sets of shorts and T-shirts are laid out on each of our platform beds. T-shirts with Lucifer's logo.

After dinner, I notice Mr. Bilovski mopping the

living-room floor. It's an almost compulsive behavior. Like he's required to keep busy, even if there's nothing to do.

He rubs his hip as if he injured it. Maybe he slipped on the tile, or maybe he was punished for forgetting to distribute the gym clothes.

Both of his pinky fingers have been chopped off.

I don't ask him about that. Instead, I say, "Thanks for your help with the mops."

I don't mention the hell dogs or rescuing Kieren, but Bilovski's gaze darts to the diabolical print over the fireplace like he's afraid it heard.

I lower my voice. "Sometimes that devil design flickers within Ulman's image."

Bilvoski doesn't hesitate. "He's peeking through."

"But it can't be Lucifer," I say. "He can't have independent power here. The classroom is well above earth's surface. Even the subbasement isn't that far down."

"I first arrived not long before the little horned bastards hauled the rock up," Mr. Bilovski says, leaning against his mop handle. "Hundreds of 'em. The tile in the floor, in the showers, the rock they crushed into gravel and then into cement. It all came from the netherworld itself. The devil blurred the lines, grabbed some territory. This entire building is a hell gate."

Caves in Nicaragua and Greece, a volcano in Iceland, doors in Egyptian tombs . . . Hell's gates aren't that rare, and—unlike heaven's gates (which are literal and polished daily)—they're largely metaphorical. I should've expected one on SP grounds.

If it's true, Lucifer can work his sorcery here. He can not only peer through a descended soul and peek through hanging pictures.

He can walk—fully present—among us.

–⁂◦ Miranda ◦⁂–

SEATED IN A RATTAN CHAIR next to a koi pond in the
Penultimate lobby, I'm amazed when Kieren manages to
dress himself and limp to class. It's 11:15 A.M. Thus far,
everyone has survived the morning without incident or
injury.

Alchemy & Incantations was a review of how to ascer-
tain the best language for a given spell, a more in-depth
discussion of what Nigel had explained the day before.

Demonic History is a comparative discussion of early
fey, shifter, and vampire societies. Ulman says, "Even
today, the fey remain the most successful in maintain-
ing their privacy and security. They are unrivaled in
their diversity and distribution throughout the globe.

Yet no faerie has ever been sold, dissected, or publicly displayed—"

Lucy raises her hand. "I object to werepeople being lumped in with magical creatures. They're natural species, and—"

"Shape-shifters have dabbled, if not excelled, in sorcery," the teacher counters. "Furthermore, their societies are not sanctioned by mainstream mortals."

"They can be dangerous." Bridget turns her whole body away from Kieren. "The predators, anyway—like that Hyena who was caught here in Vermont. He was a baby eater. I saw it on the news."

Bridget sounds the way I used to. Lucy would reprimand me for being a bigot.

Evelyn leans forward. "He was most certainly *not*—"

"Anyone can be dangerous," Vesper says. "Even me."

What was that supposed to mean? I dislike Vesper. It's not jealousy, I hope. I had the wealth that she has, if only in undeath. My preternatural status gave me greater allure. Moreover, I had Zachary's true love, and he only tolerates her.

Yet having ruled over the eternal court, I recognize a gauntlet tossed when I hear it. None of the other students seem to take her words seriously, perhaps because of the way she so often bitches and preens. They're foolish to underestimate her.

The ghostly teacher calls their attention to the topic

at hand—something about a faerie congress. In passing, she mentions eighteenth-century ballot issues involving human-size faeries versus those three inches tall or less.

It's remarkable how adaptable people are. The students have already processed that they have to play along in order to survive.

The guys—Nigel, Kieren, and my angel—have been quieter today than usual. The Wolf may well be in more pain than he was yesterday. Poor thing. I don't know whether the six beers he consumed last night helped or hurt.

"*Tsk, tsk,* Your Highness," Harrison scolds, pulling up a chair beside me. "What did I tell you about spending all your time staring at your monitor-com?"

"You haven't checked on your brother, Freddy?" I reply, slipping the gadget in my pants pocket. "Or what's happening in Vermont? Kieren was nearly devoured by hell dogs."

Harrison tucks his jacket tails under as he sits. I'm amused that he's chosen to appear not just in formal wear, but in a different ensemble every day.

I'm happier in this baby-blue turtleneck sweater and matching pants that tie at the waist. They're not made of anything, of course, but they feel like cashmere.

I can tell from the way his gaze sweeps me that Harrison misses my ball gowns. Of course, he's never had to suffer through a padded or push-up bra. That I know of.

I tell him about Cissy's visit, and Quincie calling down Joshua, and what's been happening at the academy.

"Demon versus angel," I conclude. "Hell versus heaven. Scholomance versus Penultimate. The last— they're both places for the dead en route to somewhere else."

"You know the difference." Harrison waves dismissively. "Don't get sucked in to moral relativism. It's appallingly wishy-washy."

I consider that for a moment.

Harrison wrinkles his fine nose. "Haven't you been doing anything fun? I met Michelangelo. *The* Michelangelo. I took his class yesterday at the art museum."

I knew that Penultimate employees like Huan had already passed through the pearly gates, only to return here to work (at least for a certain number of hours a week). It never occurred to me that heaven provided an art-appreciation program.

Imagine a grand master crossing back to this side to reach out to newly ascended souls! Yet Michelangelo's class seems an odd choice for Harrison. "Since when are you so interested in classical painting?"

"Sculpture, my dear. Sculpture. As in Michelangelo's *David*." Harrison holds up a photo image on his monitor-com. "In marble. Very naked, very attractive, currently on display in Florence."

"I've heard of it." I don't recall Harrison's being such an art aficionado.

He clasps his hands together. "Michelangelo brought his model along to meet the class. The *actual* model! Well worth dying to see, believe me."

So that's it! I recall mentally comparing Zachary to David when he first appeared in my office at the castle. My angel's shoulders are broader, his cascading golden curls more luscious.

Vesper can hardly look away from Zachary, but if there's anything I'm certain of, it's his devotion. I could hardly doubt the angel who gave up heaven for me. He's scarcely more aware of her admiration than Kieren is of Bridget's—or at least until Bridget's discovered that Kieren is a Wolf. Not that I'm in a position to judge.

"Judge what?" Harrison asks.

I didn't realize I'd spoken aloud. "Bridget, the youngest of the academy students." Nothing. "The one who went very prematurely gray and doesn't want to talk about it."

"Lawyer's daughter, poor thing," Harrison says. "What about her?"

On her first night at the school, something that looked like an old woman appeared to Bridget in her room. It scolded the girl and called her a murderer. It railed against her for disappointing her parents and God. It terrified her.

"She's lost interest in Kieren, now that she knows he's a werewolf. He's already taken, of course, but it's her reasoning—"

"Kieren of the pouting lips and bulging muscles? Too young for me, though kudos on that animal magnetism. His muscles aren't all that bulge."

"Harrison!" I scold, but he only laughs. "She's not being obvious about it," I add, "but Bridget isn't bringing him meals or asking about him or even stopping in his room to say hi." When Harrison fails to react, I clarify. "She's afraid of werepeople. Prejudiced. So is Vesper. I heard the two of them whispering about it in Vesper's room."

"Most humans have issues with shape-shifters." He brushes his lapel. "A few hunt them for sport and sell their heads and skins to the highest bidder. So what?"

"I was, too." Still nothing. "Prejudiced. Before I started to become evil, or at least before I was infected with vampirism."

"The Penultimate is full of imperfect people," Harrison replies with a sweeping gesture at the lobby and surrounding promenade. "We've been forgiven. 'To err is human, to forgive, divine.' Once we forgive ourselves and each other, we can enter—"

"Do you think souls make love in heaven?" I ask, taking the monitor-com from him to focus more fully on David's . . . endowments or lack thereof.

I've never seen Zachary in the nude. Not in person, anyway.

"Well." Harrison leans back in his chair. "Far be it for me to underestimate the complexity of the formerly undead adolescent female mind."

"It's like bacon-fried rice," I reply. "Grandpa Shen makes the world's best bacon-fried rice, and he knows I love it." At Harrison's puzzled look, I add, "In heaven, will Grandpa be able to stir-fry me a steaming plate of bacon-fried rice? Or because it's an earthly pleasure, have I lost my chance at bacon-fried rice forever?"

"You've eaten fried rice in the past—"

"Harrison," I say. "Metaphor."

"Oh, right!" He smirks. "Can we agree that sex with Zachary equals bacon-fried rice?"

"Forget the rice!" Come to think of it, the image of Grandpa in this particular conversation isn't helping either. "Why don't we simply say—"

"Earthly pleasures," Harrison declares as a black-and-blue butterfly lights on his perched finger. His smile is wistful. "I wish I knew, Your Highness. Between you and me, I find it hard to imagine heaven without stir-fry. Or, for that matter, bacon. However, it's not as though we're without sensation here in the Penultimate. I can feel this chair." The butterfly launches into the air. "I can see that gorgeous insect."

"We can see and hear," I say. "We can touch."

"Not to get too personal, princess, but from a technical perspective—"

"What about smell, taste?" I cut in. "It hit me after I visited Joshua in the stables. The experience felt incomplete, muffled. When my angel and I are reunited . . ." I would swallow hard if I were corporeal. "*If* my angel and I are reunited, I want . . ."

"Of course," Harrison agrees. "Well, yes. Valid point." Lowering his voice, he mutters, "You'd think I was the virgin."

I return his monitor-com. "Recent apocalyptic portents aside, I may be a virgin for eons. Perhaps forever. As a wholly souled eternal, Quincie could remain on earth, under Zachary's guard, for centuries. Even when he finally returns to the Penultimate, Michael could redispatch him within a blink." I feel guilty saying it, admitting to my selfishness. "I don't want to root for the End Days. That's not a very ascended-soul thing to do."

"Ah, Miranda, you're too hard on yourself." Harrison laughs again. "Think about bacon-fried rice instead! Call me an optimist, but I say that heavenly pleasures sound even more tantalizing than earthly ones."

He seems bemused by the concept. "In any case, we'll find out soon enough, Your Highness, what blessings eternity holds. I'm itching for a cigar myself."

~Kieren~

THE SCREAM AT MIDNIGHT seeps into my nightmare. The shouts that follow wake me up. By the time I make my way down the hall, Bridget is already in Lucy's arms. Her neck is bleeding from two fang marks. She's babbling something about Mr. Bilovski's saving her life. I notice Andrew's head on the hallway floor. His body lies not far away.

Mr. Bilovski is standing outside Bridget's open doorway. He's holding my battle-axe. There's blood on the blade. I wrench it away from him. "I'll take that back now."

"No weapons allowed," he insists.

He smells like piss. "Come and take it," I reply.

Mr. Bilovski might be a friend. He might be an enemy. I'll feel better thinking it over with a weapon in my hand.

The handyman gestures to Andrew's remains. "It *was* a vampire, wasn't it? I wasn't wrong this time, was I?"

Zach grabs Andrew's head by the hair and lifts it. We can all clearly ID fangs.

"Bridget could use some room to breathe," Lucy says, guiding her into the kitchenette. Away from the corpse. The other students follow, except Nigel. He's nowhere in sight.

What if someone bit him, too? I backtrack to knock on his door.

It takes a couple of minutes. Then he answers in his robe. His eyes widen at the sight of my axe. "What the hell, man?"

It's past time to stop coddling him. "The 'what' is this: Bridget was attacked by Andrew, who was a vampire. Bilovski beheaded him. She'll be fine. But she screamed her head off. Everybody started hollering. Did you hear *any* of it?"

He belches. "I was out cold."

I tossed back a couple of beers after I was mauled by the hellhounds. But that's not the point. "None of us can afford to be less than one hundred percent alert. I'm sorry about Willa. I am. But your drinking is not only endangering you. It's also putting at risk whoever you might be able to save if your reflexes were sharper. Or if you were, you know, conscious."

Nigel rubs his eyelids. "Where's Bridget?"

"Kitchenette."

"Be there in two minutes," he replies, shutting the door.

I limp back down the hall. I've already investigated the kitchenette. The glass-fronted cabinets are fully stocked with tea, coffee, and cocoa. Instant noodle soups, microwavable miniature pasta dishes, and an array of snack food. Granola bars, yogurt-covered pretzels, raisins, crackers, chips. A number of processed pastries that could survive the total destruction of the sentient population. Inside the full-size refrigerator: a couple cartons of 2 percent milk; various sodas; an assortment of deli meats, cheeses, and bagels; a head of iceberg lettuce, some fruit, and several jellies and jams.

"Can we agree that vampires are bad?" Vesper asks as I stroll into the room. "Oh, wait. Never mind, the werewolf is dating one."

"Shut up, Vesper," Zach says. He's a forthright guy. But I've never heard him take that tone with anyone before. Then again, he's almost as attached to Quince as I am. And in a mission-from-God kind of way.

Bridget is seated with Evie and Lucy at the table. She's pressing a wet paper towel to her fang wounds.

"Andrew didn't commit suicide," Evelyn says.

"He didn't hang himself?" Nigel asks from the entry.

"He hanged himself." Zach reaches into the refrigerator for a pear. "But it didn't matter because he was already undead."

"He probably fixated on Bridget on the drive from New York," I add. "Vamps do that. Prey are fairly disposable to them. They tend to obsess over those they intend to curse. You didn't drink any of his blood, did you?" I ask Bridget.

She wrinkles her nose. "No, and ick."

"Who knows what will happen next?" Vesper says, toying with her nail file.

I pitch the idea that we all bunk together. Sleep in shifts.

At first, nobody argues. They're scared. The fact that I'm the werewolf with the axe makes me more convincing.

Then Vesper glares up at me. "How do we know that you're not in on it? You're the one with knowledge of the demonic. You're the one with the vampire girlfriend. And you're the one with a massive double-fang scar on your neck. How many people—excuse me, *werepeopl*e—walk away from something like that?"

The scar came from Quince's bite. Brad, the vampire who cursed her, wagered that she couldn't drink from me without taking my life. He lost. He retreated. At least for a time. But I don't owe these people an explanation.

"You're accusing me?" I shoot back. "You're the one who was raised by alumni."

"Not a secret," Vesper clarifies. "What about you and Zachary, though? Dr. Ulman did that kill gesture at him, and nothing happened."

"If he were a bad guy, why would Dr. Ulman try to kill him?" Lucy asks.

"Maybe she wasn't really trying," Vesper suggests.

"I know why the administration did it." Nigel steps more fully into the kitchenette. "Why they're doing all of it. To turn us against each other. To make us doubt each other. So we'll be weaker. Willa's parents did the same thing to the two of us. We have to be stronger and smarter than that."

The kid's not half bad when he's sober.

Zachary nods and hands me a cup of hot cocoa. "Easier prey."

~ Zachary ~

"OOMPH!" NIGEL EXCLAIMS, helping Evelyn wrestle the last mattress into position in the first-floor casual lounge. We've roughly divided the space by gender. Kieren and I are closest to the entryway.

"I'll keep watch tonight." Kieren props his axe against the wall. "In fact, I can keep watch half of every night. As a Wolf, I can get by on four hours of sleep."

"You're still healing up," Lucy says from a mattress across the room.

The Wolf narrows his eyes at her. "The axe makes you uncomfortable."

I missed that completely. Must be one of those shifter-instinct things.

"Guns make me uncomfortable," Lucy replies. "Knives. Things designed for killing people. But we're defending ourselves against homicidal demonic monsters, so I say, rock on with your bad axe. Really, I'm good with it."

Vesper unfurls what she's referred to as a Persian-plum sheet. "Still, why does Kieren have exclusive control over our only weapon?"

"It's my axe," he replies. "I've taken out a vampire with it before. And I'm strong enough to hold on to it."

Besides, as a werewolf, he *is* a weapon. He's learned how to handle that.

Evelyn brought a container of raisins from the kitchenette. She passes it around.

Vesper dabs her forehead with a cold washcloth. The temperature has settled in the mideighties. It's less bothersome to the southwestern students than to those from up north.

"At least for tonight," I say, "the question of watch is pointless. I doubt anyone is going to be getting much sleep."

Nigel, stretched out in front of the fire, begins snoring.

"I stand corrected."

"About the axe," Vesper begins again.

Kieren holds the weapon out to her. "Try it."

She grips with both hands. When he lets go, her knees buckle. "Uh, never mind," she says.

He takes it back and gives her his flashlight instead. "This axe was forged for a vampire, the vice principal at my high school. I beheaded him with it."

Nobody mentions that Bilovski was able to wield the weapon. The old coot is stronger than he looks. Or maybe it was like Evelyn said about Kieren: adrenaline.

Bridget hugs her knees. Her voice is tentative. "Kieren, I'm glad that you have vampire-hunting experience, but given that your girlfriend is undead—"

"You want to hear the story?" he asks, grabbing a fistful of raisins.

Everyone does. Kieren doesn't start by explaining that neophytes are still redeemable. Or by noting that Quincie is an exception to all the rules. Instead, he passes around her junior-year photo.

He lounges, one hand propping up his chin. "It was my ninth birthday. Dad set up a treasure-chest piñata in my backyard. Quince's swing tore it open. She ignored the candy. The confetti horns. The plastic doubloons.

"She put on an eye patch. She ran up to me and bellowed, 'Ahoy, matey!'

"Quince was adorable. I loved her, even then. I didn't care when other boys teased me about having a girl as a best friend. After everyone else went home, I told her the whole truth about what I was. My parents had warned me to trust no one. Every day. Like a mantra. A prayer. I put my faith in Quince anyway."

The girls are hooked. I excuse myself to go to the restroom.

I stroll through the formal living room and foyer toward the restroom past the Bilovskis' apartment. I can't hear any voices or see any light beneath their door.

In the men's room, I splash my face at the sink. When I look up in the mirror, the devilish face is superimposed on mine. Like with Ulman, only the fit is better. As if it's a custom-made mask.

"Dude!" whispers a voice. A hand clamps on my shoulder.

"Gah!" I exclaim, turning to face Joshua. "You scared me."

"Yeah, I got that from the way you jumped and the girly shriek."

"I did not shriek." I glance back at the mirror and my face looks normal again. "Where have you been? Can you tell me—"

"Where have *I* been?" He folds his arms across his chest. "I am not your genie. I'm not your feisty redheaded assignment's genie either. I'm an angel of the order guardian and deserving of some respect. You and your young ladies"—he uses air quotes around "young ladies"—"got me into this mess, and—"

I shush him. "What are you talking about? I'm the one who's—"

"Yeah, uh-huh, it's all about you. The famous, fantabulous, slipped Zachary."

While he's ranting, I peek outside the restroom door to make sure no one's eavesdropping. All clear. Except maybe for whatever the hell that was in the mirror.

"Well, I've got news for you, dude. It's just a matter of time before Michael hauls my ass into his office for a full review of your file and shows up to check on you himself."

That would be bad. "Can you stall him?"

"What do you think I've been doing? Meanwhile, I'm trying to babysit your—"

"Is Quincie okay? I thought she was watching movies at the B and B."

"Now you ask. It's been three days. She's conniving a way into this place so she can rescue you and her hirsute honey, or try to anyway. Kieren told you this would happen. You know as well as I do that you can't expect that girl—"

"I warned her how dangerous the school could be. Especially to a neophyte vampire, wholly souled or not. She doesn't belong here."

"Neither do you. Find a way out, Zachary. Get back to Quincie, and start doing the job you're supposed to do. Now."

At about 2 A.M., Bridget whispers, "Why do bad things keep happening?"

"We're being schooled," Vesper replies. "It's all part of the curriculum."

"I was under the impression," Lucy says, "that they're trying to graduate the strongest, the survivors. Like some unholy reality television game."

"If that were true," Bridget counters, "why would Dr. Ulman be teaching Physical Fitness and Combat, of all things? She doesn't even have a physical presence."

"Why only one faculty member?" Kieren asks, as if surprised it didn't occur to him before. "Granted, we're not a big class. Maybe only ghosts are eligible to teach because we can't fight them."

I see what they're getting at. "How hard could it be to find a gym teacher in hell?" I ask.

"Not very," chimes in every other student in the darkened room.

I fall asleep sometime after four. Bridget shakes us awake before the alarm goes off. She brought her Bible from home. She suggests holding a makeshift church service.

"You may want to carry that with you," Kieren suggests.

Lucy joins them in an impromptu prayer group.

Meanwhile, Vesper announces that she wants to take

a shower. Evelyn goes along so Vesper won't be alone on the second floor.

Nigel and I duck in to the kitchen. Mrs. Bilovski has laid out her traditional breakfast spread. "What are you children all doing downstairs?" she asks.

"Safety in numbers," Nigel says. "We thought—"

"There is no safety," the cook replies. "There is only prodding the Beast or not prodding the Beast. I'm warning you: do not provoke it. Do not invite it further in."

Transcript of Call:
Vampires Quincie Morris and Queen Sabine
1/9, 7:43 A.M.

Sabine: What is this about another letter of reference?
After what I said when we last spoke, you nevertheless
dare to invoke my name with the Prince of Darkness?

Quincie: What are you so nervous about, Your Majesty?
He's a prince. You're a queen. Doesn't that mean you
outrank him?

Sabine: Do not be insipid. You know it does not. It occurs
to me that, because I graced your quaint little restaurant
with my royal presence on Halloween night, you assume
we are friends. We are not. Whatever your heavenly
associations, you are still a vampire, and that makes me
your sovereign.

Quincie: I thought you'd kicked me out, waived my taxes
and everything.

Sabine: I have reconsidered.

Quincie: Because?

Sabine: I have news for you, young gentry-woman. My

consort Philippe spoke personally to a Scholomance representative. In an unexpected turn of events, the administration is, and I quote, "delighted" by your application and "honored" by my recommendation. In fact, you were described as having been targeted as "a prospective student of highest interest" for some time, and your application approval process is being expedited.

Quincie: So it's a trap. Fine. I'm going in anyway.

⎯⎯⎯⎯⎯⎯ Zachary ⎯⎯⎯⎯⎯⎯

THIS MORNING, Kieren decides not to risk Ulman's wrath by bringing his axe to class. Using shifter strength and hardware from our luggage, he mounts it in the chimney of his room's fireplace. He singes the hair on his arms in the process.

In Underworld Governments, we've been assigned to do semester-long independent studies, to culminate in oral reports. I pick the old-school Chicago mafia as my topic. Now that Kieren's Wolf heritage is public knowledge, I want to make a point about what *human beings* are capable of. Besides, Moran and Capone feuded as much over acquiring demonic knowledge as they did over money, territory, and bragging rights.

Evelyn backs me up by choosing the National Council for Preserving Humanity, and Lucy does the same by selecting the Ku Klux Klan. Kieren calls Wolves. Nigel, the kingdom of hell. Bridget and Vesper defer their decisions.

Ulman herself seems at a loss in Physical Fitness & Combat. It isn't just that she has no corporeal presence. I suspect she's never physically faced off against anyone or, if she did, won. For the last two days, she's assigned us to do calisthenics and to jog around the track.

It makes me wonder about her employer. Lucifer is known for his ego, Michael for his work ethic. My angelic performance may be short of the archangel's expectations, but I'm sure he carefully considers each mission he assigns. From what I can tell, the adversary stuck Ulman in this class, without a whole lot of thought, to fend for herself on his behalf. She doesn't matter. The class doesn't matter. This so-called school is a joke.

"Kieren," Ulman calls as he limps around the far curve, "your performance is insufficient. Minimum standards must be met." Without further warning, she extracts her lace-trimmed handkerchief from her bodice. "My available discretion is limited."

Crap. For a moment everyone freezes, remembering what happened to Willa. The Wolf is on the opposite side of the room. If Ulman flicks her wrist, there's no way I can make it across the gym in time to block her attack with my immortal body.

Lucy's hand shoots up. "Dr. Ulman, I, um, I . . . have a green belt in tae kwon do. I volunteer to share my knowledge with my fellow classmates."

For the first time, Ulman smiles. "Very good. Do take over. I will supervise."

I don't remember Lucy studying tae kwon do. It's possible that she took a class or two after Drac Radford made off with Miranda. I can see where that experience would inspire her to learn more about self-defense. Plus, she went through an obsessive period of watching the entire *Buffy the Vampire Slayer* TV series in back-to-back episodes during the summer after seventh grade. But Lucy's never been much of a student.

On the other hand, she gets an A in distracting the teacher.

We gather in two staggered rows, a few feet in front of the parallel bars. Nigel, Kieren, and Bridget in back. Me, Evelyn, and Vesper up front.

Lucy faces us as Ulman hovers above the track behind her and to the right. Ulman hasn't tucked the handkerchief away, but she doesn't seem mindful of it either.

"Tae kwon do," Lucy begins with only five minutes of class left, "is a Korean martial art. It has an emphasis on kicking. . . ." She glances at Kieren's bandaged calf. "And punching." She grimaces at his shoulder injury. Still, she's kept him alive this long.

Trying to mimic Lucy's demonstration, we punch thin air. I can't see Kieren in back of me, but I hear him suck in a sharp breath on the first punch.

Nigel whispers to the Wolf, "You're bleeding again."

"Kieren." Glancing at the cloth in her hands, Ulman apparently remembers what she was saying when Lucy's arm shot up. "Your performance is insufficient. Minimum standards must be met. My available discretion is limited."

A wave of her wrist, and he's gone. Completely. Unlike Willa, whose body remained after her life was extinguished, there's no trace of him left in the gym.

"You killed him!" Evelyn exclaims as the initial shock begins to dissipate.

"I did no such thing," Ulman replies. "I merely relocated him to his personal quarters. His situation did not parallel Willa's. He did not willfully defy me. My available discretion is limited, but I do have some."

Ulman vanishes. The digital clock on the wall reads 2:45 P.M. We're excused.

Everyone sprints for the elevator. We're silent as it rises to the second floor, and then we all trip over each other, barreling to Kieren's room at the end of the hall.

Lucy tries the door—locked. She and Evelyn beat their fists against it. Seconds pass, a moment, then the door opens.

Kieren's blurry, confused. Swaying a bit. "What?"

225

Everyone crowds in, laughing, cheering. Nigel calls the Wolf bro. Bridget wraps her arms around him from the back and bursts into tears.

In light of Mrs. Bilovski's warning, the students voted four to three to sleep upstairs tonight, though Bridget, Lucy, and Vesper are all staying in Vesper's room.

A couple of hours after dinner, I find Nigel alone downstairs. He's positioned himself in a chair in front of the fireplace in the formal living room. As usual, he has a beer in one hand and a cigarette in the other. He's wearing his slippers, and his silk robe reminds me of a smoking jacket. Hugh Hefner Jr.

I wonder if Nigel has, even for a moment, had a stimulant-free system since he staggered through the front door. Has he always been this way? Or is this a self-medication strategy?

"Want one?" he asks, holding up an unopened bottle from the table beside him.

"Sure." He's grieving Willa. Silently. Privately. Trying to man up or some such nonsense. "You loved her. As in, you were *in* love with her."

"It wasn't mutual." He shrugs. "Anyway, she turned out to be every bit as disposable as I was. Like a live mouse that you buy to feed to your pet snake. Not that I'm surprised."

"Because?" Assuming you knew what was in store, sending your kid here is the de facto equivalent of infanticide. Someone like Vesper may have been raised to compete in this environment, but Willa was fragile.

"Her parents, the Wimberleys, they were a piece of work. They had this prenup where if Mrs. W. ever topped 105 pounds, Dr. W. could divorce her free and clear, including child support."

"Doctor?" I prompt.

"Plastic surgeon," Nigel explains. "You know, Las Vegas. There's a lot of money to be made off the showgirls alone. The doc did all the work on his wife and Willa, too. She got breast implants for her last birthday. The procedure was mystical or maybe just experimental. I'm not sure. But when something went wrong with them, Daddy took the originals out and put in new ones."

I'm disgusted by the thought of a father cutting into his own child that way, putting her at risk for no good reason. "You two had some idea of what you were walking into. Why didn't you—?"

"Run like hell?" He takes a puff. "You can't run away from this place. Or at least, you can't run from where it leads. Or at least, I can't."

I twist off the cap. "What makes you say that?"

"Destiny," he replies, like it's funny somehow.

"Crystal ball?" I stroll around the room to make sure no one's lurking around a corner. "Psychic?" I snap my fingers. "Let me guess: somebody read your cards."

No reply. "Tea leaves?"

Once I'm satisfied we're alone, I take the chair across from his. The beer would taste better cold. I'm surprised that Nigel's stash wasn't confiscated like our weapons.

I gesture to his cigarette. "There's a reason people call those things coffin nails."

He meets my gaze. "Is it time for me to go? To finally meet my maker? Is that why you're here, to take me to him?"

The way Nigel is looking at me, I wonder if Lucifer's face has manifested over mine, the way it did in the restroom mirror just before I talked to Josh.

I shake my head. "I have no idea what you're talking about."

He elects not to explain.

For a while, we sit in companionable silence and drink. I can hear the girls' voices upstairs, but I can't make out what they're saying. Finally, I can't help myself. I'm curious. "How do you know what's destined?"

It's possible that the boy has precognition, second sight.

Nigel takes a long drag, puffs the smoke out in rings. "I've died before. Nothing supernatural about it. I'd turned ten a few days earlier. Willa's parents—the Wimberleys—had put in a pool the month before and already hosted two parties to christen it—one for their business associates, one for their coven or whatever it is.

"I hadn't been allowed outside much," Nigel goes on. "A tutor came each morning. Willa didn't have an easy life, but she got to go with her parents to the country club, shopping. She got to leave for sleepovers at her friends' houses. It didn't bother me as much as you'd think. I'd become vaguely agoraphobic."

"But you wanted to swim?"

"I didn't know how," Nigel says. "Maybe because it was forbidden . . . They had this fear of my being around water, fire—"

"There's power in the elements."

"Long story short," he adds, "I drowned. The backyard neighbor saw me go down. He brought me back, or maybe it was the EMTs. I remember a shadowy whirlpool. A voice called to me." Nigel blinks at the sinister-looking print above the fireplace. "He said I already belonged to him. He said that I always had."

"The voice lied." I finish off my beer. "Because of this near-death experience you think you're damned?" When he doesn't reply, I lean forward. "Don't you see? It's the opposite. Nigel, you were *sent back*! You got a second chance."

He gives me a long, measured look and snuffs out his cigarette on the glass coffee table. "You know, I never thought about it like that." Nigel glances at his watch. "It's five till ten. We'd better get upstairs while we can still see where we're going."

On the second floor, Nigel says goodnight. "I still catch sight of him sometimes," he tells me, "the man with the voice."

"The voice from . . . ?"

"When I died. It's strange. He looks a little like me and a lot like you. Not your coloring or features, but he's tall like you. Taller actually, and broader. Like a gladiator."

I wonder if Nigel's memories are more psychological than metaphysical. "There are a lot of big guys in the world."

"True." He lets himself into his room. "But how many of them have wings?"

Whoa. "You can see my wings?"

Nigel reaches into his shirt pocket for a fresh cigarette. "Can't everybody?"

SP goes dark. I hear his latch click shut and the dead bolt slide into place.

I would've never guessed. Nigel is pure of heart.

~⚶ Kieren ⚶~

FREEDOM, FOREST. One, the same. I run. I seek pack, home, meat, mate. Escape the trap, still bleeding. Blood scent prey. But where?

Open. Out! Prey fleeing. Lunge to bite. It gets away.

Chase blocked. Wind shifts. Puzzling, puzzling.

There! Paws slip. Tumble, bruise, tear. Yelp.

Prey gone. No matter. Heat, ache, heavy, straining.

Mate here. Tongue, teeth. Hers, mine.

Slap! "Kieren!" I'm midshift. Quince is shaking me. "Kieren, can you hear me? Do you know who I am?" She shakes me harder. "Do you know who you are?"

Quince struck my cheek. My whole face radiates pain. I catch her forearm before she can slap me again. "I'm back."

My half-shift retracts. I pull her into my arms. "How—"

"Sabine," she whispers, showing fangs. "You're hurt. God, Kieren, your face."

"Shh." This kiss is as tender as the last one was fierce. I wish she hadn't come after us. But I'm not surprised. I try to lighten the moment. "I don't suppose you thought to leave the front door propped open?"

Quince frowns. "Was it a nightmare? A spell?"

Both? It felt so real. Except when I shift, I'm more me. I maintain my human mind. That was a seriously wolfy experience. "I thought I'd found prey. . . ."

"That would be me." Evie staggers in.

Oh, God. In my haze, I mistook her for prey. I bit her left hip.

"I made it to the elevator," she explains. "Came out when I heard voices."

Running a hand through my hair, I move to help her.

When Evie shrinks back, Quince goes to support her from the other side. "Kieren tends to suppress his Wolf nature," she explains, her teeth normal again. "Sometimes his subconscious gets frustrated, and he loses control."

"You think?" Evie winces.

It's a valid explanation. Except I've had full control

over my shift since the first time I managed to go all the way to Wolf and back last fall. "I'm not saying this to excuse myself," I begin. "But I think somebody's yanking my chain."

Quince tracks my gaze to the portrait above the fireplace. "Freaky," she says.

THE ARCHANGEL MICHAEL
The Sword of Heaven
The Bringer of Souls

To: Joshua
From: Michael
Date: Thursday, January 9

Your last several A-127B forms have been uncharacteristically vague in reporting on your principle assignment, the angel Zachary.

Effective immediately, I require more thorough updates. Be mindful of this in future reports.

~❦ Zachary ❦~

WHEN I STROLL into the bedroom, after my morning
shower, Quincie tosses me my robe. "You'd better put this
on," she says. "My Wolf man is very understanding about
our being such good friends, but—"

"Quincie," I say, not even trying for the catch.

Dressed in a Scholomance uniform, she's ready for
class.

I'm mad at her for being here. I'm furious at myself
for creating a situation where she felt compelled to come.
Not that hand-wringing will help now.

"Robe," she reminds me. She points at it from beside
the window wall.

As I slip the robe on, she explains how Sabine vouched for her admission and tells me what happened last night after the taxi dropped her off.

"Evie is moving slowly," Quincie says, "but given Otter healing rates, she should be almost back to normal in a couple of days. The rest of the students don't know, and Evie insists that they don't have to."

Understood. If word gets out that Kieren's Wolf went rogue, he'll lose the others' trust. As awful as it is that Quincie is here, at least she can help keep him in check.

"And Kieren?" I ask.

"He reopened the wounds from the hellhounds, but it could've been worse. Mostly, he's freaked out and embarrassed about having bitten Evie on the butt."

"Evelyn escaped through the elevator?" I ask.

Quincie nods. "From what she said, it was right there."

"It always is after lights out." I vaguely recall Mr. Bilovski telling me that.

"Try to stay clear of the handyman," I warn her. "His wife, too." I grab my Scholomance uniform and go back in the bathroom. Keeping the door cracked open, I fill Quincie in on Bilovski's beheading Andrew. Then I return to the main room and gesture at what was my locked door. "How did you get in here, anyway?"

"Broke the lock," she replies. "I can't budge the front

door, the walls, or the windows, but the interior doors aren't as tough."

It would be hypocritical, as her GA, to complain about boundaries. Besides, the room locks couldn't stop Ulman. Bridget's didn't stop Andrew. If anything, the blasted thing would just slow me down if somebody screamed. If I'd slept with the door open, I might've heard Kieren wolfing out down the hall last night.

I sit on the corner of the bed to pull on my socks. Then bend to tie my shoes.

"Zachary," Quincie begins again. "You're acting so . . . not you."

When I stand up, she takes a step closer. "Do you need a hug?"

"Yeah," I say. "I do."

Ulman materializes in the seminar room promptly at 9 A.M. "Good morning, students. I see our tenth scholar has arrived. Class, this is Quincie Morris."

At breakfast, Evelyn, who's convinced Quincie saved her life last night, sang the neophyte vampire's praises as best she could without actually revealing what happened.

The other girls, except Lucy, looked horrified to have a known vampire among them. They compensated by being overly polite. Vesper included. Nigel, on the other hand, nearly fell out of his chair because he was so wowed by Quince's preternatural sex appeal.

Ulman clasps her ghostly hands together, preening. "I was a tenth scholar, too," she says to Quincie, which doesn't help.

I recall Van Helsing's words: ". . . the devil claims the tenth scholar as his due."

Kieren demands, "What do you mean? There are only eight of us here."

"You're forgetting Willa," Ulman replies. "And Andrew."

"I'll never forget Willa," Nigel puts in.

I clench my fists. "Andrew never even made it to class."

"Nevertheless," Ulman counters, "he was an enrolled student. Lucy, Vesper, Andrew, Evelyn, Zachary, Kieren, Bridget, Willa, Nigel, and Quincie. That's the roll call for the first class of Scholomance Preparatory Academy. Those were the names given to me when I was initially assigned to this post."

I've known since my dream—or hallucination—of Miranda that it was no coincidence, Lucy coming to the school and my following her here. But until this moment, I didn't fully appreciate how contrived the whole Scholomance experience has been.

Quincie is special. Her refusal to give in to her

bloodlust should serve as an inspiration, especially to others who are demonically infected.

I get how that threatens Lucifer. I can see where he'd personally throw his full devious energy to orchestrate laying claim to her soul. Too bad for him.

Quincie isn't just my assignment. She's the little sister I never had.

I'm not giving her up to the adversary. I'm not giving up any of these kids.

~⚶ Zachary ⚶~

AFTER PHYSICAL FITNESS & COMBAT, Ulman disappears again and Quincie lingers in the gym and chats with Evelyn. They'll wait until everyone else has left. Then Quincie will help the injured Otter to her room.

The other girls wander toward the stairs, Nigel trailing them.

I motion to Kieren to follow me to the elevator so we can talk on the way up.

He begins. "About Quincie being the tenth—"

"I know," I whisper. "If we could get to the roof, I could fly everyone to safety, one at a time. But I've gauged the width of the halls. My wings are useless inside."

"Hey, guys," Nigel calls. "Hold the door. I'll ride up with you."

I'd hoped to talk to Kieren in private, but Nigel is starting to grow on me.

Once he's inside, I hit 2 and ask Kieren about trying a reversal spell. "That way, if someone tries to ring the bell or knock on the door, they won't be magically electrocuted."

"Electrocuted?" Nigel echoes. "Like, *electrocuted*?"

"Unless you're an enrolled student, faculty member, or staff member," Kieren explains. "It's not exactly electrocution. It's flashier than that."

According to Quincie, Scholomance's communication efforts on behalf of its students aren't all that convincing. Sooner or later, somebody—like Kieren's mom—is going to show up to check on him. I'd rather she not lose her life over it.

"Returning the building to its normal state should be easier than imposing a paranormal condition on it," the Wolf explains. "My knowledge base is academic, though. Not practical. We have Lucifer's library upstairs. But we can't trust what's in those books."

The look on Kieren's face says he's doing good to trust himself. It occurs to me that this must be especially hard on him. He's always turned to books for answers.

"About the resurrection spell," Nigel begins, "the one we tried for Willa. It might've made a difference if the dragon eye had been fresh."

"Because fresh dragons are lying around everywhere." I regret the words as soon as they're out. Sarcasm isn't helpful. "Ignore me. I'm frustrated."

"We all are," Kieren replies.

The elevator doors open, and the three of us step onto the second floor.

On our way to the kitchenette, Kieren adds, "Dragon eyes are rare. Powerful. It might've been used in enchanting the building. In raising Ulman from hell. Or even in creating the mystic fires in the fireplaces."

As we pass Bridget's and Lucy's rooms, I reply, "You're saying there's a chance that the dragon eye was key to the security spell on the outer building?"

"It doesn't matter," the Wolf reminds me. "The eye has been confiscated, too. I think we should visit the Bilovskis' apartment. It's a stone unturned."

Lucy says, "Howdy" as we join the girls in the kitchenette.

"Kieren!" Bridget exclaims, drumming her fingers on the cover of her Bible. "Ask Vesper why she hasn't started her term paper for Underworld Governments."

He indulges her. "Vesper, why haven't you started your term paper?"

The other girls are seated at the table. (Somebody broke out a deck of cards.)

Vesper is doing leg lifts. She's using the counter like a ballet barre. "Because my topic is zombies."

Nigel laughs. "Zombies don't have a government. They just shuffle around."

Vesper raises her free arm, rises on her toes. "That's my thesis statement."

The visit to the Bilovskis' first-floor apartment is a strictly volunteer mission.

"No pressure," Kieren emphasizes.

In the end, it's decided that all of us together might be overwhelming, but nobody should go alone. So, it'll be me, Kieren, and Lucy.

At our knock, Mrs. Bilovski opens the door. "Problem?" she asks. "Toilet overflowing? Lightbulb burned out? The mister isn't here right now, but—"

"This is a social call," Lucy says. "I'm sorry we're unannounced. If you'd like, we'd be happy to reschedule." She presents a tissue-wrapped package. "Regardless, I hope you'll accept this hostess gift."

It's a shockingly effective southwestern-lady social pitch.

Mrs. Bilovski invites us in. "May I get you something

to drink?" She takes a step toward a kitchenette similar to the one we share on the second floor.

"Please don't go to any trouble," Lucy replies. "You already do so much for us."

Mrs. Bilovski fidgets with the gift. She takes a seat in a chair next to Lucy's. On the sofa across from them, Kieren and I trade a look. We'll let Lucy do the talking.

The décor matches the rest of the house. Unlike the students, though, the Bilovskis have a separate bedroom and the in-unit kitchen.

A gray sheet has been tossed over the print above the fireplace.

The bedroom door is open. I'm not surprised that the outward-facing, floor-to-ceiling window wall doesn't include a building exit. But I feel that remote hope squashed.

Then I'm distracted by the framed family photographs. They cover nearly every visible inch of every surface. A mix of black-and-white and color pictures. Individual and group shots. Depicting babies, children and teens, boys and girls. Snapshots and school portraits. Taken at births, birthdays, holidays, and every days. Every kid has either Mr. Bilovski's hooked nose or Mrs. Bilovski's pointed chin, or both.

Four boys and six girls. They're always well groomed, wearing clean clothes. At least two had braces. Firmly middle-class. The Bilovskis aren't that old—late forties, maybe early fifties. With such a big brood, I doubt the kids would all be grown by now.

"While you're here," I begin, "who's taking care of your children?"

Lucy glares at me. "What he means is, you have a beautiful family."

"Each one my darling," Mrs. Bilovski replies, carefully removing the tissue wrapping. "Each one my precious, precious babe." She unfolds a red scarf with the image of a multicolor winged horse printed or painted on it.

"It's a Hermès," Lucy says like that means something. "From Paris."

Mrs. Bilovski rubs it against her cheek. "Silk."

The scarf was donated by Vesper. So was the tissue.

"Have you ever been to France?" Kieren asks.

"Me?" Mrs. Bilovski exclaims. "Gracious, no. I had my babes to look after, and George and I were so involved in the church. It was our pastor who warned us about the Nosferatu. George took it to heart, bless his soul. Bless all of their souls."

Mrs. Bilovski glances at the digital clock above the door. It's 4:30 P.M.

"Thank you for the scarf." She stands. "I should get started on dinner. It's not easy, feeding so many young people. If anyone knows that, it's me."

Lincoln Bee-Gazette, June 16
BEHEADED CHILDREN DECLARED HUMAN
By Diana Larkin

Three medical examiners have independently confirmed that the bodies of ten murdered siblings, ages six to sixteen, were human beings. The children were found beheaded and hanged from a barn ceiling by their ankles Friday night outside Lincoln, Nebraska.

Although most experts on the supernatural concur that vampires have been extinct since the mid-twentieth century, a media frenzy arose when it was leaked that the word *Nosferatu* had been spray-painted in red several times on the walls at the murder scene.

Law-enforcement officials have not been able to locate parents Gladys and George Bilovski. Mr. Bilovski's sister, Shirley Fieldman, has been quoted as saying that the handwriting matched that of her brother. She also claimed that he was mentally unstable and she had long feared for Mrs. Bilovski and the children's safety.

~❦ Miranda ❦~

I WATCH FROM MY HAMMOCK as my angel joins the others after dinner in the casual lounge. They're gathered in a circle on their mattresses. Mrs. Bilovski's warning hasn't been forgotten. But after last night's events, sleeping separately doesn't seem like such a bright idea either. They're discussing how to reverse the spell on the building. Having run out of ideas for escape, they're trying to bolster their hopes of rescue. It's all they have left.

"Undoing magic that powerful will come at a cost," Kieren says. "I'm thinking of paying with the heart of a hellhound."

"Kieren!" Evelyn exclaims. She's seated cross-legged in front of Bridget, who's braiding her hair. "Last time, those things nearly killed you."

"Last time," he replies, "they caught me by surprise."

Quincie starts to say something—either to protest or to offer help when, in a loud, clear voice, Lucy declares, "That was then. This is now."

Only it's not Lucy's voice, it's mine! Not an imitation, *my* voice. Not that I've ever talked like that. The tone is menacing, sexual, like it wants to seduce them all.

"It's not possible!" Zachary gapes. "She sounds like Miranda. Exactly like her."

The not-Lucy, not-me leaps to her feet. "Anything is possible with faith."

The demonic force is using me, my angel's love for me, to lash out at Zachary.

"That's not Miranda," Kieren exclaims. "Zach?"

The other students recoil. Kieren and Quincie position themselves to protect the rest.

Mumbling in—is it Latin?—Lucy peels off her T-shirt, reaches to unhook her bra.

My angel stands, gripping Lucy by the shoulders. "Leave her alone."

Lucy—or whoever it is—knocks his hands away and lands an uppercut on his chin that sends him crashing into the wall. It's the possession, giving her strength.

Lucy spreads her arms wide. "You all think you were

recruited. Chosen. My, what high self-esteem!" She swings her hips to one side, then another. "It was you who chose me. Or at least came close enough to catch my interest."

She slides her hands up her bare stomach. "It was you who said or thought or acted in such a way that put the fate of your souls in play. You revealed that you might give up anything, even the promise of heaven . . ." She cups, squeezes her breasts. ". . . for whatever it was that you wanted most."

God is always with you, but the devil watches sometimes. Waits.

It's a sobering thought.

Lucy sashays in a tight circle and meets each student's gaze in turn.

"Kieren wanted to be wild, the predator untamed.

"Lucy wanted to know what happened to Miranda.

"And Zachary wanted Miranda in his bed."

Bridget holds up her Bible in an attempt to ward it off.

The possessed Lucy throws back her head and cackles. "You, Bridget, wanted to be a winner. Nigel wanted to know where he comes from. Vesper—"

Quincie grabs the holy book from Bridget and smacks it across Lucy's head.

Lucy's mouth falls open, and six tiny gray snakes slither out. They're hissing, tangled, falling to the black tile and onto her Fighting Coyotes T-shirt.

Vesper screams, and Nigel yells, "Not again!"

Suddenly, the serpents disappear.

Lucy drops to a mattress, unconscious.

"You can't let it into your head," Kieren says. "The demonic is built on lies—"

"They weren't *all* lies," Bridget says.

"We may have been tempted," my angel acknowledges. "But that's not what matters. What matters is that we each ultimately turned back to the Light."

"Once," Nigel whispers. "Or twice. Who knows how long that'll last here?"

An hour later, I'm relieved that Lucy doesn't remember anything about what happened. She appears unharmed, seated in the circle on her mattress. She keeps inundating everyone with questions, using *The Exorcist* as her point of reference.

When Nigel alludes to Lucy's stripper routine, her hands cover her face.

That's when Vesper says, "The devil didn't mention what you wanted, Quincie."

"Or you," Quincie replies. "Or, for that matter, Evie."

Evie is in the restroom, but I know what she wanted: to be wholly human. She confided as much to Kieren on the first night.

When Vesper won't stop staring at Quincie, the neo-phyte gives her a half smile—just for kicks—and asks, "Why? Do you have some O positive to spare?"

"Willa wanted to matter," Nigel declares. "She wanted to become more than something her parents could cut out, cut up. More than their paper doll. She wanted to matter to someone besides me."

Desperate to clear my head, I stomp down the promenade. How dare the devil do that to Lucy—using my own voice! What I wouldn't give to crush his horny, scaled head under the heel of my incorporeal tennis shoe.

I'm about to declare that—loudly and proudly—to anyone who'll listen when I spot my victim in the ARTEMIS GYROS T-shirt. He's sitting off by himself next to a koi pond.

He looks heartbroken.

My anger drains away and is replaced by guilt as I duck behind a palm tree.

I'm probably the last person he wants to see, but I do know him. In a manner of speaking. In the sense that I drained him to death.

I step down into the lounge and approach. "Hello."

He gapes at me. "You're her, aren't you?"

No point in denying it. "I'll leave if you want me to, but it looks like you need a friend." Out loud, the words sound even more ridiculous.

Yet he pats the chair beside him, a clear invitation. "Why are you here?"

"I . . ." Sometimes I'm still not certain. "I was redeemed, forgiven."

"*You* were?" he asks. "For killing me like you did?"

Among other sins. "Yes."

"*Really?*"

Didn't we just cover this? "Yes."

"Ha!" He kicks up his heels and kisses my cheek. "I am Demos, your new friend. My thanks to you for having ascended! My thanks, my thanks, my thanks!"

"What did I do?" I ask, flustered. "What did I do that was . . . good?"

"All this time, I have felt tortured, unworthy to cross through the pearly gates. It's YaYa, you see. My grandmother. I did not come to her bedside when she died. My sister Deira said, 'She is rallying. There is no need.' I believed Deira, but she was mistaken. An honest mistake, but . . .

"When my grandmother lay dying at the hospital, I was eating hot dogs and drinking beer at the Cubs game. I have wondered, 'How I could face YaYa on the other side?' But if you, the monster that took my very life, are embraced here and in heaven beyond, how could YaYa not forgive me?"

~⚜ Miranda ⚜~

MY ANGEL SLUMBERS near the entry to the casual lounge.
So does Kieren, one hand on his axe and the other around
Quincie. It's little more than a gesture, these heroes pos-
itioning themselves as if to defend the others from an
intruder. The next attack is more likely to materialize from
nothingness or to rise up from within.

It's unlikely that they'd all be asleep at once. I'd blame
it on exhaustion, the toll of confronting what must've
been the devil, filtered through Lucy's form and my voice.
Yet I'd expect such trauma to leave them wide-eyed and
vigilant, especially the angel, the eternal, and the shifters. I suspect that this good night's rest is the result of an
enchantment.

As if to confirm my suspicions, Quincie slips away from the Wolf, and he doesn't flinch. It's past lights-out, and the reception on my monitor-com is still sketchy. But I can make out her standing — sleepwalking? — by the fireplace glow.

As Quincie exits the casual lounge, her previously bare right foot, suddenly clad in a red satin pump, lands on a gold-infused black stone dance floor. Her CELL PHONES WILL BE EATEN T-shirt and borrowed cotton boxer shorts have given way to a red satin evening gown. The neckline drapes at an angle to show off her left shoulder, and a side slit in the skirt reveals most of her left thigh. The ponytail is gone, and the curls, too, as if a stylist blow-dried them out. The effect is straight, sleek, and sophisticated.

Worried as I am about Quincie, I can't help thinking how I've envied her curls.

The Scholomance formal living room transforms into a ballroom, and she's suddenly awake. She lifts the skirt of her gown and abruptly drops it.

I can focus my viewer on the students sleeping only feet away in the casual lounge. Or I can see from Quincie's vantage point that the lounge seems to have disappeared. The ballroom in its place appears to be five times the size of the living room. It boasts three magnificent crystal chandeliers and gold leaf on the ceiling and walls.

Here, in the Penultimate, I'm safe from the Evil One's mental machinations. Yet as with Willa in her shower, I can see what Quincie sees. It's not only minds that Lucifer toys with. He can alter the appearance, the experience within his domains, if not reality.

"Hello, baby." A handsome rogue greets Quincie from across the dance floor. He raises his wrist to check two watches. "You're fashionably late."

Speaking of fashion, it's the very image of Bradley Sanguini, modeling a black suit with a white shirt and a dark red handkerchief, tie, and buttoned vest.

Bradley is the charming, nefarious eternal chef who blessed—cursed—Quincie with his own demonic blood, turning her undead.

"Hello, baby?" she snaps. "That's your best sales pitch? You're not even Brad."

He snaps his fingers, and the voice of Eartha Kitt begins singing *"C'est Si Bon."*

"Of course I am." He dances her way with Fred Astaire grace. "Didn't the mongrel explain where you are? What the school is? Hell gates swing both ways. I've returned to renew our love."

Quincie pauses, apparently acquiesing, until he's within range. Then she kicks him in the throat. The blow knocks back the Bradlike creature. The music stops. The ballroom melts away, and he collides with the Scholomance living-room fireplace.

As he struggles to his feet, Quincie says, "I personally launched a holy sword into Brad's heart and turned him into a thirty-foot bonfire. He couldn't return from hell, at least not any more corporeal than Dr. Ulman, and you're solid. I can kick your ass."

The not-Brad's eyes burn red. "Insolent child, you will regret—"

"Oh, please," Quincie replies. "I've dealt with Carpathian magic before, and I'm so over this cheap 3-D mind crap." She glances at herself, clearly pleased to see her T-shirt and Kieren's boxers again.

As the monster disintegrates, she adds, "At least the *real* Brad realized that a sinfully delicious marinara, sautéed with farm-fresh basil and oregano, is the way to woo me. You run a lousy school and a worse kitchen. Those tuna sandwiches Mrs. Bilovski served for lunch? The iceberg lettuce was wilted, and the fish smelled overripe."

Quincie has faced down what may be Lucifer himself and has emerged unscathed.

Where her soul remains gloriously whole, I squeaked into the Penultimate a mere sliver of my former self. Yet I wonder if I've begun to heal, if I could be whole again, too.

Because I'm bursting with pride and love for Quincie.

⤚❧ Kieren ❧⤙

WHERE'S QUINCE? I push up. Grab my axe. Sprint to the
living room. She's alone, seated in front of the fire.

"Hey, you all right?" I cross to join her. "Are you
thirsty?"

Quince threads her fingers through mine. "I brought
a couple Thermoses of porcine blood with me from the B
and B. They're hidden behind the milk in the kitchenette
refrigerator upstairs. If I'm careful, I should be okay for a
few days. Maybe a week."

That deadline could be trouble. We still have no escape
route. Mr. Bilovski has a serious hate on for vampires. So
we can't ask his missus to serve Quince animal blood.

I'll offer my neck if Quince needs me. It's something we've done once before. Under duress. It was as erotic as terrifying.

The repeated portrait of Lucifer gazes down on us. It bides its time.

~∙∙∙ Kieren ∙∙∙~

AFTER BREAKFAST, Quince stops me in the foyer. She glances back at the elevator. "Where're you going with that axe?"

She knows I plan to take out a demon dog. Use its heart to try to defuse the mystical charge on the building's exterior. "Quince."

"Take the weekend to heal," she says. "There's no immediate reason to push it. Freddy knows better than to charge in. Your family is still in Hawaii."

I hate being caged. I want to *do* something. It sounds whiny even in my head.

"Stay smart," Quince urges. "Stay alive. The students need you. I need you. Don't let this place make you crazy. No suicide missions, *capice*?"

I let the axe fall to my side. "What're we going to do all weekend?"

Quince's lips curve. She plants them on mine, licks my top lip.

Hoots and whistles come from the others, peeking out of the dining room. Scholomance Prep isn't conducive to privacy. "Plan C?"

"Homework," she suggests.

We elect to focus on our Demonic History reports. In the library, Bridget helps me pull and organize stacks of research materials. One for Nigel on hell. On the Mantle of Dracul for Quince. On the KKK for Lucy. On the mafia for Zach. And on Wolves for me.

"I have to pick a topic," Bridget says. "I don't want to fall behind."

"How about werearmadillos?" I suggest. "One of my best friends was a 'Dillo. Travis. Sweetest guy I've ever met. You could research the werearmadillo royal family."

"There's a werearmadillo royal family?" she asks, clearly charmed.

"Books on shifters are over there." I gesture. "I flipped through. They look okay."

Bridget skips off. I'm glad she's more open to were-people. I see no reason to mention that Travis was murdered by a fellow wereperson—a Cat.

By midafternoon, everyone has claimed a spot at the tables. Except me and Vesper. She's flipping through a fashion magazine in a plush chair. Looks like her zombie report is going as well as expected.

I tell Evie, "I still can't find anything on the NCPH."

"No worries," she assures me. "I intend to be my own first-person resource."

I don't need to research Wolves. I've been doing that my whole life.

Bridget and Lucy duck out to go to the restroom down the hall.

Quince motions me over. She whispers, "How do you know Ulman's not a regular ghost? How did you figure out she was—"

"Previously descended. At first, it was just a hunch. But given her power level, and the way the devil's image seems to flicker within her own, I'm as sure as I can be."

Quince is ignoring the Dracul stack to study a book on wraiths. "Could we send Dr. Ulman into the Light?"

Zach, seated across from her, shakes his head. "The Light won't take her."

After a moment, Nigel asks, "Could we banish her back to hell?"

"We could try," I say, "but incantations take time. She's quick with that hankie."

"What if we trigger the spell the second Ulman appears for Alchemy and Incantations?" Evie puts in from next to Quince. "You know, surprise her."

I think it over. "It wouldn't be easy. If we could get by the hellhounds . . . I remember smelling sweetgrass and sage in the storage area. But even if we succeeded, we'd still be trapped inside the school. Lucifer could toss Ulman right back up at us."

Vesper is the one who says what we're all thinking. "All it would accomplish is pissing her off. And she's such charming company already."

~❀❂ Zachary ❂❀~

THE ALCHEMY & INCANTATIONS assignment on Monday morning involves making a firecracker sound. It requires whistling a jaunty tune while pouring sea salt over the carcass of a hairy-necked tiger beetle. Only Kieren, Nigel, and Lucy manage to pull it off.

When the bald guy strolls in two minutes before Demonic History, I recognize him right away as an angel. It's the way he holds his shoulders squared, like he misses his wings. He's not an archangel. I know all of them. But there are many guardians.

He's wearing SP gray. The blazer with the Lucifer logo dresses up his uniform. If he's still full status, I'd eat my halo. If I had a halo.

"If it isn't the man of my dreams!" Vesper launches herself into his arms. "Seth!"

I wonder how literally she means that. Seth makes a show of French-kissing her, and I remember Lucy mentioning him. The school's head recruiter. Some parent-alumni combo pulled in Nigel, Willa, and Bridget. Kieren, Quincie, and I came on our own. Andrew, who knows?

But Lucy, Evelyn, and Vesper dealt personally with Seth. He lured them here. Or at least, in Vesper's case, convinced her to honor her alumni parents' wishes. Evelyn heard of the program through a friend of a friend of a friend, but it was Seth who talked to her—who chatted up all of them—on the phone.

Over Vesper's shoulder, Seth calls, "Evelyn, enjoying your second chance?" His gaze moves to Lucy. "Finding the answers you wanted?"

I hate him. I'm about to say so when the digital clock flashes 10 A.M.

"Please be seated," Ulman begins. "It is time for class to commence."

Vesper giggles at whatever the traitor is whispering in her ear.

The shifters, who can hear for themselves, look aghast.

"It is time for class to commence," Ulman says again.

We all take our seats, except Vesper, who gently urges Seth into her chair first. Then she plants herself provocatively on his lap. "Aren't you cozy?" she coos.

I'm not shocked by Vesper's swing in loyalty. I am disappointed.

"Seth," I begin. "I don't think we've met. I'm Zachary."

"Mornin', brother," he replies. "How're you liking your education?"

"Silence," Ulman orders. "Today, we have a guest speaker. Seth will be talking about Nigel's independent-study subject: the history of angels in the kingdom of hell. Nigel, you'll want to be sure to listen carefully and take notes."

As Vesper stands to let Seth up, she shakes her wrist and a metal rod falls from her left sleeve. Catching it in her right hand, she turns to jab at his heart.

He's too strong for her. Seth intercepts Vesper's weapon. With his free hand, he flips up the table, which knocks down Nigel, Quincie, and Kieren. Then Seth drives the rod through Vesper's heart and runs out the door.

I chase after him.

From behind, I hear Bridget scream, then Evelyn. I hear Ulman ranting about Scholomance policy. Almost to the elevator, Seth makes a 180. "You see, baby brother, you're following me already. Practice saying it: 'Hail, Lucifer, my king!'"

He dematerializes before I can reach him. That was no ordinary fallen angel. That was the Enemy himself.

He's been here the whole time.

Screw him. The others need me.

The table has been set back upright. Lucy is cradling Vesper on the floor. The other students have gathered around them.

Ulman urges us all to our seats. Despite her power, no one cares. This isn't like what happened to Willa. Vesper isn't dead yet.

Nigel and Bridget make room for me, and I move in closer to smooth Vesper's hair.

"I came here to destroy this place," she whispers. "That's what I wanted, more than anything. I would've burned it to the ground, if you all weren't trapped inside."

"You had me fooled," I say. "I didn't—"

Vesper's grin is more of a grimace. "I make a believable bitch, don't I?" Her laugh is weak, bloody. "You're pretty, Zachary. Not real bright, but pretty."

One more breath and she's gone.

Over Ulman's protests, Lucy says, "We'll try the resurrection spell again and—"

"Forget it," Kieren declares. "Willa's death was magical. Vesper was killed with something of this earth."

Not by *someone* of this earth, but it's the means—not the actor—that matters.

The Wolf yanks the rod out of Vesper's body, and more blood pours out and pools below. I recognize it as a towel bar. From her private bathroom, I bet. She had that metal nail file. She could've used that to unscrew it.

"Be seated," Ulman insists. "This is Demonic History,

not Alchemy and Incantations." She turns toward me and ceremonially announces, "During class time, you may not leave without my express permission. Zachary left class without being excused."

She jerks her wrist my way. I'm not sure if she's trying to kill me or relocate me. Again, nothing happens. "Zachary, you are hereby expelled. You will leave alone. Mr. Bilovski is holding the elevator for you. He is authorized to take you to the roof."

Bridget exclaims, "Bilovski is going to throw Zachary off the building?"

"Don't be ridiculous," Ulman says. "You all will go to observe and write a two-page report for tomorrow on what you see. Consider this a field trip."

The roof is *outside*. The roof means my wings are back in play. Quincie and Kieren are already on their feet and headed around the table. I feel guilty for abandoning Vesper's body, but nothing can bring her back now, and this is the first break we've had.

It's a race to the elevator.

⊸⊛⊙ Zachary ⊙⊛⊶

IN THE ELEVATOR Kieren hands me the towel bar. It still has Vesper's blood on it.

The students look less shell-shocked than they did after we lost Willa.

They're adapting. Accepting, or at least compartmentalizing. I hope it's a sign of strength, not resignation. We're not out of here yet.

The doors open to the roof. Cold hits like a physical blow. It's ten, maybe twenty degrees below zero. I'm ready to bust out my wings. Then I look up.

I'm facing a twenty-foot-tall, slate-colored dragon with a spiked head frill. It's missing its right eye. It's trapped a squirming, sobbing, very *alive* Willa beneath one of its front paws. They're both wet, which is risky at this temperature. At least for her.

Shaking its enormous head and scales, the dragon tosses water in all directions. Up front, Kieren, Quincie, Lucy, and I get the brunt of the spray.

The winter wind blows, making it worse.

"Good morning, Zachary," Ulman says, materializing as the others stumble out of the elevator. "This dragon has come to take you away."

I glance at the blood-stained towel bar in my hands. A toothpick would be about as effective.

When I loosen my grip, Nigel snatches away the bar and charges the dragon's paw as he shouts Willa's name.

The dragon swings its head, knocking Nigel off the building.

Before I can think twice, I fly up and intercept the kid in midair.

If I set Nigel down by himself on the ground in these hills, in this weather, it would be the equivalent of a death sentence. Besides, he'll never run away from SP now. Not without Willa.

Nigel squirms. The bar slips away. "Whoa!" he yells.

"Be still so I don't drop you on your head." It's not the most angelic thing to say.

Lucy runs to meet us on the roof, and she gives Nigel a quick hug.

Kieren and Quincie stand shoulder to shoulder in front of the other girls, who're gaping at my wings. Kieren never takes his eyes off the dragon.

"Zachary," Ulman says, materializing by the dragon's side. "You have been expelled for leaving class without permission. I seem to be incapable of killing you. Therefore, this fine fellow will escort you directly to hell."

"That's not what *expelled* means," Evelyn shouts. "It means—"

"Not in accordance with your contracts," Ulman informs her. "You agreed to abide by the rules of this institution. Leaving class without permission is forbidden. My available discretion is—"

"Limited," Kieren finishes. "We've heard it before."

I think back on what the devil said to me in the third-floor hallway, that I would hail him as my king. Has this been his plan all along, to trick me into joining his army of fallen angels? Did he recruit Lucy simply to lure me through Scholomance's front door? To get me to subject myself to his rules, tempt me to break one?

If so, it worked. I would've done almost anything for someone Miranda loved.

I wasn't an easy catch. My slipped status has made me more wary of evil.

What I don't get is, why bother?

What about *me* was worth so much trouble?

Bridget draws papers from her pants pocket. She unfolds them and begins to study them.

"Zachary," Ulman begins again. "It's no longer a secret that you're a flight risk. If you come willingly, Willa will be released."

What else can I do? "Fine."

The dragon lifts its paw. Willa struggles to her feet. Nigel charges forward again, this time to assist her. Evelyn starts to follow.

Then Quincie raises a warning hand, urging the Otter to stay back from the dragon. Smoke is rising from its nostrils. If that thing can breathe fire, there's nowhere to go except back inside SP. The fact that I'm immortal doesn't mean I can't be barbecued.

I escort Lucy to the group. Nigel half-carries Willa behind Kieren and Quincie. There's no reason to prolong this. Willa needs a hot shower and blankets—stat. I'm about to say my good-byes when Bridget runs up to me.

"Did you *sign* your contract?" Bridget asks. She's holding her fistful of paperwork. "The one in that manila folder of forms on your desk when we first arrived?"

The forms looked standard, boring. "I never signed or turned anything in."

"Me neither," Kieren adds, reading over Bridget's shoulder.

"You can't take Zachary," Bridget informs Ulman.

"Or, for that matter, Kieren. You have no right to them. They didn't consent to this overly vague, tiny-print, boilerplate provision allowing 'special disciplinary action in accordance with the traditions of this and its affiliated institutions.' So, tough luck."

"It makes no difference if they actually signed," Ulman counters. "They applied and were accepted and—"

"Except," Bridget interrupts, "it says here, lower down, in even tinier print, that subjecting oneself to the contract requires express consent."

Otherwise, the literally Highest Court can step in and toss out the whole thing. Bridget is right. Fate isn't running a free-for-all. There are rules of engagement between heaven and hell. Free will is what makes one's destiny.

"The rules must be enforced." Ulman zeroes in on Quincie. "You are the tenth scholar. Already tithed to the Luminous One. Who better to pay for the angel's misdeed?"

Not only was Lucy the bait, Quincie is the devil's ace in the hole.

Before I can protest, Bridget prompts, "Quincie? Did you sign?"

As Kieren reaches for her, Quincie replies, "I didn't even open the envelope."

I can't help feeling proud of her. Lucifer is used to dealing with the weak willed. He may have tempted her into becoming the tenth student through the front door, but Quincie will never succumb to his expectations for a tenth scholar. She's learned to define herself.

Ulman paces, fuming. "A student must be punished, an example set." Turning, she claps her hands beneath her bosom and tells the dragon, "Take another one. It doesn't matter which."

Fire pours from the dragon's mouth and scatters us to either side of the elevator.

I can't fly the students to safety, not all of them. Not at once. I should save Quincie. She's my assignment. But Lucy, she's Miranda's best friend. And Kieren . . . He'll be killed, trying to protect the rest.

Once the flame subsides, Lucy darts to press the elevator button.

The dragon bounds forward, quick for something so huge. It scoops Lucy up into the air with one paw and then catches her in its claws.

"Not Lucy!" Ulman screams at the beast. "I need her to TA gym!"

"The elevator," Kieren shouts as the door opens. "While it's busy, go!"

Ulman points at Nigel. "What about that one? Why don't you want him?"

"I didn't sign," Nigel says. "Willa's parents filled out the forms for both of us."

Everyone but the Wolf and Quincie hurries inside

the elevator. The doors close, shielding them. For now.

Carrying Lucy, the dragon takes flight, but it's not the only one with wings. I'm diving after it into the lake.

I ditch my wings a second before hitting the water. I understand now why it hasn't frozen over. There's a fire-breathing dragon living here. I can't see anything below the surface, except some lava rocks along the SP foundation.

My lungs burn. I can't hold my breath much longer.

I can't believe this. I've lost Lucy, lost her to him.

Up top, Quincie and Kieren are on the roof with Ulman.

When I rejoin them, the ghost says, "Get inside the school, or I will kill the werewolf."

The thought of walking back in is physically painful, but what choice do I have?

First I glance to the heavens. I imagine my Miranda, my girl, looking down. "Pray for us," I tell her. "We need all the help we can get."

~ Kieren ~

THE GIRLS HURRY WILLA into a hot shower. She's changed into a school uniform in time for Underworld Governments. By then, Vesper's body has been removed.

We gut our way through the rest of the morning. Losing Lucy. Willa's return. Zachary revealed as an angel. It's a lot to process. Nobody says much, even at lunch.

Then, in Physical Fitness & Combat, Dr. Ulman announces that, starting tomorrow, we'll pair off in blood matches. Forget that.

Forget the reversal spell on the building. We're not waiting for rescue.

We're leaving. All of us. I have faith that we'll find a way.

But come hell or high water, this was our last day of class.

"Since we arrived," I begin in the first-floor living room, "we've been reacting. Playing by the Scholomance rules. Or paying the price. Although . . ." I nod to Bridget. "The devil clearly underestimated one member of our team."

Willa is snuggled under Nigel's arm on the sofa.

"What else *can* we do?" Nigel asks. "We're up against a ghost who can kill or relocate someone with a flick of her hankie. Whatever possessed Lucy. Then there's that really tall, bald guy who looks like Zachary and murdered Vesper."

"He does not look like Zachary," Quince insists from the chair closest to the fireplace. "They're both more than six feet tall, appear to be about the same age, and they have a similar build. But Seth's coloring is much fairer, and he looks sunburned."

"Don't everybody freak out." Zach sips his Dr Pepper. "But I think Seth *is* the devil. If you see him again, don't trust anything he says."

Nobody freaks out. But they take a couple of minutes to consider that.

"Isn't Lucifer a fallen angel?" Evie asks, glancing at the fireplace print.

"A fallen archangel," I say. "Zach is a guardian angel."

Bridget moves in from the window wall. "Are *you* a bad angel?" she asks Zach.

"I am not a bad angel," he assures her. "I'm just not great at my job."

Willa stands. "I first came to near a stream by the storage area in the subbasement. Then I blacked out again. For days, I guess. Finally, I woke up in a cavern by the lake. The dragon grabbed me and brought me out through the water."

"Do you know who resurrected you?" Quince asks.

Willa shakes her head. "I don't remember."

"It took Lucy to hell by diving back down," Evie reminds us.

"So the lake leads to both hell and freedom," Nigel points out. "Maybe."

"The water isn't that cold," Zach adds. "If we could find a way to dry off—"

"We packed blankets," I say. "They're in the SUV."

"Hang on," Bridget says. "The cavern opening to the lake could be separated from the subbasement by tons of rock. It's possible that Willa wasn't carried there, but instead Ulman magically teleported her like she did with Kieren that day from the gym."

At Willa's baffled look, Nigel whispers the story to her.

"A lot of things are possible," I reply. "We have to try."

"Uh, guys?" Evie begins. "You're forgetting the three hell dogs."

"If there were only three originally," Willa informs us, "then they're down to two. I saw one with its heart cut out. The other two were eating it."

Someone beat me to the hunt.

Odds are, whoever it was took that fresh heart as a sacrifice. Used it in a spell to restore Willa. The Bilovskis? I haven't seen the handyman lately.

"I see no reason to wait," the angel says. "Kieren, with your nose, you can smell those hellhounds coming. You lead everyone else out."

"Where are you going?" Quince asks.

"To bring back Lucy," Zach replies, "from hell."

-&& Zachary &&-

I'D EXPECTED TO WANDER a while with the others through the caves. Fighting off devil dogs, in search of our respective paths.

Instead, when we step off the elevator, there's a new signpost. One arrow points toward the warehouse area. It reads: VERMONT. The other points back at an angle, as if around the elevator car. It reads: THE KINGDOM.

Because as long as you're evil incarnate, why not be pretentious about it?

"This is where we part ways," I say.

"I've been thinking," Quincie says. "I'm the one with preternatural power. I should go with you and—"

"You should leave with Kieren," I reply. "If you value what I try to do as your GA, honor that by leaving this place." Truth is, the Wolf guards her better than I do.

"Don't you think the devil is out to get you?" With his good leg, Kieren kicks down the sign. "And cocky about it? Why give him what he wants?"

"With every second that passes," I say, "Lucy is in torment. I don't care what she signed. It's my place as an angel to bring her home."

It's not total BS, unless you factor in that GAs are supposed to have nothing to do with the demonic. Or, for that matter, battle. But to hell with the rules. Literally.

I take what may be my last look at the remaining students. They're armed with one battle-axe, a pack of matches, a bottle of aerosol hairspray (from a nearby shelf), two mops, and Vesper's Persian-plum sheet. The idea is that the alcohol will function as an accelerant in case they encounter the hellhounds again.

Nigel pulls me aside. "Take me with you."

I'm surprised that he'd separate from Willa, but I've got no time to deal with adolescent male posturing. "Give me one good reason I should."

"I'm Satan's son," he replies.

-❧ Miranda ❧-

USING MY MONITOR-COM in the lounge, I can't see my angel or Lucy at all. I lost sight of Lucy only seconds after the dragon plummeted into the lake. I lost sight of Zachary once he stepped into the subbasement. I can't see any of the students now.

Frantically, I zoom around the building. Nothing.

Shutting down my monitor-com, I slip it in my pocket. For days, I've taken comfort in the idea that, if something fatal happened to Lucy, we'd be reunited in heaven. Now, she's—as a mortal—been sentenced to hell. What does that mean? Does the devil have claim to her soul, too? And what of my angel?

I wonder if Zachary and Nigel will cross paths with Vesper, and I feel a stab of guilt at having misjudged her, though she was putting on a good act. I wish we'd had a chance to meet, if only so I could've shown her the proper way to assassinate a dark lord.

Wondering what to do next, I regard the bloom of a nearby bird-of-paradise flower.

"Miranda Shen McAllister?" calls Renata, the reunion coordinator.

I stand up from the rattan chair. "Is it Lucy?"

I don't know if I hope so or hope not.

"No, another young lady. Tamara O. Williams. Do you remember her?"

"Yes." She's the young weredeer I drained at the Edison Hotel. My last victim.

Renata gestures. "Please sit. You are by no means required to agree to this meeting. Her counselor from the Ascended Souls Mental Health Board, while acknowledging that such an exchange may be cathartic, is concerned—"

"That I'll say the wrong thing?" Tamara interrupts, coming around the nearest palm tree. "That I'll upset the darling serial killer? That she'll have to deal with having ripped away my dreams of being an artist and marrying Corey?"

"Ms. Williams," Renata begins, "you were warned—"

"What are you going to do," she asks, "send me to hell?"

"It's fine," I reply. "I'll talk to her."

"Perhaps somewhere less public," Renata urges as two elderly ladies and one animal-form werehog retreat from the conversation area. "I can provide a private, neutral room and a qualified therapist to facilitate—"

"It's fine," I say again. Since the moment I died, this is the confrontation I've been waiting for. I didn't know it would be Tamara, yet someone would have to hold me accountable for my crimes. I summon up the last vestiges of my royal composure. "We don't need a babysitter."

Clearly taken aback, Renata excuses herself.

Tamara tears a long leaf off the closest fern and begins shredding it. She tells me about how she began as a painter and then started doing collage, but decided to go into arts education after teaching at a summer camp for disadvantaged kids.

She tells me about her fiancé Corey, how they met at the Indianapolis airport and ended up seated next to each other on the flight to Boston. She explains how by the time they landed, she was certain that she'd marry him someday. He was a Deer, too, and in animal form, he had the most attractive set of antlers she'd ever seen. "You took all that away from me, from us. I can't let go. I can't move on. I watch over him day after day."

I stay still, penitent, my hands folded in my lap.

Tamara bursts into tears. "He . . ." She gulps. "He kissed my cousin Ellen in the funeral limousine."

That was not what I was expecting her to say.

"Grief," I begin. "They were both hurting, and, for a moment, that drew them together. I'm certain they're both embarrassed and regret—"

Gulping, Tamara shakes her head. "No, they're dating now on the sly. Our friends, my family, they don't know. My mother knitted him a scarf for Christmas. They were screwing around behind my back before I died, even after we got engaged. I heard them talking about it." She sinks into the chair beside mine. "She does things with him in bed, sexual things that I wouldn't do, if you know what I mean."

I don't. I nod anyway and risk petting her shoulder.

"If you hadn't killed me," Tamara concludes, "I would've married the jerk."

-⁓ Zachary ⁓-

NIGEL AND I take cautious steps on a narrow rock path with steep drops on either side. I considered flying down, carrying him, but I don't know how long the trip might be. The curves and corners are unpredictable. I don't want to wear myself out or break one of my wings or crash. We have enough to worry about.

"Do you want to talk about it?" I ask.

"I've always known," Nigel says. "For as long as I can remember, Willa's parents emphasized to me that I was spawn. I tried to be evil, to live up to my legacy. It's just not me. Now you're claiming I'm pure of heart. Daddy must be so disappointed."

As we descend into darkness, I can already feel the temperature rising, the air heavier with soot. I wish Nigel would put out that cigarette.

I think we should be shimmying through crevices. Crawling on our hands and knees. Doubling back because of dead ends. Then I bang my shin against a rock.

I center myself. Then I begin to glow softly.

"Is he an angel or a firefly?" Nigel says. "Who can tell?"

Still, it's too easy. Lucifer has paved this path for us. Sent demons to clear our way with shovels and spells. He's looking forward to our arrival.

We hike for what seems like days. It may be minutes, or years. Our supply of water and honey-nut granola bars is dwindling.

At least we have water. It was Nigel's idea to wash out the milk bottles in the kitchenette, refill them, and secure them with belts that double as shoulder straps.

"What are we looking for?" Nigel asks. "How can we tell if we're getting closer?"

Lightning illuminates the cavern. Skeletal remains litter the ground, hang from rock walls. Lost explorers, human sacrifices, or both.

"We're getting closer," I reply.

The damned in hell crave blood every bit as much the undead on earth.

"Has anyone done this before?" Nigel wants to know. "Brought someone back?"

Thinking, I narrow my eyes. In the past century, there was only aviator Amelia Earhart, back in 1937. It's one thing to journey to hell. It's another to somehow locate the soul you're seeking and escape in one piece. "Not lately."

Up far ahead, I see fire along both sides of the path. Lightning flashes again. The stream we're following starts to boil.

~~◈~~ Zachary ~~◈~~

WE FOLLOW THE BOILING STREAM, our path lit by pools of fiery rock. I didn't expect to see lava this high up. Or maybe we've descended more than I realize.

"Do you know your mother?" I ask when the mud rain stops.

"Not personally," Nigel replies. "I tried to contact her by letter a couple of times. Her agent or personal assistant or whoever probably screens her mail."

"She's famous?" That hadn't occurred to me. "Like rock-star famous or car-dealer-who-advertises-on-TV famous?"

"Like red carpet, two-time Oscar winner, five husbands, miscellaneous provocative tattoos, a fake British accent, and seven kids adopted from various countries (and raised by seven nannies) that double as fashion accessories." He pauses. "I didn't get either of my parents' looks."

Lucifer is all too capable of seducing a mortal, but it doesn't sound like Nigel's mother was an unwitting dupe. I'm guessing she gained her celebrity status, money, and lifestyle in part by birthing Nigel and handing him over to Willa's family.

It's not the kid's fault. You can't pick your parents.

A demon scampers by. It's apelike in its gait. It's single-minded in its quest to reach the mortal world, to contaminate it. It's about three feet tall with a lolling forked tongue, a tail, and hooked horns that bridge from its half-desiccated nose.

"We should stop that thing," I say.

Nigel scoops up a mostly round stone and beams it at the demon. He hits it squarely on the back of the head. It drops, defeated.

"Good arm," I say.

Gas—sulfur dioxide—stings ours eyes and burns our nostrils. Our water supply is exhausted. We're thirsty. "Save your voice," I say. "Save your strength."

Nigel talks anyway. He tells me about how his dream was to try out for his high-school baseball team. He finally got Willa's parents to agree—or so he thought—over the holidays.

Given his parentage, it's no wonder he's so erratic. But Nigel keeps going. He's determined to make this journey for reasons probably even he doesn't understand.

Over the next ridge, we come upon the skyline of Lucifer's vast kingdom, the City of Punishment. It resembles a shadowy version of the classic film depiction of Oz's Emerald City. Subtract the glittering green. Ixnay the yellow brick road. Heavy on the flying monkeys. Or, rather, flying monsters.

~⚙ Miranda ⚙~

"HUAN," I BEGIN in a casual voice, "do you know where I might find my friend, the guardian angel Joshua?"

He fiddles with the microphone on his stand. "Now, Miranda, ascended souls are encouraged to make peace with the lives they've left behind, not—"

"Not associate with guardians," I say. "But you don't understand—"

"Don't I?" He scratches his chin. "I shouldn't be telling you this, but Joshua is currently the subject of a disciplinary meeting."

"Can you get a message to him?" I plead.

"Miranda," he says. "I know you mean well. But it's your messages—and what Joshua did with them—that's gotten him into trouble in the first place. It's time to accept the limits of death. Here in the Penultimate, down on earth, you're only making things worse."

As I shuffle toward my residential tower, a female voice calls, "Miranda!"

It's the guardian Idelle, coming up beside me on the promenade. "Have you caught sight of Zachary on your monitor-com?" she asks. "Rumor has it that he fell."

It's too terrible to imagine. If my angel has fallen, I've lost him forever.

~✿❀ Kieren ❀✿~

FLOWING WATER COMES from somewhere. Goes somewhere.

Our theory? Downstream is the way to hell. Upstream is the way out.

I take point. Evie and Bridget back me to either side, each holding a mop. Willa, carrying Vesper's rolled sheet, behind us. Quince at the rear with the flashlight, matches, and hair spray.

After a dozen steps, I catch the scent of blood. "Quince?"

"I smell it, too."

Evie keeps her nose to herself.

"I'll be back." Nobody objects to my military tone. It's nothing to leap on top of the closest supply shelf. Nothing to leap to the next. The one after that.

So long as I don't land on my bad leg. Or use any other muscles.

"Be careful," Evie calls. "We'll grab candles."

Good idea. I'm not sure how much power is left in the flashlight battery.

Beneath me are bottles of herbs. Dried flowers. Crustacean powder.

I find Mr. Bilovski's and Vesper's raw, leaking remains on the floor between the twelfth and thirteenth shelves. Their heads have been chewed off. Their noses and cheeks gnawed to meat. Only one of Vesper's gooey arms remains.

I pivot. I pour on Wolf speed. Ignore the pain. A moment later, I land beside Bridget. "Mr. Bilovski's dead," I say. They don't need to hear the rest.

Evie points. "The stream is that way."

We pause to stuff our pockets with river rocks. We can always throw them.

~⚘ Zachary ⚘~

THE CITY OF PUNISHMENT suffers from sprawl. Upon reaching the border, we're greeted by bellows and shrieks of the damned.

"They're descended souls," I say. "They can't hurt us. They've been expelled from the mortal plane. Ditto when it comes to the essences."

Nigel coughs. "Which are?"

"Formerly undead beings—mostly vamps—whose souls had withered away completely before they were destroyed. The essence is the will, the personality, the whatever-it-was that persisted to animate them after their mortal deaths."

Eventually, the relatively smooth rock path turns into a road paved with screaming faces. Eyes blinking, crying; mouths gaping, jabbering nonsense and threats. It's as if the heads have been partially embedded, faceup, in the lava stone.

Nigel hesitates. We both do.

We have no choice but to take another step. Then another. Moving on, crushing cartilage that will heal only to be crushed again.

"If they can't hurt us," Nigel begins again, grimacing, "why can we hurt them?"

"Because that's what hell is all about," I reply. "Them hurting."

It's the vicious genius of Lucifer's kingdom. Though no longer corporeal, the damned can feel. Like their ascended brethren up in the Penultimate, these souls have a pseudophysical presence. To each side of the road, more of the damned—filthy, bare skinned, on chafed knees and shredded palms—strain to grasp our ankles.

Beyond them, cannibals tear off flesh by the mouthful. Torture wheels shatter limbs and joints, crush shoulders and hips. Screws twist into skulls.

As whirligigs spin, the condemned wail and spew vomit.

Metal claws rip away breasts. Rake tissue from within bodily orifices.

What they wouldn't give for nothingness, an abyss.

I can't help scanning for Danny Bianchi's face, Mitch's, Vesper's. It's no use. Hell is vast. They could be anywhere. I won't fail Lucy, too. I pick up my pace. "Hurry."

Nigel, who's been chain-smoking, replies, "I'm barely keeping up *now*."

Faintly at first, music rises. It wafts through the foul air.

After a moment, I recognize "Only You (And You Alone)" by the Platters. It's one of the love songs I crooned to Miranda on our one date, as we swayed cheek to cheek on the dance floor at Chicago's Edison Hotel. When Elvis's "Love Me Tender" follows, it's clear the adversary is trying to poison the memory.

"Can anything hurt us here?" Nigel asks.

"Demons. Fallen angels. True and evil immortals."

I recall Kieren's pointing out that my pregame pep talks need work, but there's nothing I can say to lighten what awaits.

Our destination is the heart of Punishment, the headquarters of Lucifer himself.

~∰~ Miranda ~∰~

WHEN I RETURN TO MY SUITE, Harrison is swinging on my hammock and playing with Mr. Nesbit. "I never did care for these things back on earth, but he's a lovely fellow. Good company. Perhaps I should adopt a pet. How about a parrot, a red one with blue and yellow wings? Like with pirates—the kind who floss."

"Why are you talking about pirates?" I exclaim. "Zachary is missing, possibly in hell. Ditto Lucy. I'm helpless to do anything about it, and it's as though every time I turn around, I'm assailed by yet another ghost of Christmas past!"

Harrison reaches up, so Mr. Nesbit can scramble from his fingers up the rope supporting one side of the hammock. "Ghost of Christmas past?"

I remind him about Cissy and then tell him about my conversations with Demos from Artemis Gyros and Tamara from the Edison Hotel. "Even in heaven, I'm haunted."

"You're not in heaven yet." Harrison scoots to the right and gestures, inviting me to join him on the hammock. I do.

"Your Highness," he begins again, "why do you think this is happening?"

"Because I was a loathsome, bloodthirsty serial killer."

"Ah, yes." Harrison grins like he misses that side of me. "But that's not all you were. I've seen my share of soul sickness, and in my experience, never has a neophyte mourned her early victims the way that you did. In fact, you're the only case I can recall of an eternal being put on suicide watch."

"It wasn't that big of a—"

"Don't you remember the nights you spent locked in your nursery? The master fretted twice over. He nearly cleared his entire collection of knives from the castle because he was fearful that you might get a hold of one and impale your own dear heart."

Mr. Nesbit slips, and my open palm shoots out to catch him.

"My dear princess, you were the kind of girl who adored furry animals. Who—even in death, undeath, and ascension—is too concerned with her loved ones to embrace her own, hard-earned happily ever after." He winks. "Remarkable that we're friends."

I smile at that. "Be right back," I say, wiggling off the netted rope to return Mr. Nesbit to his aquarium in the other room.

I pause, staring out the window at the heavens. I've hardly been able to believe it, that I could belong here with my angel among the stars. Yet, here I am. It must be true.

The Miranda that he loves was once an eternal, was adopted by the eternal king, and yes, took lives. Wherever Zachary may be, whatever he's going through, he expects that same Miranda—who was both a shy human girl and a ravenous preternatural fiend—to greet him in heaven someday.

He hasn't fallen, no matter what Idelle may have heard.

I believe in Zachary the way he believed in me. I have faith.

Both of us deserve to be forgiven. I know that now, heart and especially soul.

Yet the situation is desperate. It's starting to look like I'll have to call on my inner demonic princess if I'm to have any hope of saving my true love.

~◈ Zachary ◈~

LUCIFER'S CAPITAL IS STARKLY URBAN. The damned aren't naked, but rather indistinguishable, shuffling around in filthy, ragged gray robes.

It's crass, commercial. Everyone's trying—and failing—to sell something or to promote themselves as candidates for Lucifer's court. I catch sight of a lone, lanky figure, staring at us from the doorway of Henry's Greasy Gumbo. He has two watches on.

Someone else on the corner shouts, "I am the true Rasputin."

No one cares. Except Nigel. I've shortened my stride so his steps can match mine. I've got a firm hand on his forearm. If I lose the kid, I might never find him again.

"Why does the torture end here?" he asks. "In the city?"

"It doesn't," I say. "The deeper we go, the more likely it is that the damned would enjoy physical pain, even desire it. So, the torture is directed where it hurts most— at their colossal egos. These souls idolize—"

"My dad."

"You don't have to call him that. You're a mortal, a child of the Big Boss."

"If you say so," he replies.

It's not hard to find Lucifer's headquarters. It's the tallest, most ostentatious building. Every street sign points to it.

As we reach the front steps, Nigel asks, "Do you talk to God?"

"I pray."

"Does He talk back to you?"

"Not directly," I say, matching him, up, up, up, step for step. "The Big Boss is always there, always everywhere. But, at the same time, kind of hands-off."

"Like a divine clockmaker?"

I smile at the expression. It's inaccurate but charming. "More like really into free will. We're defined by our choices."

Now I'm putting more pressure on the kid. What he needs is a distraction, even for a moment. "I've heard that occasionally the Big Boss sends a memo."

Nigel tilts his head. "A memo, really?"

"So I've heard. A memo to one of the archangels."

On the landing, Nigel does the bravest thing I've ever seen.

He knocks on the devil's front door.

~<> Zachary <>~

LUCIFER FELL LIKE A STAR, but he didn't fall alone. A third
of heaven's angels went with him. One answers Nigel's
knock, and another waves us through security.

What was it that I told Lucy? That the wings of
demons are scaly, dragonlike, clawed? That's true of the
little ones, the hell born. Flying around, tearing at the
damned mortals. But not the fallen immortals.

They're forever young, well muscled. Still sporting
white robes and gold sandals. Their beauty, it's blasphem-
ous. However, their hair has been burned away by the
fires of hell. When we angels risk showing ourselves on
earth, it's often our hair that draws eyes and awe. A petty
vanity vanquished. The obviousness of it is unnerving.

The fallen greet me by name: "Zachary," "Zachary," "Zachary." A reminder that I've slipped, that the Big Boss has yet to decide if this is where I belong.

The modern lounge-area furnishings contrast with the art-deco architecture. The chairs, sofas, and tables could've come out of the same catalog that stocked SP.

"Hello, boys," calls an enthusiastic voice from the reception desk. It's the essence of Andrew, the onetime hearse-driving, monosyllabic vamp student from Scholomance. "Welcome to Temptation Tower."

Nigel gapes. "Bilovski beheaded you!"

Not that you could tell to look at Andrew. Here, his head appears to be still attached.

"Indeed he did." Andrew presents us with a sign-in sheet and offers a pen. "Hence my landing this plum assignment—it's my dream come true."

"To be Lucifer's receptionist?" I said. "*That* was your goal in life?"

"In undeath, actually," he says. "In life, I was a peace-loving hippie child."

Wow. "We're here to see Lucifer." I almost pick up the pen to sign in, before realizing how stupid that could be. "Unless you could point us to where the mortal girl, Lucy Lehman, is being held. I'd appreciate it, and we'd be happy to leave quietly."

Andrew reaches to pinch my cheek. "No can do, golden boy!" He gestures toward the left of the desk. "But if you'll continue that way, you'll find that the Luminous One is already expecting you."

Nigel and I move on to an old-fashioned-looking elevator that resembles a large gold cage. Before the door closes, we take one last look at Andrew.

"At least he's happy," Nigel muses.

I push the button marked *S*. Not just for *subbasement*.

When the elevator doors open, we step onto the plush carpet. Black marble columns punctuate the unoccupied space. It's a study in vanity—the paintings, sculptures, Hollywood posters. Lucifer, Lucifer, and more Lucifer.

Even the chintzy knickknacks pay tribute to our host. A collection of tarot cards is displayed under glass in the central coffee table.

In repeating the *Codex Gigas* illustration at SP, he was showing restraint. I don't even think all of the art pieces were originally meant to depict him. I'd swear one is supposed to be Pan, another Dionysus.

A rear-facing chair in the seating area swivels toward us. He's holding my holy sword, the one Michael gave me. The one confiscated at SP.

It's Seth, aka the devil himself, in armor that resembles the archangels'. I'm almost insulted that he didn't adopt a better disguise. On the other hand, he did stay out of my sight until he was ready to reveal his true self.

"Welcome, Zachary." He stands to greet me. With a gloved hand, he points my weapon toward the conversation area. "Have a seat. We're all family here."

Coming around to one of two parallel sofas, I see that Lucy is seated in a high-backed chair beside his. She's not bound, though her mouth is covered with what appears to be duct tape. Her eyes are watery. She's fisted her hands tight.

"I thought I'd save you some posturing," he says. "You know, 'Where's the girl? Bring her to me!' All that nonsense. You'd end up sounding like a 1950s action hero."

I hate how civilized this conversation is. I'd love to disembowel him. But he's armed, and I'm not. He's having fun, and I've got these two kids to protect.

I perch on the edge of a sofa, and Nigel settles by my side.

"We're taking Lucy with us," I announce. "You have no right to her."

"Alas." The adversary returns to his chair. "All my efforts for naught. You have a lot of gall, making demands in my house."

I almost retort that he has a lot of gall, failing to acknowledge his own son, but I don't want to draw more attention to Nigel. I hope that meeting with the devil face-to-face and recognizing the difference between them will reassure the kid.

"I'm the one who left Ulman's classroom without

permission," I say. "You can't keep Lucy as punishment for something I did."

"Can't I?" The devil taps a contract on the coffee table. "Transfer of punishment is a standard Scholomance disciplinary measure. With Willa or Nigel here, you'd have had a leg to hop on. Their forms were signed by a parent, a legal guardian. That doesn't hold up against the Kingdom of Heaven, and your Executive doesn't entertain the notion of implied contracts. At least not where I'm concerned."

Lucifer may rule here, but ultimately, the Big Boss still calls the shots.

"You *had* to give Willa back," I realize out loud. "Spell or no spell."

"Her soul, yes. Her life? She was saved by that blasted handyman and his blasted handywench." He spins my sword. "You, Quincie, and Kieren don't have signed contracts at all. On the other hand, Lucy and Vesper—they were mine for the taking. In fact, I could go back for Bridget and Evelyn, too. I could mount their heads on my wall."

"Not so fast," I say, armed with an argument from Bridget. "This provision for 'special disciplinary action in accordance with the traditions of this and its affiliated institutions'—what's that supposed to mean? How could Lucy or, for that matter, any of the others understand what they'd consented to? It's overly vague, and you know it."

"Fine." Smug in his chair, the devil leans back. "No Bridget, no Evelyn. But Lucy and Vesper knew full well that the academy was a demonic institution. They understood that enrolling could cost them their lives and souls."

"Did you know that?" Nigel asks Lucy.

She shrugs, apologizing with her eyes. Out of love for Miranda, she risked everything and lost.

"Forget it," I tell the adversary. "You never would've had this chance at Lucy or Vesper if you hadn't laid your trap for me. Their contracts were signed under false pretenses."

"False pretenses," he replies. "How very droll. You and the boy — *only* you and the boy — are welcome to go." Lucifer pauses. "I'm curious, Zachary. How does one lone guardian hope to best my ferocious army of demons and escape with the girl?"

Claim or no claim, there's a history of souls stolen away from hell. But I haven't exactly snuck in. We can't leave undetected. It's impossible. So is my slim hope of finding Vesper, too.

What was I thinking? Crap, I *wasn't* thinking. I was leading with my heart. Again.

"Tell you what, brother." Lucifer leans forward. "I'll make you a deal. How about you stay — of your own free will — and I'll let them both go? It's not so bad here. Look at how happy your classmate Andrew is! Besides, you're the only reason Scholomance Preparatory Academy exists in the first place. It's you I've wanted all along."

"I've figured that much out," I reply. "What I don't understand is, why me? There are plenty of GAs, and I—"

"You've been saving souls marked as mine." He gestures at Lucy. "This one would've been damned back in Dallas, if it weren't for you. The undead king would've taken her, not Miranda. Now you're arguing that I shouldn't get either one."

He stands, suddenly losing his composure. "There's to be no fraternizing with the eternal queen! No rehabilitating neophytes!" Lucifer stomps his foot. "Who ever heard of vampires spurning blood? The whole point of the damned things is to drink, kill, contaminate!"

"They're not *all* damned things," I reply. "Most became undead against their will, through no fault of their own. The young ones can still achieve salvation. So, that's it, Lucifer! No more freebies."

"Every one of the formerly undead essences in my kingdom has killed—"

"Without the guidance or support of a guardian," I remind him. "We will surrender no more souls without a fight."

"'We' nothing! It all started when *you* broke heaven's rules. Why has that turned into *my* problem? You're a rebel. Heaven's bad boy. You should be on my team."

"I may be heaven's bad boy. But I'm still heaven's."

"Ha! If you think you're such a divine angel, prove it!

Sacrifice yourself so this mortal girl may return to her life with all the blessings and perils that implies."

It's the noble thing to agree, the hero's thing to do—save the dearest friend of my true love. It's also everything I've been warned against.

Miranda may hate me forever. I may be abandoning Lucy to an eternity of torment and humiliation. But the number-one rule of heaven is, no matter what the adversary asks, the answer is always: "No."

"No? *No!*" Lucifer waves my sword. "I'm the victim here. I'm the one who's lost what was owed to him."

"You?" Nigel lights a fresh cigarette. "What about me? I've been reading up on your limited dictatorship for my Underworld Governments paper. I'm sitting right here. And, oh, right! I'm your son. Aren't you going to ask me if *I'll* trade *my* soul to free Lucy?"

~❀❀ Miranda ❀❀~

HARRISON STORMS IN FIRST. He throws open the double doors of the reception area outside the Office of the Archangel Michael. "I demand to speak to someone in management! My afterlife thus far has been wholly unsatisfying. I have combed, literally *combed*, the streets of the entertainment district, and I'm yet to find one showing of Andrew Lloyd Webber's *Cats*!"

Marching to Yasmeen's desk, he adds, "If this, madam, is a taste of Kingdom Come, then I, for one, am sorely disappointed!"

Taking a brisk turn toward the hall leading to Michael's office, I'm positive that Yasmeen has never encountered such an unreasonable, ungrateful, or loud ascended soul.

Meanwhile, Idelle tosses aside her copy of *Interfaith Archaeology Bulletin*. Rushing to Harrison, she heightens the scene. "What an insensitive question!" she scolds, as I start running. "The famed werecat peace advocate, Palpate Kith, has petitioned for *Cats*'s banishment from heaven and the Penultimate as an insensitive mockery of—"

"Censorship!" I hear Harrison yell. "Who is she to suppress . . ."

At the heavy mahogany door, labeled MICHAEL in engraved gold, I reach for the handle and swing it open. "I hereby demand an immediate audience with the archangel Michael, the Sword of Heaven, the Bringer of Souls."

As Michael himself rises from behind the desk, I feel my knees quiver.

Though occasionally mistaken for a werelion because of his golden mane, Zachary can pass for human. I'd say the same for Joshua and Idelle. They're all angelically gorgeous, but the archangel is, for lack of a better word, more.

There's no wall behind him. The backdrop is a symphony of moons and stars. He's dressed for battle, and his full attention is trained on me.

"Miranda Shen McAllister," he says by way of greeting.

I resist the urge to clear my throat. "The guardian Zachary is in peril, along with six young mortals and the only wholly souled eternal. They've been lured into a satanic academy called Scholomance. It's located in Vermont and affiliated with—"

"I've heard of it," Michael replies, crossing his arms over his chest shield.

"I've been watching them," I continue, "with my monitor-com, yet they've disappeared from view. *All* of them. You know what that means."

He settles for raising an eyebrow. "Guardians are assigned to the mortals. Zachary, on the other hand—"

"How far can those other guardians follow?" I want to know. "How far down?" When Michael doesn't answer, I exclaim, "Are you the Sword of Heaven or not?"

He does not look pleased with my tone.

This is it. My redemption will be revoked. If the others are in hell, I'll soon be joining them.

The archangel takes one step onto his desk and one step down from it. "Since his creation in 1945, the guardian angel Zachary has had a spotty work record and is currently earthbound because of it. He broke the rules, which is why you became undead in the first place. His first assignment, Daniel Giacobbe Bianchi, turned out to be a crooked, petty politician, dead at the hand of a call girl with a toxic cocktail.

"He counseled his current charge, the vampire Quincie P. Morris, toward self-destruction when it turned out that she'd been wholly souled all along."

I clasp my hands behind my back. "Did you honestly see that coming?"

"I wasn't her angel!" he exclaims. "There is a reason that I delegate. And now Zachary has abandoned his post, abandoned young Quincie, on this disastrous errand—"

"The original mission—to help neophytes—was my idea in the first place," I remind him. "He's been trying. You, on the other hand, oversee all of the world's souls and their guardians or lack thereof. With the End Days nigh, do you think it's fair to assign only one angel to every demonically infected—"

"Fair?" He marches toward me. "Do you think Lucifer plays fair?"

"No, but I expected more from you."

It silences him for only a moment. "Zachary is a slipped angel. He doesn't even have full status under—"

"Again, it comes back to you, Michael. You're the one he calls his supervisor." I recall what Idelle said about Michael when we first met. That he's been given a lot of leeway. Yet he isn't infallible. He isn't God.

"You're the one who grounded him to the mortal plane," I continue. "Yet is it your place to dismiss him as fallen? Or does that decision have to come from the Highest?"

Michael closes the distance and grasps my shoulders. "What did you say?"

I will my hands to stop shaking. "Isn't it your

responsibility to watch over the guardians, to *guard* the guardian angels, like Zachary used to watch over me?"

The scowling archangel closes his eyes, for a moment, two. Then he does something extraordinary. He kisses me quickly but firmly on the top of my head.

"Lucky for both of you," Michael says, "I could use a good battle today. Now, what's this nonsense about the apocalypse?"

I find myself at a loss. "Well, you know. Everyone's talking about it. There's that Nostradamus and a super-volcano under Yellowstone and turmoil in the Middle East. One natural disaster after another. Not to mention all the movies and books and—"

"Only the Executive knows when the end will come," Michael replies. "Lucifer, I suspect, is the one stirring it up. He works through fear like we do through faith."

The archangel motions for me to follow him to his desk and hands over a piece of paper labeled PETITION FOR FULL-STATUS ANGEL REINSTATEMENT: ORDER GUARDIAN.

It's one of hundreds of different color-coded forms, citing official tasks performed by angels in heaven and on earth.

"Fill this out and give it to Yasmeen. I've got some-where else to be."

⤐ Kieren ⤏

WE DESCEND. WE RISE AGAIN. Our path narrows. The rock wall is uneven. Occasionally pitted. Steep, jagged to either side.

Nowhere to climb to safety. Nowhere to wait in attack.

"I hear water," I announce, glancing at the Otter. "Not the stream."

Evie can't swim out of here without revealing to everyone that she's a shifter. But she's taking time to psyche herself up.

"Could it be the lake?" Quince asks.

"The lake where the fire-breathing dragon lives?" Bridget puts in.

Shining the beam ahead of us, Willa whispers, "I can't swim."

"I'm a great swimmer," Evie assures her. "I'll . . . Kieren?"

"I smell it, too." Brimstone, from behind us. "Light the mops."

Evie does it with shifter speed.

I take the sheet from Willa. "Get behind me—back, *farther* back."

The approaching claws click against the rock. I unfurl the material. Quince hands Evie the matches and hair spray.

"Bridget, Willa, run! Quince—"

"Come on!" she urges the other two.

Hopefully, they won't have to battle the dragon without me and Evie.

Once they're off, I explain my plan to the Otter. "Then, with or without me, find the others. Find a way out. Let your inner animal take over. Trust your instincts."

As she finishes dousing the sheet in hair spray, Evie's eyes widen. "Kieren . . ."

I turn to confront the approaching hounds. "You know the ironic thing about our relationship?" I ask them. "I've always considered myself a dog person."

The first bounds at me.

I slam the flat of my axe blade into its skull. I try to take the head.

The hound's neck is thick, all muscle and magic.

The second one creeps closer. My blade is still stuck in the first.

Number two is about to spring but loses its footing on the slippery material.

I let go of my weapon. "Evie, now!"

She lowers the mop head. Flame flies across the material. The first hound catches fire. Its companion retreats, howling.

I catch Evie's hand, pull her forward.

"Slow down!" she shouts. "You're going to yank my arm out!"

Moments later, I see light ahead.

"Kieren, look out!" Evie pants. "We'll crash!"

We skid to a stop inches before the passageway narrows. It's nothing for Evie to squeeze through. I rip open my shoulder again.

"Quince!" I call. The cavern is big enough to house the dragon. By the firelight, I can make out Quince's silhouette. She's with Willa and Bridget. They've found the lake.

We're not a PDA kind of couple. But I lean in to give Quince a quick kiss. And linger despite the audience.

"Uh, Bridget," Evie begins. "Willa. If I sprout whiskers, don't panic."

It's not the most elegant way to declare your species. But it gets the job done.

"Hell's bells!" Bridget exclaims. "Am I the only human person here?"

"Nope," Willa replies. "What about the dragon?"

Suddenly, the cavern fills with an enormous splashing noise.

"That's it!" she adds.

"I don't think so," Quince yells. "I think . . ."

Then the Light is everywhere.

⊸ Zachary ⊸

"YOU?" LUCIFER SNEERS AT NIGEL. "I don't want you. I arranged for you to be raised by perhaps the two most twisted parents in all of the American suburbs, and you still turned out a disappointment. You're pure of heart, Nigel. Pure. Of. Heart. The only thing worse than you is your pseudo-incestuous crush, that vapid weakling you call Willa. She doesn't love you back, you know. Nobody has ever loved you. Nobody ever will."

Nigel tosses his cigarette and launches himself at Lucifer.

"No!" I yell, lunging to stop the boy — too late.

The devil swings my sword into his son's chest. The flash of pain in Nigel's eyes tells me this is the first time his life has ever felt real. It also says he has no regrets.

Nigel's body falls in two pieces onto the carpet.

I whisper, "Bless his soul."

The adversary reaches to drag Lucy in front of him. "Ready to see me kill another one? Let's be real here. You're a slipped angel, already half mine. Why delay the inevitable? Trade places. That way you can tell yourself you're a hero. Miranda's hero."

"They have a saying up on earth," I reply. "No means no."

He tightens his grip on Lucy's arm, and she whimpers beneath the tape. "Zachary, you're a vampire lover who craves earthly pleasures. Your soul isn't worth the fight."

"I managed to piss you off," I reply. "So, not a total loss, I suppose."

I stretch my shoulders, extend my wings, and blast him with my radiance.

I have no idea what, if anything, to expect. The pretense of a building dissipates. The furniture and art disappear. The carpet returns to lava stone. A final lie revealed.

The surface beneath my feet isn't wider than fifty feet in any direction. The drop on all sides is endless. Lightning flashes. The damned wail. Millions of them, millions upon millions, naked and desperate, try to claw themselves to the platform.

The tape over Lucy's mouth is gone. She turns her wrist, so I can see that her SP key is threaded between her first and second right-hand fingers like a claw.

It's another useless but valiant effort. I already see Satan's army of hellions rallying to his defense in the distance. We'll lose. That's a done deal.

But maybe it's *how* we lose that matters.

"You're barely more than a child, Zachary," the adversary sputters, raising my blade to rest against Lucy's neck. "Hardly old enough to make me break a sweat."

Suddenly, lightning erupts across the sky. The wind shifts. The damned tremble.

"What about us?" calls Michael, riding in on the devil's own one-eyed dragon. Chariots driven by Gabriel and Raphael flank him to either side. Soldiers of heaven—some on flying horseback, others via their own wings—swoop in behind. It's a veritable tidal wave of holy forces, of glory and light.

Because Michael is just cool that way.

Satan's jaw hangs open in fury.

Then as he orders his soldiers to war, Lucy slams her SP key into his balls.

He howls, dropping my sword.

I scoop her up, take to the air. "I can*not* believe you did that!"

"Couldn't reach his eyes," she replies. "He's too damn tall."

I could've tried for my weapon, too, but Lucy is far more crucial. Not just because she's a mortal or even because of her long history with Miranda.

Lucy is my friend now, too. If only I could somehow find Vesper. . . .

"Zachary!" Michael yells, as the dragon careens closer. "Retreat!"

"On it!" I dive toward heaven's approaching soldiers.

A bat-size winged demon rakes its claw across Lucy's cheek. She throws her hands up, beating it away.

"Hold on!" I strain my wings against the winds. I fly us away from the fray.

The Big Boss created me to serve as a GA. Offscreen. Off the grid.

How did I end up like this? Ego. The temptation to step onstage.

That's what I did, that night in the cemetery, in showing myself in full glory to Miranda. That's what I did, abandoning Quincie in an attempt to save Lucy. First from SP and then from hell itself.

I wanted to play by my own rules. I wanted more power than the Big Boss allows GAs.

I ended up with far less.

Miranda nearly lost her soul. I can only pray that nothing horrible has happened to Quincie. Michael had to lead his premier battalion here to rescue my ass.

I've been wrong about a lot, but I've learned something: being a good GA is a tougher, more important mission than I ever realized.

I'm flying Lucy to the life that she deserves. Then I'll pay penance to all that's holy. I'll fall—hopefully no further than my knees—and beg to keep my job.

From now on, I'm going to respect the wisdom of the Big Boss, embrace the limits of being a guardian, and probably end up doing a lot less damage.

~⊰⊱ Miranda ⊰⊱~

WHEN I BOOT MY MONITOR-COM in Michael's office, I still can't see anyone at Scholomance. Yet the reception is better. I can even make out the fourth floor. It's largely unfinished, unfurnished. However, there is a small office with boxes stacked against one wall. I suspect Lucifer used the space to meet with the Bilovskis and Dr. Ulman, perhaps even to make recruitment phone calls.

Then I attempt to locate Zachary. No luck. Next, I try Quincie.

"Do you think I should dive in after her?" the neophyte asks.

"Give her a minute," Kieren says, his arm around Quincie's shoulders.

My monitor-com shows a subterranean space, bordering a lake. It's shadowy, but I can make them out, along with Bridget and Willa, standing at the edge of the water, by the light of two flaming mops. The maps are propped up between rocks, like torches.

Where's Nigel? Lucy? Is Zachary still in hell?

"It's been at least three minutes," Willa says.

"I don't see any bubbles," Bridget adds, shining the flashlight over the water. "How long can Otters hold their breath?"

Suddenly, Evelyn, midshift, pops her head out of the lake.

Willa jumps back, startled.

"No sign of the dragon," Evelyn announces. "I can't see the glow anymore either . . . whatever it was. But, awesome news! If you swim to the far wall and dive about ten feet down there's a huge opening that leads to the outside."

"We should go now," Kieren says. "Swim for it while we can."

"You don't have to tell me twice," Bridget says. She drops the flashlight and plunges in.

Evelyn reaches for Willa, who's frozen in place. "It's okay," Evelyn assures her. "I'm stronger than I look and the fastest swimmer you'll ever meet. All I need you to do is trust me and, when I say so, hold your breath."

Willa stands there. "Are you sure—"

"Your chances of success are best in a full-immersion setting," announces Dr. Ulman's voice, as she materializes behind them. "Therefore, you will not be leaving the building or contacting the outside world until you graduate."

Kieren tosses Willa into the water. "Evie—"

"Got her!" the Otter calls, and a moment later, both girls submerge.

The ghostly teacher tries her handkerchief trick on Quince. It's no use. Quince is undead. That's more than enough to mess with the magic.

"Dr. Ulman," Mrs. Bilovski interrupts, emerging from the crevice into the cavern. "These are my children now." She strikes a match and lights up a bundle of what appears to be smudge. "Each one my precious, precious babe."

She begins chanting in Latin. At least I assume it's Latin. Blood is streaming from both of her wrists and palms. To pay for the magic, she's offering up herself.

"Kieren," Quincie whispers. "Go!"

"We can't leave Mrs. Bilovski," he argues. "She's a human being."

"I'll protect her," the neophyte replies. "Dr. Ulman can't hurt me."

The cook's mystic repellant appears to be working. The Scholomance teacher fades in and out, in and out again, almost to nothingness.

Then she returns one last time, her handkerchief ready, and zeroes in on the Wolf. Her available discretion may be limited, but she's going to use it to kill him.

She waves her hand, and Kieren crumples, dead, to the ground.

⊸⚏⚏ Miranda ⚏⚏⊸

DR. ULMAN IS GONE, banished to hell where she belongs.

"Kieren's death is a magical death," Mrs. Bilovski calls to Quincie. "You have an hour to reverse it. Get the boy to safety. With river stones, the scent of lavender, and the fresh eye of a dragon, you can bring him back."

Quincie, in shock, stares at the cook. She has the presence of mind to say, "Come with me. We—"

"George is dead," she replies. "Let this be our final resting ground."

Quincie doesn't waste time debating. She stands, lifts Kieren, and hurries into the water.

⌒

Outside the academy, Kieren's lifeless body rests on the snowy lakefront.

Bridget has surrounded him with smooth river rocks and lavender candles.

Willa runs to her with a pack of matches. "I found these in Andrew's car."

They begin lighting wicks.

Evelyn pushes herself out of the water. "No luck," she announces. "The dragon is still gone." She blinks rapidly. "How much time is left?"

"A couple of minutes," Bridget says. "Is Quincie coming up?"

Evelyn shakes out her fur, retracts her shift. "Not yet. She . . ." The Otter glances at Kieren. "It's no use." Visibly pulling herself together, she takes a gulping breath. "But Quincie is desperate, and she doesn't have to breathe."

The girls stare at the smooth lake. Then, suddenly, the academy is ablaze. Glass explodes from the fourth-floor windows, smoke billows, flames lick the night sky.

The front door falls out and slides down the outside stairs.

My angel appears with Lucy in the doorway. He's carrying Kieren's battle-axe.

He's returned—victorious—from hell.

The floors begin crashing down, one onto the next, and Zachary lifts Lucy with one arm. They land in a heap near the SUV.

A moment later, the other girls are helping Zachary and Lucy to their feet.

"Nigel?" Willa asks in a tight voice.

Zachary's voice is raw. "He's gone."

Willa did love him. She collapses into Bridget's embrace.

That's when Zachary sees Kieren, laid out on the cold ground.

"It was Ulman," Evelyn says. "Quincie's fishing for a dragon eye in the lake. I can't reason with her. She won't talk to me at all."

My angel hobbles over. He half-sits, half-falls in the circle of candles and stones, next to Kieren's body. "The dragon is busy. There's a war raging in hell."

Quincie climbs slowly out of the water. "It's too late anyway."

When Zachary moves to comfort her, she says, "Not now." The neophyte stands. "I'm glad you're okay," she assures him. "Lucy, too."

"Heads up!" Evelyn shouts as a flaming metal beam spins off the building.

They all duck as it crashes into what was Andrew's hearse.

I have to *do* something! Biting my lip, I scan the stacks of color-coded forms on Michael's desk.

~❦ Zachary ❦~

WITHOUT WARNING, the dragon bursts out of the lake. It's carrying Michael, who launches himself off its back. As his boots touch snow, I notice that the archangel is wearing two scabbards. In one smooth motion, he draws a sword—my holy weapon—and formally presents it to me. "*Try* to hang onto this," he says.

I will. "Quincie, this is the archangel Michael."

"The wholly souled vampire!" he exclaims.

I've never seen Michael smile at anyone like that. He's impressed by her.

Quincie, on the other hand, is barely registering him. She moves to sit vigil beside Kieren's body. She takes his cold hand in her own.

I introduce the other girls. Michael praises Willa for her bravery and Bridget for her intelligence. He assures Evelyn that the Big Boss loves her, whiskers and all.

They're all starstruck. Bridget is annoyed that she can't get her waterlogged phone to boot so that she can take a picture.

Then Michael says, "Lucilia Castillo Lehman, stay out of trouble from now on."

Her reply is a sharp "Yes, sir."

"Michael has come to take Kieren's soul to heaven," I explain.

"No," he replies. "I have not."

I'm outraged. It's not my place to question, but there must have been some kind of administrative mix-up. "That boy is a hero. He is one of the finest—"

"Silence!" Michael thunders. "Quincie Patrizia Morris, stand back."

"Forget it," she replies. "If you're taking him to hell, I'm going, too."

The archangel's hand falls to the hilt of his sword. "I do not take anyone to hell." He pauses. "Except occasionally heaven's warriors, but only to rescue wayward angels and troublesome mortal girls who do not leave Fate well enough alone! At least lately."

"He's telling the truth," I assure Quincie. Which

doesn't explain why Kieren's translucent blue soul isn't already cradled in the archangel's arms.

But I just resolved to be more trusting of my superiors, to have more faith. Apparently, it's a work in progress.

"Let it be known," Michael begins, "I did not file the requisition on this particular holy act. Despite the fact that, traditionally, only an archangel may file it. Despite the fact that it bore my official seal." He kneels, placing one hand over Kieren's heart and raising the other toward heaven. He begins to glow, radiating warmth.

For a moment, the Light blinds us all.

When it fades, Kieren's body is still here, but the archangel and, for that matter, the dragon, are gone.

"What did he do?" Bridget exclaims, reveling in the experience. "What was that?"

Kieren moans. He begins coughing, sputtering. He rolls to his side and throws up water.

Quincie gasps and bends to rub his back. She starts laughing, a little hysterically.

"He's alive!" Willa cries. "He was dead, truly dead, and now he's . . . not."

"An archangel can do that?" Lucy asks me. "Bring someone back to life?"

"Not with his own power. This is coming from higher up. The Highest. What just happened here, that was Michael acting as a conduit for the Big Boss."

Ha, *ha*! Somebody filed a freaking Z-777Z on Kieren and initialed the Lazarus provision. Somebody capable of bullying, sneaking, or otherwise invading the Office of the Archangel. It might be Joshua, but my money's on my girl, my love, my Miranda.

~⚜ Kieren ⚜~

IT'S A HALF HOUR PAST SUNSET. Sanguini's is filling up. I'm in the manager's office with Quince, doing homework.

Tonight all proceeds will be donated in Mitch's name to local organizations serving the homeless. It's been just over two weeks since Zach struck Mitch down on the lakefront. Only three days ago, halfway across the country, the archangel Michael raised me from the dead.

Almost as miraculous? I beat my family home from Kona. Barely, but still. I plan to tell my parents the whole story. After my thirtieth birthday.

Bridget is home in San Jose, and Lucy is back in Dallas. Evie moved in with her girlfriend in Montpelier.

Meanwhile, Freddy has taken Willa under his wing. She's living in an apartment over his new boyfriend's garage. Freddy's training her for a position at Sanguini's Catering. She'll transfer to Waterloo High next week.

We're already moving on. But before we left Vermont, Zach, Quince, and I drove back to Scholomance Prep. We erected markers in memory of Vesper and Nigel.

For a while, we were a pack. A better, tougher pack than the Wolves I met in Michigan. We, the Scholomance students. I'll always miss them.

"Hey, Wolf man," Quince says. "What are you thinking about so seriously?"

"How sexy you look in those overalls," I reply. Enough Dante.

I shove our English textbooks off the desk. I lift up Quince and indulge in some serious animal passion. I've been given a second chance at life. I'm gonna enjoy it.

~⚬ Zachary ⚬~

AT HALF PAST ELEVEN, Kieren and Quincie finally come out of the locked manager's office. Kieren announces that he's starving. Yani, at the hostess desk, replies that she's had one cancellation, in case they want to eat at a table like real guests.

At one of my tables. They're happily underdressed.

Quincie is sipping warmed porcine blood from a wine glass.

Kieren naturally orders from the predator menu. He's already inhaled the carnivore taster — wild boar prosciutto, venison blood sausage, duck liver pâté. His crimson drink, cranberry herbal tea. Nora is a stickler about not serving alcohol to minors.

I drop off the main course: little javelina chops with rosemary and olives.

"How am I doing, boss?" I ask Quincie. "How's that tip coming?"

Tonight I'm wearing the outfit that she gave me for Christmas: a long-sleeved blue shirt—she calls it sapphire—with black leather pants.

Kieren glances sideways at me. I have this theory that it's only because of his respect for me as a holy being that he resists mocking my work wardrobe.

The Wolf makes a show of swallowing a bite of mouth-watering javelina. "One more question about Michael—"

"For the last time," I tell him, "Michael is a colossus. The example we GAs strive to emulate. And he manages to secure his own weapon."

"As opposed to you," calls Joshua, strolling our way.

He's always been a GA fashion trendsetter. But when it comes to Goth glam, Sanguini's is a stage unparalleled. Josh is sporting a knee-length black cape over a black vest, high-necked white satin long-sleeved shirt, black satin pants with black dress shoes, and an ascot with a steam-punkish bat tie tack.

"News flash," he says to me. "Our man Michael is reassigning you to the front lines."

As a waitress passes by, I hand off my tray to her. "What are you *doing* here? In Sanguini's dining room? In that outfit?"

"Grounded, big-time," Josh says, presenting me with scrolls tied with gold ribbon. "But hey, you're upstairs bound. Congratulations, dude! When Miranda—"

"You're earthbound?" I reply, struggling to understand.

"Call me earth angel, second string." Josh points to Kieren's plate. "Can I have what he's having?" Rubbing his hands, he adds, "Hello, earthly pleasures, this meeting is *long* overdue."

"Crap," I reply, realizing what happened. "Because of me and Miranda, you—"

"Cheer up! Eternity is too short." Josh gives Quincie a quick hug. "Great to see you, cutie!" He offers his hand to the perplexed-looking Wolf, and they shake.

Then Josh plucks a bowl of kumquat sherbet off of a nearby tray.

As Quincie assures the waitress that it's fine, I tug at the gold ribbon, and Kieren stands. "Did your friend say that you're headed upstairs?" he asks. "Upstairs as in . . ."

The parchments unfurl. I scan one, then the other.

"Zach?" the Wolf prompts. "Zach, are you okay?"

Nodding slowly, I point up, as if to heaven.

Kieren's generous brows draw together. "You're going home to Miranda?"

"Miranda," I repeat. "And there's more."

THE OFFICE OF
THE ARCHANGEL MICHAEL
The Sword of Heaven
The Bringer of Souls

To: Zachary
From: Michael
Date: Thursday, January 16

Be advised that the Petition for Full-Status Angel Reinstatement: Order Guardian, filed on your behalf by ascended soul Miranda Shen McAllister, has been denied.

In fact, you are no longer a guardian angel at all.

The guardian Joshua will be assuming your current assignment. Henceforth, he will watch over the vampire Quincie P. Morris.

P.S. Thank you for your years of service, such that they were.

THE OFFICE OF
THE ARCHANGEL MICHAEL
The Sword of Heaven
The Bringer of Souls

To: Zachary
From: Michael
Date: Thursday, January 16

Be advised that the Word from On High is
that you have been promoted to archangel.

You shall hereby be assigned to the deploy-
ment and supervision of guardians who will
be assigned, one-on-one, to every neophyte
vampire still in possession of his or her soul.

Report in your new uniform at your first
available convenience to your new office at
the Penultimate.

You'll recall that archangels not only provide leadership to the lower ranked, but also

on occasion lead heaven's forces into battle. Consequently, a chariot has been reserved for you at the stables. Sword practice is Tuesdays and Thursdays at 8 A.M.

P.S. Congratulations, Zachary! You are now middle management with a legion of your own guardians to supervise. I could not have conceived of a more fitting punishment.

⟶ Miranda ⟵

WHEN I HEAR RENATA'S VOICE over the sound system ("Attention, Miranda Shen McAllister! Attention,
please!"), calling me to the reunion desk, for a moment I'm
certain it must be Zachary at last. Then I realize, no, I'm
off to meet another newly ascended soul.

Guardian—I mean, *arch*angels—don't arrive and
depart through the Penultimate processing system. My
boyfriend, an archangel. Imagine that!

According to Idelle, it means he'll have to spend qual-
ity time in his office at the Penultimate, yet he's no longer
limited to this way station or earthly service. His place of
work will be here. He'll come. He'll go.

Yet from the time he returns, heaven will be his primary residence.

His. Mine. *Ours.*

I'm surprised when Harrison meets me at the reunion receiving area.

Then I catch sight of Renata, escorting Nigel forward. He's complaining that no one will let him have a cigarette.

"Dear boy," Harrison begins, "I can't have a cigar either. It's part and parcel of the Penultimate experience." My fellow former eternal grins. "A final cleansing of the soul before passing through heaven's gates."

Nigel glances at Renata. "I don't know these people. I don't have any family or friends. I don't even know why I'm here. My father is—"

"I'm Miranda." I take Nigel's hands in mine. "Zachary's girl. This is Harrison. We're your family now."

At that very moment, the chariot of the archangel Gabriel touches down on the nearby promenade, and the crowd scatters.

"Hey, Nigel!" Vesper calls, climbing out. "Who're your friends?"

Two days later, the "doctor" on stage with me in the theater raises his chin. "Hark! she speaks: I will set down what comes from her, to satisfy my remembrance the more strongly."

I tap in to my inner eternal, the moments when the madness took me. "Out, damned spot, out, I say! One, two—why, then 'tis time to do't. Hell is murky! Fie, my lord, fie! a soldier and afeard? What need we fear who knows it when none can call our power to account? Yet who would have thought the old man to have had so much blood in him?"

"That'll do," calls the director, making a note on his chart. "Next."

I'd been hoping for a "Brava, Miranda!"

Exiting the round theater, I scan the entertainment district for Harrison and Nigel, who promised to toss rose petals at my feet as I descended the stairs.

Did they forget?

About halfway down, I let the loneliness soak in. I feel foolish in the period Scottish nightdress I'm wearing for the audition.

I'm not utterly self-absorbed. I understand that my angel couldn't return home right away. He took Willa out for ice cream. He called to check on Bridget and Evelyn and Lucy. He gave Joshua tips on being earthbound, raised his glass to toast Freddy, indulged one last time in Nora's bacon-wrapped prawns. Zachary went howling with Kieren. He flew Quincie over Mount Bonnell and told her she's his hero. He took a day, two, to say his good-byes.

The tick of each second resounds like a gong.

"Miranda?" calls a voice from above.

"Zachary?" Glancing up at him in battle gear, I lose my balance on the stairs.

No chance of my falling anywhere, except more profoundly in love. My angel spins me, and it's as if I'm flying, too. Weightless, we dance among the stars.

We glide above the Penultimate, away from the stables and the arts district, past the honeycomb-shaped towers. Blue-and-black butterflies flutter behind us like a bridal train. Finally, we land at heaven's gates. We're laughing, giddy.

Touching down, he says, "Hold out your hands."

My angel reaches for a pouch tied to his belt and opens it to nudge Mr. Nesbit into my palms. "I've searched everywhere for you." He gestures to the side. "And Grandpa Shen is so excited. He's waiting beyond those clouds. He wants to cook us bacon-fried rice for dinner tonight."

Yes! I set my gerbil on my shoulder and give my angel a kiss that makes Saint Peter blush. I revel in the feel of his lips against mine, thread my fingers through his gold mane, and caress his feathers.

Touch, only touch, and for this moment, it's enough.

On the other side of the gates, we'll build our eternal

lives, lives blessed with a whole new array of tantalizing and heavenly pleasures. If there's bacon-fried rice in heaven, who knows what other possibilities await?

I remember the first time I saw Zachary. He appeared as if ripped from Eden. Yet he was heaven-sent, and now he's home again. We both are—almost.

"Ready for ever after?" he asks, offering his arm.

I rest my fingertips in the curve of his elbow. "I am now."

With my angel at my side, I cross into the divine.

The Scholomance in this novel is inspired by a school of the same name mentioned in Abraham Stoker's *Dracula* (1897). It was Stoker's work that spawned this and three of my previous books — *Tantalize, Eternal,* and *Blessed* — which feature characters that appear herein.

Each sequential story inches closer to that classic novel, and in *Diabolical,* we touch on a landmark from Dracula's own history. He was once a Scholomance scholar, though I reinvented and updated SP for my own fictional purposes.

Beyond that, in reference to his battle-axe, Kieren challenges Mr. Bilovski to "come and take it," if he dares. This expression was used as a slogan in the Texas Revolution and appears on a historic Texas flag.

Careful readers may also notice nods or tributes to Kathi Appelt, Animal Planet ("Hellhound"), Fred Astaire, Stephen Vincent Benét, Dante Alighieri, Sir Francis Bacon, L. Frank Baum, Helen Eileen Beardsley, Otto Binder, William Peter Blatty, Bob Carroll Jr., Chris Carter, Warren Casey, Madelyn Davis, William C. DeMille, Charles Dickens, Amelia Earhart, Douglas Fairbanks, William Friedkin, Sigmund Freud, Bruce Geller, Fred Ebb, Sarah Michelle Gellar, Emily Gerard,

Laurell K. Hamilton, Katharine Hepburn, S. E. Hinton, the History Channel ("Gates of Hell," *Hell: The Devil's Domain*), Washington Irving, Jim Jacobs, John F. Kennedy, Fritz Kiersch, Stephen King, Rudyard Kipling, Jack Kirby, Eartha Kitt, Mort Lachman, Noel Langley, Stan Lee, Jonathan Lemkin, C. S. Lewis, Astrid Lindgren, George Lucas, Elliot S. Maggin, Judith Martin, Vera Matson, John Milton, Andrew Neiderman, Michel de Nostredrame, William Paley, Luciano Pavarotti, Al Plastino, the Platters, Alexander Pope, Elvis Presley, Buck Ram, Gene Roddenberry, Florence Ryerson, Walter "Jack" Rollins, John Romita Sr., Tom Schulman, Melville Shavelson, Charles M. Schulz, William Shakespeare, Anthony Trollope, Mark Twain, Mies van der Rohe, Andy Warhol, Andrew Lloyd Webber, Len Wein, Peter Weir, Joss Whedon, E. B. White, Oscar Wilde, and Meredith Willson.

That said, *The Blood Drinker's Guide, Eternal Elegance, Baba-Yaga's Junior Encyclopedia, Interfaith Archaeology Bulletin*, and a number of other media references or (mis)representations sprang completely from my imagination.

In terms of locales, Sanguini's: A Very Rare Restaurant in Austin and Scholomance Prep in Vermont are both fictional. So is Chrysanthemum Hills Cemetery in Dallas and both the Edison Hotel and Artemis Gyros in Chicago.

Likewise, you'd be hard pressed to find Norma & Harry's B and B in Montpelier, but if you did, there would be wild, wonderful gardens and soup with bread for dinner. I set the academy outside Montpelier because it's one of my favorite places, where I'm on a faculty myself (though I usually lack Dr. Ulman's disciplinary flare).

As to the question of an original Scholomance in the Carpathians, some say it does exist. Make of that what you will, dear readers, and travel safely.

I'm putting my faith in the angels and in you.

THANK YOU

For research and other support, my thanks to Salima Alikhan, Ann Angel, Gene Brenek, Alissa Cornelius, Lynne Kelly Hoenig, John Kandler, Anne Mazer, Steve Nelson, Susan Robertson, Leda Schubert, Christy Stallop, the Vermont College of Fine Arts family, and City of Montpelier planning and zoning assistant Audra Brown. Special cheers to the children's-YA creator community, especially here in Austin.

Moreover, my undying appreciation goes to my editor Deborah Wayshak, the whole team at Candlewick Press, my agent Ginger Knowlton, and her assistant Anna Umansky. For everything else, here's to my very cute husband Greg Leitich Smith as well as our kitty cats, Mercury, Bashi, Blizzard, and Leo. I love you guys.

P.S. I promised to name Evelyn's wereelk girlfriend, Ollie, after author Ann Hagman Cardinal. So, let it be known that the character's full name is Olinda Ann Cardinal.

*T*rouble brews when Quincie Morris and her uncle decide to remodel the family restaurant with a vampire theme. One month before the grand reopening the chef is mauled to death in the kitchen and the murder suspect is … a werewolf!

Quincie has to transform Henry, the new chef, into Sanguini's vampire extraordinaire – and fast. But strange things are happening to her boyfriend, Kieren, and a deadly love triangle forms.

"Readers will be tantalized by this dark, romantic, and disturbing fantasy … fans of Stephenie Meyer will eat it up." *School Library Journal*

At last, Miranda is the life of the party: all she had to do was die. In the afterlife, she goes from high-school stage wannabe to vixen vampire-princess overnight. Meanwhile, Zachary, her reckless guardian angel, goes undercover in a bid to save his girl's soul before all hell arrives – quite literally – on their doorstep.

Sink your teeth into a dangerous love story played out in a dark eternal world where vampires vie with angels.

"Stephenie Meyer, honey, watch out.
Twilight **fans, you are gonna LOVE** *Eternal.***"**
Dallas Morning News

*Q*uincie Morris, neophyte vampire, is in the fight of her life – or undeath. She must clear her true love, the hybrid-werewolf Kieren, of murder charges and thwart the apocalyptic ambitions of Bradley Sanguini, the seductive vampire-chef who "blessed" her.

But with hundreds of new vampires on the rise and Bradley assuming the powers of Dracula Prime, can the preternaturally beautiful Zachary help her staunch the bloodshed before it's too late – *and* save Quincie's soul?

"A hearty meal for the thinking vampire reader."
Horn Book

UNDER COVER

READ BETWEEN THE LINES

READ
- Sneak previews
- Author interviews

DISCOVER
- Trailers
- Behind the scenes footage

WIN
- Review copies
- Signed books

COMMENT

Have your say on the books that you want to read

Scan the code to watch our book trailers*

Discover more at
WWW.UNDERCOVERREADS.COM

CYNTHIA LEITICH SMITH is the acclaimed and best-selling author of *Tantalize*, *Eternal*, and *Blessed* as well as *Tantalize: Kieren's Story*, a graphic novel illustrated by Ming Doyle. About *Diabolical*, she says, "Angels slip. Souls waver. Not every Wolf howls with the pack. Yet we all deserve a second chance, even if it might be our last." Cynthia lives in Austin, Texas, with her husband, author Greg Leitich Smith.